D1530580

# THE MIRACLE OF MISS WILLIE

ALMA J. YATES

# THE MIRACLE OF MISS WILLIE

**Deseret Book**
Salt Lake City, Utah

© 1984 Deseret Book Company
All rights reserved
Printed in the United States of America

First printing March 1984

Library of Congress Cataloging in Publication Data

Yates, Alma J.
    The miracle of Miss Willie.

    I. Title.
PS3575.A755M5  1984        813'.54        84-1864
ISBN 0-87747-996-8

# Chapter One

STANDING IN THE CORNER of the church cultural hall, I brushed the back of my hand across my forehead and brought it away wet with perspiration. I wrinkled my nose as I took a breath of hot air, wondering if I should chew it before breathing it. It was rank and stiff with the smell of sweating bodies and a touch of Old Spice cologne.

My ears rang painfully with the cacophonous twang of a hundred old-fashioned tunes that Brother and Sister Hatch were cranking out on the old gray phonograph perched up on one end of the stage.

I gulped and glanced around, checking to see if any of the windows were still closed. Every door and window was pried open, but in the late August heat of Snowflake, Arizona, conditions demanded more than just a few opened doors and windows.

Desperate, I began creeping toward the side door, but Bishop Williams spotted me. He was standing guard at the door, his massive hairy arms folded across his barrel chest. While the Hatches stood in front of the stage and shouted directions to the complaining youths, all the Mutual Improvement Association teachers and priesthood advisers rushed about trying to chase the guys into the

1

girls' corner. The bishopric had assumed their usual sentinel posts at the three doors. The bishop glared at me and nodded toward the dance floor. Escape past him was impossible.

"Great!" I muttered to myself, sneaking back to my corner. "This is supposed to be the Mutual's biggest summer party. And what do we do? Dance in this oven! And right outside there's a perfectly good basketball court going to waste."

Suddenly I spotted Rita Flake and Sue Willis marching toward me. Panicking, I backed into the wall.

"Don't worry, DJ," Rita sneered, as she flounced by, "we're not going to ask you to dance. We're going for a drink of water."

I fumed and railed at myself for allowing my presumptuousness to show so plainly. Just as I was recovering from their first cutting remark, the two girls brushed past a second time and Sue flung over her shoulder, "Still waiting for someone to ask you for a dance?"

I pressed my lips together and glared after them.

"DJ, don't you have a partner yet?" Sister Hollingsworth, the Mia Maid teacher, cackled as she thundered toward me, her jowls bouncing and her corpulence stuffed into a thin cotton dress.

"Dang!" I muttered.

"We're going to do one more Virginia reel," she grinned, grabbing me by the arm and dragging me onto the floor.

"Not again," I moaned, trying to hold back.

Sister Hollingsworth's face was a flushed, perspiring pink. Like the other adults, she had spent most of the evening chasing Scouts and Explorers and dragging them over to the girls. I wanted to jerk my hand loose, but Sister Hollingsworth was a big woman and I didn't know if I was up to that kind of a battle. Besides, with so many other adults patrolling the premises, I didn't have much chance of effecting any kind of an escape.

"Oh, I spy a good partner for you," she called out with excessive enthusiasm. I cringed, knowing I was in for one of the disastrous mismatches for which the Mutual was so infamous. "Amy Thomas doesn't have a partner."

"Amy!" I groaned under my breath. "She doesn't ever have a partner." Amy was the littlest Beehive girl in the whole Church.

She was almost two feet shorter than I and at least seventy pounds lighter. Every time I saw her at Mutual I couldn't help feeling that she was AWOL from the Primary.

"Amy," Sister Hollingsworth panted, "DJ's coming to ask you for this dance."

I managed a sick smile, my way of asking a girl for a dance. Amy, her face draped by two long braids and sprinkled with freckles, blushed and grinned up at me. I'd already danced with her three times, and each time I had, I hadn't known if I was supposed to dance or baby-sit. I looked away to hide the disappointment and boredom drooping from my wilting face.

"I thought the Church outlawed dances like these with all these little Scouts and Beehives," I murmured to Sister Hollingsworth.

"Oh, this isn't a dance dance. This is just a fun way to teach you some steps. When you're older you'll be glad you came to these Mutual parties and danced with the Beehives."

I rolled my eyes and muttered, "I wish I was glad right now."

Standing next to Amy, I watched the other incongruous pairs around the cultural hall. Sam Richards, the Scouts' newest recruit, was paired with Sandy Williams, who was big enough to play for the Los Angeles Rams. Betty Linn, who was a petite ballerina, was thrown together with Ben Bush, who couldn't have walked in a straight line without tripping over his shadow. Roy Farrell, who was the high school's star center at six-foot-five, was given Tina Larsen, who could have walked between his legs without so much as bending over. But the adults didn't ever seem to notice any of these incongruities. They were too busy chasing all of us and shouting about how much fun we were having.

Sister Hatch tossed another record on the phonograph, and Brother Hatch began stomping his foot and hollering about swinging your partner and promenading the hall. All the guys began to groan, but Sister Hatch clapped her hands and punctuated each round with a shrill whoop that was supposed to fire us up and help us forget that we were prisoners here and that the bishop had confiscated our basketball and forbidden us to return to the basketball court outside.

I clamped my jaw shut and tried to endure, wondering how my

dad had ever talked me into coming to this circus. After all, missing my allowance for a month, as he had threatened to make me do, wasn't nearly as torturous as doing a fourth Virginia reel with Amy Thomas.

After the Virginia reel there was a short break. Waiting for an opportunity to fade into the crowd and ditch Amy, I heard some-one growl in a hoarse whisper, "Hey, DJ, let's get out of here. This thing's a joke."

I turned to find Jefferson Judd, tagged by Becky Thomas, pant-ing next to me. I grinned at Jefferson and said, "You too?"

Jefferson nodded and hiked up his pants. Jefferson and BB Bunderson were the best friends I had in Snowflake. Ever since I'd moved to Snowflake from Eager, Arizona, after my mom's sudden illness and death, I'd been running with BB and Jefferson; how-ever, the first time I met the two I wasn't sure whether they would be friend or foe. I was miserable sitting in my front yard, glumly contemplating life in this new town without mother or friends. Then BB and Jefferson came ambling down the street, kicking a battered soda-pop can before them. They stopped in front of our house and glared at me for a minute. None of us spoke for some time, choosing instead to communicate our eight-year-old disdain through angry, beady eyes. Then Jefferson asked in a challenging way, "Who are you?"

I stared back and replied defiantly, fully expecting to defend myself against these two strangers, "Who are *you?*"

"I asked you first," Jefferson sneered.

"Well, I don't have to tell you because it's none of your busi-ness."

"Do you live here?"

"Maybe."

"Maybe you just don't know where you live."

"I do too," I snapped. "I live right here, and if you don't get out of here I'm going to get my big German shepherd police dog after you."

BB and Jefferson took an involuntary step backward and looked around for the dog, which of course was a desperate fabrication. BB spoke for the first time, asking cautiously, "Where is he?"

"Oh, he's around," I said boldly.

"You don't even have a dog," Jefferson guessed correctly. "You're just the new kid that moved in." He said *new kid* like it was some loathed disease.

"I have a dad and he'll knock your block right off if you don't get out of here."

"I ain't afraid of your old dad. Besides, he's not even here. I saw him drive off this morning, and I sure ain't afraid of your big sister."

It was a stand-off. For almost fifteen minutes we threw threats and insults at one another. At the end of our verbal jousting, when we had exhausted our imaginations as well as our vocabularies, we stared at each other for a moment and then I said in the same challenging tone of voice, "There's a sack of cookies inside." BB and Jefferson licked their lips. "I can eat as many as I want. It don't matter. I can have all the cookies I want, whenever I want," which was a blatant untruth.

"Can we have some?" BB asked hungrily, suddenly submissive and friendly.

I stood and marched into the house as though this were something I did every day. My heart was pounding and my hands were shaking, but I didn't retreat. I only hoped my sister, Sharon, was occupied so I wouldn't be made to look foolish in front of BB and Jefferson.

I found the cookies hidden in the top of the cupboard and took them out into the bushes, where the three of us ate every last one. As we lapped up the crumbs, a tacit truce was made. That was our inauspicious beginning as a threesome.

Now Jefferson stood next to me. He hated Mutual dances more than I did, and the only other person who hated them more was BB.

Jefferson's face was beet red under a thick crop of sandy hair that hung down limply into his blue eyes. Jefferson was a couple of inches taller than I, almost five-ten, but he was narrower through the shoulders and chest; we both weighed exactly one hundred and fifty-seven pounds. He had a fair complexion and was probably the most handsome of the three of us. In fact, people said his face was almost angelic; however, the angelic traits ended abruptly on the surface.

Jefferson ran his tongue over his lips. "Let's ditch this joint," he grumbled.

"I got to stay a little longer," I replied under my breath so Amy wouldn't hear. "Dad told me if I ditched one more Mutual, that was it. I think he means it this time. Ever since you and BB tore the screen door off the hinges last Tuesday, he's really been down on me."

"But that wasn't our fault. How were we supposed to know Sharon had latched the screen? Who latches a screen door in the middle of the afternoon?"

"That's what I tried to tell Dad," I sighed, "but he said we weren't supposed to be having a water fight in the house."

"Well, when me and BB saw you coming with Sharon's dirty mop water, all we could think about was getting out of there."

I smiled, remembering last Tuesday. "You sure blew that screen door to bits, though. Maybe if you hadn't both hit it at the same time— Man, there wasn't enough left to make a screen door for a dollhouse."

"I thought Sharon was going to claw our eyes out, especially after we stomped all over her waxed floor. It looked dry to me."

"You're lucky you weren't there when Dad got home and saw the door."

"Are you going to have to pay for it?" Jefferson asked.

"Dad said so, but I'm still paying for the kitchen chair we broke last month. If he has me pay for everything we've broken, I'll be paying for the next thirty years." I sighed and shook my head ruefully. "I heard him tell Sharon he's afraid to come home from work anymore. He says he can't bear to find out what else we've destroyed."

"Are we that bad?"

I shrugged. "Maybe we ought to spend more time at your place."

Jefferson puffed out his cheeks and blew slowly. "Well, actually, Uncle Roy isn't too crazy about us over at his place either. Hey, there's BB," Jefferson called out, pointing to the opposite end of the hall.

We could easily see BB's mop of straw-straight red hair. Like everyone else in the building, his round face was flushed and speckled with beads of perspiration, but the redness didn't erase the freckles. His face was plastered with them. Even from where we stood, the freckles were BB's most prominent feature. His eyes were bulging from heat and exhaustion, and his mouth was gaping open. There were sweat rings under the arms of his light blue polo shirt, and his slightly ample hips and thighs were squeezed tightly into a pair of faded Levi's. As usual, his belt was cinched two notches too tight, cutting into his soft stomach and making him appear a little on the pudgy side.

Jefferson and I laughed when we saw he was dancing with Ruby Waite, the ward's only girl redhead. BB saw us about the same time. Without checking to see if Ruby was going to follow, he charged through the panting throng and hustled our way. Ruby, not wanting to chance being ditched, stumbled right behind him.

Jefferson grinned as BB came up. "Looks like you found your old honey," he whispered in BB's ear, then winked and jabbed BB in the ribs with his elbow.

"Ah, lay off," BB growled. He mopped his face with his hand and moaned, "This place smells like a gym."

Sister Hatch began screeching into the microphone about practicing the waltz one more time before taking a break. Jefferson, BB, and I groaned our displeasure, turned our backs on our partners, and convened a quick conference.

"Haven't we been here long enough?" BB whined. "I'm suffocating. I just promised my dad I'd show up, not that I'd dance with Ruby Waite six times." He gulped some stale air and winced. "The next time Dad says I can either go to the Mutual party or stay home and clean out the horse stable, I'll take the horse stable. Those two horses of ours never ask me to dance with them."

"Well, we've made it this long," I remarked, "we might as well stay a while and find out what they're going to feed us."

"It'll probably be just cold cauliflower and carrot sticks," BB grumbled. "You never can trust the refreshments. When we stay, they don't serve nothing. If we leave early, they end up having something real good." Suddenly BB's eyes lighted up. "You know, I think Old Man Harrison's melons are ripe. I saw him out there thumping 'em around this afternoon, and he picked two. I've never seen such big melons, even from his patch. We ought to head over there and get us each one."

"Do you think we can get past the bishop?" I asked. We all turned and looked toward the side door. The bishop stood in the doorway watching us.

"Looks like we're boxed in, all right," Jefferson remarked.

"What about the windows? There's a window off the stage. We could sneak out there."

"If we could just get our basketball out of the bishop's office, we could go out and finish our game," BB said.

"Yeah, then we could sneak back in for refreshments—if there's anything good."

Just then the music started for the waltz. We had missed all of the instructions, but that didn't matter much. I couldn't ever understand Sister Hatch's little jigs no matter how many times she went over them. I just wasn't born for dancing.

My inabilities didn't stop Amy, though. She grabbed my hand, jerked me around, smiled up at me, and started stomping around in front of me. I had no idea how to follow her so I just shuffled along, dragging my feet and trying not to get in her way or trample on her toes.

"Come on, DJ," she complained. "You have to pick up your feet. It's easy."

I could feel the hot blood of a blush flood my cheeks. With my head bowed in concentration, I gaped at her strange gait, unable to make any sense of it. "Why don't you just do it, Amy," I mumbled, "and I'll kinda watch and pretend that—"

BB jabbed me in the back with his thumb. "Hey, would you look at that," he gasped, pointing.

Into the cultural hall from the kitchen staggered Brother Hill and Brother Smith, carrying a long table heaped high with pies.

There were apple and cherry, blueberry and boysenberry. Sister Flake and Sister Briggs followed, each carrying a two-gallon bucket of ice cream. Two Scouts tagged along lugging a huge silver kettle—must have held ten gallons—of pink lemonade. My mouth broke out into a delicious watering.

"I think that's worth waiting for," I grinned as the refreshment table was set right in front of the stage.

"Forget about Old Man Harrison's melons," BB whispered. "They'll still be there tomorrow."

"Look at that one in the middle," Jefferson said, pointing. "I didn't know you could make a pie that big."

Ruby, who overheard our whispered comments of profound admiration, remarked, "That big one's Sister Hatch's."

"Sister Hatch's!" The three of us gasped.

"It's cherry," Ruby added.

I despised Sister Hatch's cackled dance calls, but I knew she could whip up one good cherry pie. I think I would have danced with Amy all night for a generous slice of one of those famous cherry pies.

"What I wouldn't give for a piece of that cherry pie," BB drooled.

I nodded. Jefferson merely growled, "Don't count on it. They always let the girls go first."

"I hate being a gentleman," BB muttered.

"By the time we get there, all that'll be left will be Sister Briggs's old apple pie."

"I didn't know Sister Briggs made apple pie," I said.

Jefferson shook his head in disgust. "She doesn't. It's just a rough imitation. You're never sure if she's used last year's potatoes or this year's sawdust. It's not worth waiting around for, that's for sure."

"Well," I retorted, "if anyone thinks I showed up to this cattle stomp just for a slice of Sister Briggs's imitation apple pie, they're crazy. We came and we've suffered right along with everyone else. We've suffered a heck of a lot more than the girls. They kinda like this tromping around. The least they could do is let us have our choice of pie."

"You get near that table," Jefferson said, "and one of the old fogies will chop your fingers off."

"There's got to be a way," BB said.

Just then I spotted Timmy Turley and got an idea. "I think there just might be a way," I stated smugly, "if we can just smuggle Timmy outside."

We ditched the three girls and cornered Timmy.

"You know where the main electrical switch to the building is, don't you?" I demanded.

"Huh?" He gaped at us.

"The switch—do you know where the main switch is?"

"You mean the one on the other side of the basketball court?"

"That's the one. You'll have to climb over that fence to get at it."

"What you guys talking about?"

"There's a pie in this for you," I explained.

"I can get my own piece of pie right here," he said, backing away from us. "You guys will get me in trouble."

I grabbed him by the arm. "I didn't say *piece* of pie," I replied. "I said *pie*. Whole pie, all to yourself. Your choice. Any pie on the table is yours. You just point it out to us."

"Any one except the big one in the middle," BB added. "That one's spoken for."

"I don't want to steal a pie," Timmy protested.

Jefferson smiled. "We just want you to throw the main switch. We'll do the rest. And you get a pie for your trouble. Which pie?"

Timmy looked at us, then at the table of pies. "How about the blackberry on the end," he said hesitantly.

"The one with the fancy design?" I asked. He nodded. "It's yours. Want any ice cream?"

Timmy shrugged. "Sure, I guess. Is that extra?"

I held up my hands. "It's all in the bargain. Throw the switch and then count to one hundred, real slow. Then throw it back on."

"And you get a whole blackberry pie for your trouble," Jefferson added.

"But how do I get out of here?" Timmy asked, looking at the guarded doors.

"We'll get you out. You just throw the switch," I said.

While Jefferson, BB, and I acted as a screen in front of one of the windows, little Timmy Turley crawled out of the cultural hall into the black night. As soon as he was safely on his way, the three of us began ambling toward the refreshment table.

"You grab the blackberry," BB said to me, "and I'll get the cherry."

I stopped and faced BB and Jefferson. "As long as we're going to pull this off, let's pull it off good. We'll take the whole works."

"Everything?" the other two gasped.

"Even the kettle of punch," I said, grinning.

In fifteen seconds I explained my revised plan to BB and Jefferson. Then the lights died. All the windows in the cultural hall faced west and there were no street lights on that side of the building, so as soon as the main switch was thrown, the cultural hall was drenched in darkness.

The three of us flew into action immediately. While Jefferson ran interference, dashing about the room shouting, pushing, pinching, banging metal chairs, and causing all the commotion he could in the dark, BB and I groped our way to the refreshment table. The whole room exploded into shouts and squeals. Bishop Williams's deep voice thundered above the bedlam, "Everyone be calm. Calm! It's just a blackout," but everyone ignored him and the blind confusion heightened.

"Get some candles," someone shouted.

"Everybody stand still and stop shoving."

"This screaming must stop!" a woman screamed.

There was mass confusion, just what BB and I needed. The refreshment table was right in front of the stage. The curtains on the stage were drawn. We grabbed the ice cream and punch and shoved them under the curtains and then lifted the table up onto the stage and pushed it behind the curtains. We then hid everything behind last year's roadshow scenery, which was heaped in one corner of the stage. The pilfering was effected in a matter of thirty smooth seconds.

As soon as BB and I finished our work, I whistled shrilly, my signal to Jefferson, and the three of us bumped our way through the screaming, panicky mob and calmly took our places on the opposite end of the cultural hall, as far from the scene as we could get. As soon as we sat down, caught our breath, and masked our faces in beatific innocence, the lights blinked on.

Almost immediately the screaming and shouting changed to nervous laughter. There was a chorus of chatter for a moment, and then suddenly a silence that was almost deafening descended over the hall. All eyes in the room were riveted to the spot in front of the stage where the refreshment table had been only moments before.

For the longest time no one uttered a word. Then the most singular phenomenon occurred. As though the whole movement had been rehearsed many times before, all eyes left the mysterious spot, drifted about the room in a frantic search, and then fell with heavy suspicion upon BB, Jefferson, and me. We sat frozen in our chairs with our legs crossed and our arms folded, and returned the stares with bold indifference.

Suddenly the silence was shattered as Sister Hollingsworth stomped toward us and shrieked, "All right, where is it?"

I pointed at myself. "You talking to us?"

"You know perfectly well who I'm talking to." She jabbed a trembling finger toward the stage. "Where's the refreshment table?"

"Are you accusing us?" I asked indignantly, standing and facing the menacing mob. Everybody nodded, even down to little Amy Thomas. I laughed weakly. "How could we walk out with a whole table loaded with pies?"

"We've been sitting here," BB whined, appearing hurt by the accusation.

"That's the first bit of evidence against you," Sister Briggs called out, stepping forward to join Sister Hollingsworth. "That's the most abnormal thing that's happened all night. You've never once sat through a blackout without pulling something."

"But we ain't done nothing wrong all night!" BB insisted, brushing his hair from his eyes.

"That's right." Sister Briggs smiled. "No girls were tripped tonight, you didn't try to break into the bishop's office to retrieve your basketball, you didn't play hockey with one of the girls' shoes during the Virginia reel, and there weren't any water balloons. Apparently, that was just the calm before the storm."

I shook my head. "I can't believe this," I said, doing my best to chuckle, but my laugh was a little shaky. "How could we possibly make off with a whole table full of pies? I mean, be realistic."

Brother Hill shook his head and sighed deeply. "I have no idea, DJ," he muttered. "I don't even want to know. The whole scheme would probably be too complex for my middle-age mind."

Jefferson stood up. "I'll admit we've pulled some tricks in the past," he confessed. "But does our past condemn us now?"

"Didn't he give us this same argument last summer when all the watermelons for the watermelon bust came up missing?" Brother Smith asked. "I even remember believing him that time. Then we found them down by the creek gorging themselves on the hearts of our eight watermelons."

The three of us blushed a deep purple.

"And what about the time last winter when . . . ."

"All right," the bishop's deep voice called out, "let's not dredge up the past." He came forward and stood before us. "DJ, why don't you just bring back the pies. We'll call this whole thing a mistake and try to forget about it. Like the other times," he added wearily under his breath.

"Bishop, you don't really believe we did this?" BB asked, his mouth dropping open.

The bishop looked at the floor. "We won't go into what I believe. Let's just get the pies."

"But, bishop, we don't have the pies," BB pleaded. "Search us."

The bishop turned to Jefferson. "Jefferson, did you take the pies?"

Jefferson sighed sadly, and for a moment I thought he was going to make a full confession and condemn us all. "Bishop," he said, his voice full of fake emotion, "I didn't touch those pies. I wasn't even near that table. That's a promise. And I didn't see who did take them."

"Nobody saw who did," the bishop said. "The whole place was pitch black."

"I didn't touch those pies," Jefferson repeated, "and I didn't see who did, but as long as you're looking for somebody to pin it on, I'll accept the blame."

"We don't want a confession," Brother Hill growled. "We don't want you to play the martyr. All we want is the pies."

The mob was pressing toward us, and I suddenly had the distinct impression that I smelled burning tar and chicken feathers coming from the kitchen. No one was smiling. In the past we had at least coaxed a chuckle from the Scouts. They usually had a greater appreciation for our tactics and humor, but there were no friends among that group this night.

Just then, over the heads of the pressing crowd, I spotted Timmy Turley. He was looking on in confusion, having no idea what had happened, but knowing BB, Jefferson, and me well enough to know that he didn't want to venture into the cultural hall and associate himself with us.

"Okay," I called out, pushing through the crowd toward Timmy, "we'll take responsibility for the whole thing, but everybody will have to help look for the pies. Everybody look," I commanded. "They can't be far."

By then I had my arm around Timmy's shoulders. Out of the corner of my mouth I muttered so that only he could hear, "Throw the switch! Quick!" Then, so all could hear, I shouted, "Let's search this whole building! That table's got to be here someplace. Timmy," I said, pushing him toward the back door, "you check outside."

BB and Jefferson suddenly grasped my intentions and scrambled toward me. Our only hope was to return the table as soon as possible. I definitely didn't want to have the infamous distinction of being the first casualty of a Snowflake Mutual party.

Just when it appeared our cause was lost, Timmy hit the main switch and, cloaked in darkness, the three of us raced for the stage while everyone else began shouting at once.

"Don't let them go."

"Somebody grab them."

"If they get out of here we'll never see those pies."

"Somebody light a candle."

"Lock the doors."

Ignoring the shouts behind us, we leaped up on the stage, ducked under the curtains, and tore away the roadshow scenery.

"Just a second," Jefferson panted. "Let's take Sister Hatch's cherry pie." He groped about the table and then grunted, "I got it. I'll set it right outside the window on the ledge."

BB and I grabbed the two buckets of ice cream and pushed them under the stage curtains while Jefferson lugged the kettle of pink lemonade and set it on the edge of the stage. BB and I then raced back for the table. We each grabbed an end while Jefferson held up the curtain for us.

It was so dark, however, that we couldn't see where Jefferson was standing holding up the curtain; consequently, we charged blindly, hoping we'd hit the opening. Instead, we plunged into the curtains to the left of him. That wouldn't have been too bad, but just as I got to the edge of the stage, I stepped into one of the buckets of ice cream. Though I almost stumbled and fell, I did manage to catch myself in time; however, at the same moment BB's head got tangled in the curtains. He became frantic and jerked himself free, only to stumble forward and smash into the kettle of lemonade, knocking it off the stage. There was a loud clatter as the kettle plunged to the hardwood floor. A muffled splash followed as gallons of pink lemonade washed across the floor in a wave.

BB teetered on the edge of the stage, desperately fighting for balance. He might have been able to save himself had Jefferson not charged through the curtains to see what was happening. He bumped BB, sending him tumbling to the floor. As he fell over the edge, he dropped his end of the table. I tried to steady the tilting table, but with my foot in a bucket of ice cream, my attempt was futile. I heard the horrible scraping of pie tins as they slid across the table and then the sickening splat as they fell to the floor three feet below.

Forgetting about BB's plight, I realized my only chance was to make it to the window on the stage, take Sister Hatch's pie, and race to safety. But our cause was lost, and I with it. When I had told

Timmy "Quick," he had misunderstood me. Just as I was about to dive under the stage curtains, the lights blazed and our crime was bathed in a humiliating light.

All eyes were riveted to the three of us. BB lay on his back in a huge puddle of pink lemonade. My right shoe was milky with melted ice cream, and I was still grasping one end of the table. Jefferson stood a few feet away from me, gaping down at the mushy pile of demolished pies.

Slowly BB sat up and pushed himself to his feet, shaking the lemonade from his hands and trying to brush away the lemonade that had soaked into his shirt and pants. He gulped and faced the glowering Mutual mob slowly inching toward us.

"We found the refreshment table," BB grinned, his face a sickly yellow under his red hair. "Somebody stuck it up on the stage. We were up there looking around . . ."

"BB," I called out, stopping him before he went any further. He looked up at me and then at Jefferson. Both Jefferson and I, our faces white and pinched with apprehension, shook our heads. I cleared my throat and tried to explain. "It was just a little joke," I rasped. "I mean, we're sorry. You don't think we *wanted* this to happen, do you?"

Sister Hollingsworth crept over to the pile of pies, being careful not to step into the punch or pastry. She didn't say anything, just stared, the horror of the sight darkening her every feature.

The bishop was the first to speak. He moved between us and the rest of the Mutual and announced forcefully, "Nothing can be helped now. Nothing anyone can say will bring anything back." He glanced at us and then back at the others. "Everyone move out to the basketball court. I think there's still a little more punch in the kitchen. Maybe even a pie or two."

No one moved for a moment. The bishop moved toward them, his arms spread wide, and called, "Come on, let's move on outside while the boys clean up their mess."

When the cultural hall was finally empty except for the bishop and the three of us, Bishop Williams pointed to the left door of the cultural hall and said, without looking at us, "The janitor's closet is down the hall. There are some buckets and mops there."

"We're sorry," I said, my voice cracking slightly.

The bishop held up a hand for silence. Wagging his head, he responded, "Don't say anything. Please, don't say anything. Just clean up the mess as soon as possible, and we'll hope the floor doesn't warp."

The bishop left, and the three of us stared down at the disaster smeared on the cultural hall floor. BB finally broke our shocked silence. "Do you think any of them pies would still be good? I mean the ones on top, the ones that aren't on the floor. Like that apple pie there. It looks in pretty good shape."

"That's Sister Briggs's pie," Jefferson grumbled.

"Dang!" BB groaned. "Hers would be the one saved."

"I think we'd better get this mess cleaned up," I cautioned, "and forget about eating pies. I think we've done it this time. I think we'd be hanging from the rafters right now if the bishop hadn't herded everyone out of here."

"But we didn't mean to," BB whined. "I mean, we were trying to put everything back. We didn't want this to happen. We just wanted Sister Hatch's . . ." He grinned widely. "Hey, we still have our pie. We saved the best one. Let's hurry and get this mess taken care of and then go have some cherry pie."

"I'm not touching that pie," I countered, getting a little irritated by BB's cold attitude. "We'll take it right out there for the others to eat. That's the least we can do."

"You mean give it back?" BB gasped, his mouth dropping open incredulously. "After all we've been through?"

"I wouldn't touch that pie," Jefferson stated. "For the next day or so we'd better lay kinda low."

Armed with buckets, mops, and old rags, we attacked the puddle of punch and pile of pie. BB and I clawed the pie off the floor with our hands and dropped it into plastic garbage bags while Jefferson slopped the mop about the floor to soak up the punch. It really wasn't a big job because everything was in one place, but it was sticky and messy, and it about killed us to see all that good pie go to waste.

After we had cleaned up the biggest part of the mess and all that was left to do was to wipe off the floor with a clean wet mop, I returned to the janitor's closet to rinse out my mop and get a clean bucket of water. The closet door closed behind me, and a moment later, just as I was about to leave, the bishop, Brother Hill, and Sister Hollingsworth came down the hall discussing BB, Jefferson, and me in subdued voices. Nervously grasping my clean mop and bucket, I stood and listened.

"Bishop, something has to be done about them," Sister Hollingsworth insisted. "I used to think it was a stage that they would outgrow, but that was years ago. When I had them in Primary, I promised myself that as long as I taught them I wouldn't say anything bad about them. But every time I turned around I was biting my tongue to keep back the negative comments. Finally I had to be released. My tongue was chewed to hamburger."

"Granted," the bishop said, "they are a little mischievous."

"So that's what they are," Sister Hollingsworth cried. "Did you know that I had the chair jerked out from under me three times, once by each of them? And each time they gave the same innocent pitch they tried tonight: 'It was just a little joke, Sister Hollingsworth.'"

"Sister Hollingsworth is right," Brother Hill corroborated. "I've had the Explorers for five years. I loved it—until those three came. I shudder every time I contemplate an overnighter—or an evening at the church, for that matter. It's one travesty after another. I mean they're habitual. It just comes natural for them. They can't seem to help themselves."

"Bishop," Sister Hollingsworth cut in, "it's almost sacrilegious to let them in the church."

"But they're not bad," the bishop defended us. "They come to church, they're not Word of Wisdom problems, they haven't started dating before they're supposed to, they—"

"There isn't a girl that would go with them," Sister Hollingsworth cut in. "That's what the Mia Maids say."

I could hear the bishop sigh. "I know they get into trouble, but there's an aura of innocence about them."

"Innocence!" the other two gasped.

"Well, maybe it is a corrupted form of innocence," the bishop admitted, "but they're not malicious. They're not intent on making life miserable for everyone."

"It doesn't matter what their intent is," Brother Hill retorted. "The fact is they *do* make life miserable for everyone."

"What I'm saying," Bishop Williams tried again, "is they're not *bad* bad. They're not hardcore bad. Sure, they'll take off with refreshments, torment the girls, or disturb a Sunday School class, or—"

"Do you realize how many Sunday School teachers they've been through in the last year?" Sister Hollingsworth demanded.

The bishop cleared his throat. "Sister Hollingsworth, I call those teachers."

"I hear you have to almost bribe whoever takes the class."

"Oh, I don't know if it's that bad."

"Well, Martha Bushman told me she'd go completely inactive before facing that Sunday School class."

"Well, they've had a hard time," the bishop pointed out. "DJ doesn't have a mom, and his dad has a terrible work schedule at the paper mill. Jefferson's parents are divorced, and he's been left with his aunt and uncle. And BB—well, I'm not sure what BB's problem is."

"He's just BB," Sister Hollingsworth said dryly. "That's all the excuse he needs."

"But I can't help thinking that there's some good under all their tricks and carelessness."

"I'm afraid the good—if there really is any—is buried too deep. No one will ever get at it," Sister Hollingsworth predicted.

"I'm sure if we try hard enough there's a way to find the good in them. There's potential there. Anybody who could make off with a table full of pies without anyone seeing them—well, there's capability there."

"Bishop," Sister Hollingsworth sighed, "I believe in miracles, even big miracles, but not fantasy. And what you're talking about is pure fantasy."

"Oh, I don't know, Sister Hollingsworth. But I guess we won't solve anything tonight. We'd better see how the rest of the Mutual is doing. Were there enough refreshments to keep everybody happy?"

"Brother Smith went down to the Frost-top for some more ice cream, and we made more punch. Sister Hatch has been keeping everybody busy with some games. I think we've taken the kids' minds off this other."

The voices soon faded as the three continued down the hall, and I sneaked out of the closet. I was quiet when I returned to BB and Jefferson.

When the floor was finally clean, Jefferson said, "All right, let's go get that pie and take it out."

"Can't we have part of it?" BB groaned.

Jefferson and I didn't even answer. We went up on the stage to the window and Jefferson groped about on the ledge. "I know I put it right here," he mumbled. "I wonder if someone else found it. Do you think Timmy came back here and . . ." Suddenly Jefferson cried out, "Get out of here, you mangy, dirty mutt! Give me something to throw. The pie must have slipped off, and that black and white stray dog's down below. He's eating our pie!" Without another word Jefferson tumbled from the window. A dog yelped and then Jefferson muttered, "Dang!"

"Is it messed up?" I hissed out the window.

"Messed up?" Jefferson growled. "He ate the whole thing. He was just licking the pie tin clean."

"You mean it's gone?" BB almost choked. "Wait till I find that thieving mutt. How low can a dog get, to steal the last pie we got!"

Muttering angrily, BB and I pulled Jefferson back into the building and returned to the cultural hall with the empty pie tin just as Sister Hollingsworth came in. Her mouth dropped open as she saw the empty pie tin in Jefferson's hand. It took us a moment to realize what conclusion she had drawn.

All three of us started shaking our heads furiously. "It isn't like you think," Jefferson stuttered, pointing down at the empty pie tin with a trembling finger.

"Yeah," BB added, his face suddenly white. "Some dirty dog just ate it."

"How about three dirty dogs," she suggested, her eyes blazing, her lips drawn tight, her hands on her hips.

I knew there was no use explaining. Our credibility, if we'd ever had any, had faded into nothing after our night's escapade. I reached for the pie tin, handed it to the simmering Sister Hollingsworth, and said with humble resignation, "Sorry about all this." Then, with Jefferson and BB tripping along behind me, I headed for the door.

The air was dark and cool outside the building as we headed for home. It felt good to be away from the stuffy confinement of the cultural hall. Basking in the knowledge that we had really escaped with our lives, we walked in silence until we reached Jefferson's place. We dropped down on the lawn, and for a long time we just lay back and stared up at the misty canopy of stars. It was peaceful, so unlike what we were accustomed to.

"I'm still hungry," BB complained.

"There's always Old Man Harrison's melon patch," Jefferson suggested.

"I don't think we're riding a lucky streak tonight," I remarked forlornly. "Maybe we better just let things settle down."

"It's my dad's fault," BB grunted. "I didn't want to go in the first place."

"I guess that's what you're going to go home and tell him?" Jefferson sneered.

"Well, not exactly."

I turned over and asked the other two, "Do you guys think we're bad?"

"Us?" BB asked, genuinely surprised. "What've we done?"

Jefferson chuckled. "I don't know if we can help it. I mean, we've always been like this. Maybe not as bad as tonight. People wouldn't know how to treat us if we reformed. Can you just see Brother Hunt giving his Sunday School lesson without some help from us? I think he has his 'Sit down and shut up' built right into his lesson. He only prepares fifteen minutes of lesson. We're the ones that stretch it out for him. Besides, I'd probably feel like a stranger if I changed too much."

"Do you think we could reform?" I ventured hesitantly, re-membering the conversation I had overheard. "I mean, if we really wanted to."

"I'd sure like one of Old Man Harrison's melons," BB groaned.

Jefferson cleared his throat. "I guess we could if there was a good reason. Sometimes I think about it. But," he added quickly, almost angrily, "it would take a heck of a lot more to reform me than old Sister Hollingsworth sticking her nose up and hollering at us."

"What do you think it would take?" I asked, much more serious than I was accustomed to being.

Jefferson laughed weakly. "That's a good question, but I really don't think we'll find the answer tonight."

## Chapter Two

THE NEXT DAY WAS FRIDAY, August 29, 1966. The day settled on us like a plague. Our disaster of the night before had already been wagged about the town on the tips of a hundred gossiping tongues, but as we lay on Jefferson's lawn, we didn't have time to concern ourselves with past mistakes and public opinion. Now, all our thoughts were riveted painfully to the discouraging reality that come Tuesday, the day after Labor Day, we were to abdicate our freedom and return to the drudgery—the terrible enslavement— of the public school, a place where dreams were squelched, whims like ours frowned upon, and all idleness and mischief supposedly banished to a future and far-distant summer.

"It wouldn't be half bad," mused BB with a blade of grass protruding from his mouth, "if we wasn't going to be sophomores. Just when we was used to being the big guys at school. Now it's back to the bottom of the pile."

Jefferson and I nodded.

For a whole year we three had ruled supreme at the junior high. We had swaggered down the halls, the girls eyeing us longingly. At least we had convinced ourselves that they did. Our appeal was not necessarily the result of our singular charm, good manners, or comeliness. There just wasn't much to choose from. In the big towns and cities, away from our little community, we might have been average or below, but here, where competition was minimal to nonexistent, no one could be too choosy. We were it. Or at least we had been.

Snowflake High School was another hierarchy, another world, and in that world sophomores, especially sophomore boys, didn't count for much, bordering between the subhuman and the peon. The seniors, especially the senior boys, reigned with impunity. For the most part, the sophomores' responsibility was to become inconspicuous, a real challenge for us after junior high, where we had attempted to be as visible as possible.

"I wish there was some way we could go to high school without being sophomores," Jefferson whined. "It's going to be just like being creepy seventh graders again." He stamped his foot angrily. "Do you think the seniors will do much to us the first week of school? I hear that's the worst time."

"Sharon said they make you carry their books, open doors for them, and shine their shoes," I volunteered as I pulled at a blade of grass and laid it on my tongue. "She said a little of that would do us three good. I told her to mind her own business."

"Last year they made Matt Harris push his books down the hall with his nose," Jefferson reported. "People kept stepping on him and tripping over him."

"Why'd he do it?" BB asked, his question an indignant protest.

"He had to," I explained. "It was that or something worse."

"Sometimes they even sit you on the fountain," Jefferson whispered. "Right there in front of everybody. And they don't let you change. That's the way you go all day."

"Sometimes they do worse than just set you on the fountain," I added. "Last year after they finished with Sam Reed, he was wishing he had some pants to get wet."

We all shuddered and were silent for a moment.

"Maybe we'd better go in groups," BB suggested. "They wouldn't dare do anything to a gang of us."

"They'd be in groups too," I countered, "and besides, there's always a time when you're alone. If they think you're running from them, then they really lay for you, and good."

"I say we ditch the first week," BB said, glancing over at Jefferson and me. "After the first week, most of the bad stuff's over."

Jefferson shook his head. "I'd rather face the whole senior class than face Uncle Roy if he ever caught me ditching. I might get away from the seniors, but Uncle Roy would catch me for sure. No thanks."

I nodded dejectedly. "Yeah, that goes for me too."

There we sat, pondering the awfulness of our fate. Then we saw Miss Willie for the first time. We had heard that a new teacher was moving in across the street from Jefferson's aunt and uncle, but we hadn't thought too much about it. We had heard that she was single and taught English. Anyone moving to Snowflake under those circumstances had to be at the end of the road. Only abject desperation would bring a single woman to that. The only step lower was suicide.

We already had one woman English teacher who was single. Miss Paine. Her name told just the beginning of the story. More horror stories involving Miss Paine circulated about the halls of Snowflake than ghost stories at Halloween. According to rumors she was an ornery, hard-skinned, heartless terror. No name created such dread in the hearts of the students as did Miss Paine's.

Even the seniors behaved themselves around Miss Paine. Oh, they would talk real big when she wasn't around and say how smart they'd acted in her class and how they'd told her what they would do and when they would do it, but those were all rumors and brags. Everybody knew it. In class it was all "Yes, ma'am" and "No, ma'am."

Barney Hunt tried to stand up to her once. The class was reading *Hamlet*. Miss Paine asked Barney to read the "To be or not to be" speech. Barney was a big senior who played fullback on the football team and was considered to be the biggest, meanest senior in the entire school. Well, he got it into his head that he didn't need any of that Shakespeare stuff, so when Miss Paine asked him to read, he closed his book, slumped down in his desk, and mumbled, "This here's dumb. I ain't going to read none of that. They don't even talk normal, all them *thee*s and *thou*s and *art*s."

The rest of the class went into a coma. No one breathed. No one moved. Miss Paine was standing at the front of the class with her book in her hand. She didn't do anything for a few seconds; then she glanced down at Barney. He stared back, as much as to say, "I won't, and you can't make me." His eyes glowered in defiance.

Miss Paine, without closing her book, walked from the front of the class to Barney's desk. The class shuddered as they watched this epic confrontation. Miss Paine stared down at Barney with her dark brown eyes and gave him her best glare, and she had some pretty powerful ones. Her stares could wilt rocks. Barney tried to stare back, but he didn't last long. Her eyes latched on to him and turned him inside out. He was soon twisting and turning and fumbling with his book and turning a deep embarrassing red.

"We're waiting, Mr. Hunt," she finally said, her voice precise. "We are *all* waiting. Would you like to proceed?"

"But this is so stupid and . . ."

"Mr. Hunt, we are waiting."

He tried to protest, but the fight was out of him and the showdown was over. He started to read—and he read until he was hoarse. Every time he stopped, he would look up and face those penetrating eyes and resume his reading. When she finally relieved him, she commented, not unkindly, "Mr. Hunt, when you have read *Hamlet* carefully and you feel as though you understand it, then you may say anything you want about it. Until that time, try to appreciate it."

Miss Paine gave more homework than any three teachers combined, and it wasn't just that silly stuff a lot of teachers assign. It was the hard kind, the kind that made you think until your head ached. She made you learn, whether you wanted to or not. Everybody worked. Everybody studied. Everybody passed. Because everybody knew that if a person didn't pass, the next year he had Miss Paine all over again.

Actually she wasn't really ugly or anything like that. She wasn't fat with straggly skirts and ratty hair and warts and moles all over her face. She didn't come to school on a broom, even though a lot of kids said she did. Actually, for an English teacher she wasn't even bad looking. I mean, if you didn't know what she was and you just saw her on the street someplace, you might think she was more on the pretty side. But she was old, at least thirty or thirty-five.

Well, with a person like Miss Paine around, it was no wonder that news of another single, female English teacher didn't generate any enthusiasm among us kids. If any interest was created at all, it was speculation on whether or not she would be as fearsome as Miss Paine.

While we had been pilfering pies the night before, Miss Willie had moved in, or at least partially moved in. Her front porch was now stacked with boxes.

As we sat on Jefferson's lawn, she came out on the porch and began rummaging through the boxes. She was wearing a faded flannel shirt with the sleeves rolled up, a pair of patched blue jeans, and some white tennis shoes. Her attire looked pretty ragged for a schoolteacher, but she livened it up plenty.

She was about five-four, shorter than any of us, and she didn't look much older. She had short brown hair that gave her a pretty, boyish look, but that boyish look was just a fleeting impression. Even from a distance, we could see that she was definitely a girl. Her grace and her feminine movements made that apparent.

Now, Snowflake wasn't made up of just homely honeys and hound dogs. There were some pretty good-lookers. There wasn't an overabundance, but there seemed to be enough to go around if everybody shared, traded off, and didn't get selfish. But quite frankly, Snowflake had never seen the likes of Miss Willie—and she taught English!

"That ain't the new teacher, is it?" BB asked, sitting up straight and squinting across the street. "Can't be. She don't look like no English teacher I ever seen. She don't look like *any* teacher I ever seen."

"She doesn't even look like any *girl* you've seen, BB," Jefferson remarked.

"Do you suppose it's her sister?" I asked, coming to my feet.

"No English teacher's got a sister like that," BB argued. "She don't look half mean enough."

"I'll go ask," I volunteered. "You guys wait right here."

I started across the street, but not alone. BB and Jefferson were tripping over my heels like a couple of frisky, frolicsome pups. We scrambled up the walk, each trying to gain the advantage over the other two, until we were almost ready to tumble into a heap on her front steps.

"Well, hello," we blurted out in unison as she looked up and saw our wild approach.

She looked down at us in a mild state of shock and then smiled widely and warmly. If she looked good from across the street, up close she looked absolutely wonderful. There was a natural curl to her hair that made it crowd about the edges of her face. Her skin was a creamy, smooth tan with just a little extra color in the cheeks. Her eyes were a dark brown, and they sparkled out between long eyelashes. And she didn't color them much. Just a touch. I suppose any more paint would have only detracted from those warm brown eyes. She had a short nose that wrinkled just a bit when she smiled. Her mouth had a pleasing, teasing pucker to it, and her whole face was properly punctuated by two faint dimples. She wasn't so beautiful that you were frightened off. Her beauty was quietly attractive, the kind that pleased and yet set you at ease.

"Good morning," she beamed gaily, displaying straight white teeth. "With whom do I have the pleasure?" Her dimples showed plainly, and her voice was gentle and pleasant and laced with traces of a smile. It really wasn't a smile you had to see; it was one you could hear and feel.

BB blushed purple, dug his clumsy fists into his pockets, and became a total mute. Jefferson, almost as embarrassed, managed to say, "How are you?" before ducking his head and toeing a pebble at his feet, completely overcome. I was our last hope, even though I was fidgeting like a flustered schoolboy before his first love. I stared down at her feet, noting how small and petite they seemed. Finally I managed to smile and respond as gallantly as I knew how. "I'm Daniel Johnson. Most people just call me DJ. That's BB with the red hair. Actually his real name is Bartholomew Bradley Bunderson, but that's enough name to choke anybody so we call him BB. The other one's Jefferson Judd. We'd call him JJ but his Aunt

Betty won't let us. He lives across the street with his Aunt Betty and Uncle Roy."

Miss Willie placed her hands on her hips, and I noticed how small her waist was. It looked as if I could put both my hands around it and overlap my fingers too. "I'm pleased to meet you," she exclaimed, making it sound like she really meant it, like meeting us was about the best thing that had happened to her in a long time. "I'm Kathy Willie. I'm going to be teaching school here."

"You really are the teacher then?" BB gasped. "You're not even her sister?"

Miss Willie wrapped her arms about herself and squeezed. "No, I'm the teacher." She laughed. "Surprised?"

Jefferson nodded dumbly, the shock registered all over his face.

"Why, you don't look any older than us," BB added bluntly. "You're just . . ."

"BB always gets flustered when he meets strangers," I butted in before BB could verbally stumble into another blunder. "What he means is that . . . well, you see . . . we've never seen a teacher in blue jeans, at least not a lady teacher."

"Oh, I've seen Mrs. Turley in blue jeans," BB blurted out, "but she ain't nearly as good-looking as this one."

"What he really means," I stammered, blushing down to the soles of my feet and trying to avert catastrophe, "is that you're a lot younger than most of the teachers we get around here."

"And that's not all," BB and Jefferson chimed in. Those two did everything but drool.

"Well, I'm flattered, to say the least," Miss Willie said. "I guess you young men are going to be seniors this year."

Our mouths dropped open. This was one person who obviously saw us as we saw ourselves. We pushed our chests out and stretched ourselves upward as much as we could and tried to appear as grown-up as we felt. BB shook his head and said with obvious embarrassment, "We might look like seniors, or even graduates, but we really ain't. We're just sophomores."

"But we are . . . well, we are quite . . ." I groped for the elusive word that would convey to Miss Willie our obvious precocity.

"You're very mature," Miss Willie proffered kindly, rescuing me from my meager vocabulary.

"Yes, we're mature for our age," I repeated.

"Very mature," Jefferson said with a slight nod of his head.

"I see. You would have fooled me." Miss Willie smiled. "For a moment I wondered if you might be the principal, the bishop, and home teacher coming to give me a welcome."

"We are here to welcome you," Jefferson said. "We knew you was coming and all, and we just dropped over to see how things are going. We like to make sure the teachers are comfortable."

"Why, thank you. If you men take such an interest in your teachers, you must really be enthusiastic about school." We all nodded furiously, a pink tinge of guilty embarrassment creeping onto our cheeks. "What is your favorite subject?"

We all glanced at each other.

"Oh, we like them all," Jefferson responded.

"All of them," I agreed.

"I really like English," BB lied blatantly. Snowflake folks had done some pretty outstanding things over the years—conquer the desert, make peace with the Indians, build a town from scratch—but learning English was not one of them. In fact, well-spoken English was definitely the rarest language spoken in town; no one excelled in English, and BB was the worst to come along. Whenever he opened his mouth, his tongue wallowed in illiteracy, making a person wonder if he had ever seen the inside of a classroom.

"What do you like about English?" Miss Willie inquired.

BB dug his fists deeper into his pockets until it looked as though he would soon burst their bottoms or pull his pants right off his hips. "Actually, I like it all. There ain't nothing better than English."

"Do you like literature?"

"Yeah. Gee, I love literature." BB scratched his head and asked, "Ain't that where you draw those lines and things and put words in the right place?"

Miss Willie smiled. "I believe you are thinking of diagramming sentences."

"Oh, yeah, I like that too. It's a little tricky though."

"Do you like Shakespeare?"

"Yeah, I really like doing that. I can't really remember how you do it because it's been a long time, but I remember it was sure fun. It's a lot like diagramming sentences, ain't it?"

"Shakespeare's a man," Jefferson whispered.

"Oh, that's right," BB beamed. "Ain't he the one that writes them westerns?"

"Well, I don't know if I would call him a western writer." Miss Willie smiled.

"Do you need any help?" I asked in an attempt to rescue BB from himself.

"I could use some help with these boxes," Miss Willie responded, her eyes twinkling with delight. "That is, if you young men don't have some other obligations to attend to."

The three of us attacked the boxes. When they were put away, we started moving furniture around. From there we went to the yard, asking Miss Willie about every little thing that had to be done so that she would always be near. We made a valiant effort to sound literate and well informed so as to impress her; at least Jefferson and I did. BB was a total disaster. His *ain't*s and his *it don't*s showed him for the Snowflake illiterate he was. Jefferson had had the proddings of a strict grammarian aunt, and Sharon, who had learned her English in Eagar, Arizona, under the tutelage of my mother, had hounded me into semiliteracy and had pounced mercilessly on my careless slips of the tongue. Fortunately for Jefferson and me, we were able to recall some of those loathed corrections and polish up our speech and make a semblance of literacy, although it was terribly shallow. We slipped occasionally, but for the most part we were able to haltingly express ourselves and sound as though we had at least passed through a schoolroom, though it was obvious we had not spent our most productive moments there.

At last there was nothing more to do except bid Miss Willie good-bye and be gone. We left, amazed that there really was such a teacher like Miss Willie. We suddenly realized there was a distinct possibility some teachers might be human.

That afternoon the three of us lay quietly under an elm tree on the church lawn. That was where we generally retired in the hot hours of the afternoon to sleep, to plan our evening's escapades, or to contemplate any idea or philosophy that might meet our fancy. On this particular afternoon, after we had spent our entire morning with the educated Miss Willie, our thoughts naturally turned toward philosophy, or at least to as much philosophy as we were capable of.

BB in his characteristically blunt way broached the subject for us. "You know, girls our age are sure dumb." Jefferson and I nodded and made BB's motion unanimous. "They just . . . well, you know, they're so . . ."

"Silly," Jefferson said.

"Immature," I added, remembering Miss Willie's word. "I'll be glad to go to high school and have them chase the seniors and juniors. It'll be good to have them off our backs. And to think we used to like that kind of thing."

We all shuddered.

"Actually, I like girls to be like Miss Willie," BB blurted out. "Do you guys figure we'll get her for a teacher?"

Jefferson and I were silent for a moment, and then I answered, the disappointment apparent. "Miss Paine teaches most of the sophomores."

"Well, I guess we can say hello to her in the halls," BB sighed.

"She did say she was going to teach one class of Mexican," Jefferson pointed out. "If we took Mexican, we'd be sure to get her."

"Yeah, but who wants to go through that just to have a certain teacher, even if it is Miss Willie?" I asked. "That would be like cutting your hand off just to steal a cookie. I don't know English good enough. I sure don't want to try Mexican."

We were silent for a while and then BB pensively posed what would have been, under other circumstances, an unaskable question: "Have you guys ever thought about getting married?" He attempted to be profound but was merely absurd; however, in our present euphoric state Jefferson and I didn't notice. He sat up and looked over at the startled looks on our faces and then tried to clarify himself as best he could. "I don't mean right now. You know, we're still kind of young."

"Miss Willie thought we were quite . . . what was that she called us?" Jefferson inquired.

"Mature." I savored the word. "You know, she really is right."

BB smiled dreamily. "We really are older than we are." The smile faded. "What I mean is, do you guys ever think of getting married? I mean, what kind of girl do you think you'll marry? Have you ever thought about it?"

Gazing blissfully upward, I placed my hands behind my head and commented, "Well, I don't want just anybody, that's for sure. I'm not sure any of the girls that's grown up here in Snowflake would be what I'm looking for. They're not . . . well, mature enough for my likings."

"You mean like Miss Willie?" BB asked.

Ignoring the question, I continued. "Actually, I'd like someone who was educated. She'd probably have to be—considering my own maturity—a few years older than me. You know, some men do marry older women. They're mostly guys that are old for their age, and I sure feel old for my age. You know, a lot of people really think I'm graduated and out of school. I'd also want a wife that was good-looking. Not gorgeous or anything like that. A girl doesn't have to be gorgeous to be okay. Some of your gorgeous ones are real snots, but I'd want a beautiful girl. There's no getting me wrong there."

BB, who was less subtle than Jefferson or I, nodded in agreement and added, "Yeah, that's the kind of girl I'd like. Someone just like Miss Willie."

None of us would have admitted it then, but the three of us had fallen in love—with a teacher, no less. If anyone had ever told us that it was possible to even like a teacher, we'd have considered them utterly insane. But we had never before met anyone like Miss Willie. There was an attraction there that we didn't really comprehend. It was magical in a way, as though she'd been sent to Snowflake just for us, to satisfy a mutual need on all of our parts.

Before the day was over, we made three more visits to Miss Willie, always being as highbrowed as we knew how, which probably bordered between the inane and the ludicrous. Though our

reasons for returning were probably blatantly obvious, we con-
cocted excuses to mask our hungry looks, anything from offers to
give her the grand tour of the town, which she deferred until the
next day, to an offer to run to the store for anything. Seeing our determination to be of assistance, she sent us to the store for a quart
of milk, a loaf of bread, and a pound of butter. We ran the three
blocks to the store and then fought among ourselves to determine
who would carry what. Though the meager purchase fit nicely in a
paper sack, we discarded the sack and divided the three articles
among us so we could all share in this altruistic act.

Each time we left her place, we went down under the elms on
the church lawn and thought. Or shall I say dreamed? We had felt
many things during our fifteen years, but nothing so enrapturing
and powerful as what consumed us now.

## Chapter Three

THE NEXT MORNING, shortly before seven, BB, Jefferson, and I converged on the Judds' lawn to wait for Miss Willie to stir. BB arrived with his hair plastered down and a part carefully carved on the left side, a part that was actually straight! Ever since BB had grown too big for his mom to wrestle him to the ground, I hadn't seen his hair combed with such precision.

"What's the occasion?" I asked, staring at his watered-down hair. "You going to church or something?"

He shrugged casually as though there were nothing unusual about his appearance. "No occasion," he replied. He was walking with his neck and back rigid and doing his best to dodge every puff of wind that threatened to dislodge one of his carefully placed hairs. "What we got planned for today?" he asked, careful not to look across the street toward Miss Willie's.

"Oh, I thought we'd play a hard game of basketball," I teased with a straight face.

BB flinched and ran his hand lightly across his hair. "Basketball! Who wants to play basketball? I thought we was going to give Miss Willie the tour."

Jefferson suddenly groaned and said, "Oh, I forgot my . . . a . . . I'll be right back."

Jefferson was gone ten minutes, and when he returned his hair was plastered to his scalp. Big beads of water were still dripping down the sides of his head and onto his shoulders, and he smelled so strong of Old Spice that BB and I had to step back a pace just to breathe.

"Did you leave any for your Uncle Roy?" I asked, just a little irritated at both Jefferson and BB.

"Leave him any what?" Jefferson asked innocently.

"You're just supposed to splash on a couple of drops, not bathe in it."

Jefferson ignored me, walked stiff-legged over to BB, and sat down, keeping his head perfectly level.

"Well," I grumbled, "I forgot to brush my teeth. Be right back."

"Brush your teeth?" Jefferson asked.

"Yeah," I said defensively. "What's wrong with brushing my teeth?"

"Nothing, I guess, but we're just sitting around, not doing a Crest commercial."

"Let me worry about my teeth," I snapped. "You just worry about the wind blowing your hair." Turning, I headed for home.

Five minutes later I was locked in our bathroom dumping Skin Bracer all over me. I longed for something a little more exotic, but Dad had always been too practical for any of that fancy cologne or after-shave. I put my head under the tap and let the water run for half a minute and then attacked my dripping mop with a comb. Seeing Dad's electric shaver on the back of the toilet, I plugged it in and ran it over my jaw a few times. Just in case. I spotted a half bottle of mouthwash in the top of the medicine cabinet and rinsed my mouth out several times. When I returned the empty bottle to the shelf, my mouth was numb and my eyes were watering, but I was sure my breath was safe.

Jefferson and BB jabbed each other in the ribs when they saw me, and Jefferson called out, "Get your teeth brushed?"

I could feel my cheeks color. "I decided to use mouthwash instead," I answered lamely without looking at either one of them.

For the next thirty minutes we sat on Jefferson's lawn staring across the street at Miss Willie's house like it was our first good meal in a month. I doubt a flake of paint could have peeled off the walls without our detecting it.

"Do you suppose we ought to go knock?" BB asked after a long silence.

"What for?" I asked.

"Well, I don't know. Maybe to see if she's okay. We sure wouldn't want nothing to happen to her."

"The only thing that might be wrong with her is that she's still asleep," Jefferson mumbled, "and I sure don't want to be the one to wake her up."

"How long's she going to sleep?" BB whined.

"It's Saturday morning," I explained. "Lots of people sleep in."

"Well, some people sleep past noon," BB declared.

"That's right," Jefferson replied matter-of-factly.

"Are we staying that long?" BB asked, almost as if he was lodging a protest.

I leaned back and stretched. "Nobody has to stay," I said. "If you want to go, if you got something important to do, Jefferson and I can show Miss Willie the town."

"I'm staying," he muttered.

We continued our early-morning vigil, chomping a mountain of grass, gnawing our fingernails, and chewing our lips in anticipation. Finally, a little after eight-thirty, the drapes in Miss Willie's front window jerked open, which the three of us took to be our personal invitation.

Jumping to our feet, brushing the wrinkles from the seat of our pants, and gingerly touching our hair one last time, we all charged across the street and began hammering on Miss Willie's door.

Miss Willie opened the door a crack and stood behind it, craning around to see us. Her hair was wet, stringy, and uncombed, her face completely washed of makeup. She was dressed in a bathrobe, obviously having just come from the shower.

At first she just stared, too shocked, I suppose, to offer a greeting. Then she smiled and glanced around and shrugged with a touch of embarrassment. "I don't think I have any more work for you to do right now. You were really quite thorough yesterday."

"Oh, we're not here for no work," BB said, blushing. "We just come by to take you on your tour."

"Tour?"

"Yeah. Remember we offered to show you the town. You said it would be better to go today. You're coming with us, ain't you?"

She hesitated, just for a moment but long enough to flood our faces with disappointment. She must have sensed how crushing her hesitation was, because she smiled and asked, "Can you give me thirty minutes?" She pushed a strand of wet hair from her eyes. "I wasn't expecting you quite so early."

"Snowflake's beautiful in the morning," Jefferson explained.

"Yeah," I added, "we wanted to let you see it when it's at its best."

"Well, we'd better see it before it gets too late, then. I'll try not to keep you waiting."

Mesmerized, the three of us nodded, backed slowly across the street to Jefferson's yard, and waited, the excitement overpowering. Thirty minutes later, with her hair dried and combed, her robe replaced by tan slacks and a yellow cotton blouse, and her face touched lightly with makeup, Miss Willie came out for her grand tour. The three of us rushed across the street to crowd around her, each vying for a coveted place by her side.

Actually, Snowflake was not the kind of community that lent itself to grand tours—or any other tour, for that matter. The Mormons had settled on this lonely piece of desert in 1878, at a time when Mormon groups were tenaciously wrenching other communities from deserts, rocky hillsides, and swamps. It seemed that if the trappers, the cowboys, the Indians, and the jackrabbits had abandoned a place as too drab and uninviting, then the Mormons pounced on it, sweat, prayed, and wept over it until it blossomed. Never having seen this land before the Mormon pioneers chanced upon it, I had always assumed that Snowflake was still in the sweating, praying, and weeping stage, but on this particular Saturday morning I was dying to show it all to Miss Willie.

"Shall we take my car?" Miss Willie offered, pointing toward an old beat-up Ford parked on the street. It was a rusty, faded maroon.

The rear bumper sagged on the left side, and there was a dent on the right front fender. The underside of the car was pocked and corroded. A crack zigzagged down the rear window, and the door handle on the passenger side was missing. The only things about the car that looked new were the two front tires, which were probably worth more than the rest of the car.

"No need to take a car," Jefferson said. "You know, Snowflake's got lots to see, but it's all in one little place. You've got to see it on foot. If you drive around it in a car, you miss most of it."

I nodded, knowing that any car tour of Snowflake bordered on being arrogantly superfluous. Furthermore, if we walked, we had more time with Miss Willie.

"Besides," added BB, "that old bomb of yours don't look like it would make it around the block. It sure wouldn't make it around the town."

Miss Willie's eyebrows rose. "Are you implying that my car is a piece of junk?"

"Not exactly a piece of junk," BB answered. "Oh, no, it don't have nothing to do with your car being junk. But . . . well, you see, Snowflake's got lots of interesting things, including the world's biggest chuckholes. You could lose your bomb—I mean car—in one of them."

Miss Willie accepted BB's explanation with a smile.

This was the first time the three of us had ever bragged about Snowflake. We had complained many a time among ourselves, but we were puffed to popping with pride today, and it wasn't long before we were completely caught up in our boasting. We loved it!

"The first thing we gotta see is the store," Jefferson beamed as we strolled under the spreading branches of the cottonwoods and Chinese elms lining the streets. "Uncle Roy owns it," he added proudly.

"There's another one at the other end of town," BB pointed out. "Snowflake's got itself two food stores and a hardware store."

"But the other grocery store's not half as good as Uncle Roy's," Jefferson said in defense.

"The other one does have a kind of a snack bar," I added, wanting to give an honest picture.

40

"Well, who wants a snack bar in a store? Uncle Roy runs a store, not a restaurant. If he wanted—"

"I'm dying to see your Uncle Roy's store," Miss Willie cut in, smiling.

By then we were stepping into the parking lot. We bolted for the doors, which had been opened for business just a few minutes before. We burst inside, rushed past the two check-out stands, and began walking Miss Willie up and down the aisles.

"You can buy about anything here," Jefferson bragged.

"Can't get a burrito," BB mumbled.

"Who wants a burrito?" Jefferson snapped, glaring at BB. "This isn't a Taco Bell."

We showed Miss Willie everything from the stew meat at the meat counter to the Cheerios to the tissue paper. Jefferson even opened the cash register and showed her how much money was in the till.

Finally we left the store and headed for the bank. Being Saturday, it was closed, so we pressed our faces against the windows and pointed out the highlights.

"That's Clark Saunders's desk," BB said. "He's the president of the bank. He even drives a Cadillac, about the only one in town. It's two years old, but it was new when he got it."

"And that steel door goes to the vault," Jefferson explained. "Must have a couple thousand bucks in there. At least."

"More," BB argued. "Closer to three thousand."

"There are three teller cages," I gloated. "Just like a big city bank. Of course we only have one teller, Sally Goodman, but there's plenty of room to grow. If there was a rush on the bank, old Clark Saunders could take one of those cages and Fred Goodman the other—that's Sally's husband; he's the janitor—and this old bank could handle everybody in Snowflake."

"And the bank's already been robbed once," BB reported excitedly. "Two out-of-towners held the joint up. Got fifteen hundred bucks. Musta been one of the bank's big money days. But those two crooks didn't get away. They came running out of the bank to jump in their car, but old Fred Goodman, Sally's husband, had doubleparked his old Chevy pickup next to the get-away car, and Fred was in the bank lying on the floor with everybody else because those crooks told them if they moved they'd blow them full of holes." He took a quick breath, then raced on.

"Those two guys jumped into Fred's truck—he'd left the keys in it and the engine going—and they tried to move it. Well, as soon as they got in, here comes Bill Hancock, the deputy sheriff. Snowflake has its own deputy. Those crooks got scared and decided to split in Fred's bomb. They tried to peel out, but all they did was strip the gears, and there they was, sitting in the middle of Main, caught for sure."

"Goodness! Snowflake is a lively place," Miss Willie observed.

"Not exactly," I remarked. "That was the most excitement we've had, and that was ten years ago. We're too far outa the way for most big-time crooks to bother us."

"It would be nice," BB lamented, "if they came through a little more often to give the deputy something to do besides chase stray dogs and go down and drink pop at Dad's garage."

"And that across the street is the church," Jefferson called out, turning around and pointing. "That's where we go to church. It burned down a few years ago, when my Uncle Roy was just a kid, so Snowflake does get excitement pretty regular. And that old building on the other corner of the church block, well, that's the theater. We get lots of good movies down this way, even new ones, one *you* might even like. *Gone with the Wind* came a few years back. That's a pretty new one, isn't it?"

"It is a very good movie," Miss Willie said, seeming to be impressed.

"Let's take her to the post office," BB said.

From the post office we went to the feed-and-seed store and explained all that was available if she chose to raise beef or pigs. "Do you want to go inside?" BB asked. "They don't care none. You can watch them grind grain and stuff. It's pretty neat if you ain't seen nothing like that before. It's a little dusty, but it don't stink or nothing."

Miss Willie looked at the old building that was the feed-and-seed store. I'll have to admit that it looked like a good wind would send it tumbling to the ground. Miss Willie smiled and said, "I think I can get a pretty good idea of what it's like from here."

"The Frost-top's just down the street," I volunteered. "We'd stop and get you an ice cream or something, but two nights ago we got our funds cut off."

"Your funds cut off?" Miss Willie raised her eyebrows.

"Well," BB broke in, "we had a little trouble at Mutual, and word got back to our parents and Jefferson's aunt and uncle."

"We destroyed all the Mutual's pies," I said sheepishly, looking at the ground.

We hadn't meant to confess any of our sins to Miss Willie, but before we knew it we had explained the whole disaster. Miss Willie's lips twitched, and she pressed them together to fight back a smile, but soon it was too much for her and she was laughing.

"You think it's funny?" I asked, surprised. I could still visualize the angry stares of the Mutual, and somehow I hadn't associated anything humorous with the evening.

"Well, it is a little amusing," Miss Willie giggled. "I mean, it wasn't right. And you lost all the pies?"

"That old dog got Sister Hatch's," BB said, frowning. "That's the one I really felt bad about. But as soon as I see that mutt, the population of Snowflake is going to drop by one. That's for dang sure."

Miss Willie cleared her throat and fought back a smile. "I don't know if I can bake a cherry pie like Sister Hatch, but there are some people who say I make a mean banana-cream pie. Since you three have such a craving for pie, I'll make you one sometime."

"You'd do that for us?" I asked.

"Why, of course." She winked at me, and I almost fainted.

"We've just got to visit my dad's garage," BB said.

"What's there to see in an old service station?" Jefferson grumbled.

"A lot more than any old store."

"All there is is a bunch of—"

"I'd love to see your dad's garage, BB," Miss Willie said, ending the debate.

BB's dad was out pumping gas and checking a guy's oil, so the four of us just walked in the service station and BB acted as the knowledgeable guide. While we waded through grease, oil cans, and tools, BB praised everything from the socket wrench to the soda-pop machine.

"I'd give you all a soda," BB said, "but the machine's jammed and the repairman don't come till Tuesday. But," he added quickly, pointing to a stack of cases of pop, "if you want one of them that ain't cold, we got plenty." We all declined, but BB took himself up on the offer and began guzzling a warm root beer. He went over to a huge red tool cabinet, opened the doors, and declared, "I know the names of all them tools. Do you want me to name them for you?"

"We still have places to go," I whispered to him.

"If you want, I can give you all a ride on the hydraulic lift," he said.

"Maybe some other time we can come down and ride the lift," Miss Willie said, stepping over a patch of grease. "Why don't you show me the school?"

"We're going there last. We still got lots more to show you," Jefferson said.

Oh, we were proud of our little town that day. We showed her everything. It never occurred to us that Miss Willie had been to much larger communities—cities no less—and had seen single blocks with more commerce than all of Snowflake combined. In our backward, smug way we assumed we were opening a whole new world to her.

We finally ended at the high-school campus, a motley assortment of buildings ranging in age from the sixty-year-old stake academy to the gymnasium, which had been completed the year before. It really wasn't a campus that one would call beautiful, but we didn't know that. To us the high school represented the big world. Beauty was not a consideration there. The prestige of the place blinded us to any of its artistic deficiencies.

We gave her the tour of the football field, the track, and the baseball diamond. "We got a lot here," I explained. "A guy can get a good start right here in Snowflake. The three of us are going places."

"Yeah," BB bragged casually as we strolled across the football field. "We'll probably play for the pros when we get out of here."

"Football?" Miss Willie asked.

Jefferson shrugged. "Anything. Basketball, football, baseball. Whoever gives us the best offer."

"Do you think we can play for the pros, Miss Willie?" I asked.

She took a deep breath and glanced about the field. "I'm convinced a person can do anything he really wants to," she answered. "Some things take a lot of work, but if you want something bad enough and you work for it hard enough, it's yours."

When we had toured everything in town except the individual residences, we sat down in the football bleachers and rested.

"What do you think?" BB asked eagerly.

Miss Willie smiled and surveyed the town slowly as though she were savoring a new Eden. "It's nice."

"Some people think we're clear out in the boonies, that we don't have much here," I said with pride, "but you can see we got about everything a guy could want."

"We didn't even show you the rodeo grounds or the pig farms," Jefferson said, "but they're way out of town. They're a tour all by themselves."

"Is it as good as Salt Lake?" BB asked. Salt Lake City, we had learned, was where Miss Willie had grown up, gone to school, and taught for a year.

She took a deep breath and leaned back against the row of bleacher seats behind her. "Well, I'm not sure you can make a fair comparison. You see, they're so different from each other."

"Yeah, you're probably right," BB said. "It wouldn't be a fair comparison. Snowflake's got so many advantages, and big cities like Salt Lake are probably just a mess to live in."

"Well, I didn't mean it exactly like that."

BB's grin disappeared. He was shocked that Snowflake wouldn't automatically be the undisputed center of the world. Miss Willie saw his fallen look and added, "But Snowflake does have some things that Salt Lake can't brag about. You can certainly be proud of your town."

We were silent for a time, basking in Miss Willie's friendly shadow. Finally Jefferson asked shyly, "Did you like Salt Lake? I mean, it's so big and all. Can you like a place like that, the way you can like a town like Snowflake?"

There was a faraway look in her eyes as she stared across the football field. She was seeing something that was invisible to the rest of us. "Yes, I like Salt Lake. It's an exciting place. The fact that it's home makes it a wonderful place."

"Then what made you decide to leave?" Jefferson inquired. "If that's where your family is and you had a job there, why did you move away?"

For the first time since we met Miss Willie, her smile faded. The sparkle left her eyes and she bowed her head slightly. For a moment I didn't know whether she was going to answer.

"My mother lives in Salt Lake. She's a widow. My father died when I was quite young. I have two older brothers, one in Denver and the other in Boise, so I don't have a lot of family in Salt Lake, just my mother."

"But you don't have any family here, or even close," Jefferson said. "What made you leave Salt Lake?"

"Oh, I suppose I just wanted a change. Maybe I wanted to run away and start over one last time. I guess everybody has to run once in his life. Sometimes there are things that frighten us and we want to run away. Escape. Running away always seems to be the easiest way out." Miss Willie sighed. "But some things a person can't run from. They stay with him wherever he goes."

"Were you running from something?" I asked. "You don't have to tell us," I added quickly. "We'll understand."

She smiled wanly. "Someday I'll tell you everything. Today it still hurts a little too much. But I guess I was running at first." She paused. "I thought a lot about coming to Snowflake. I felt strongly that I should come, that there was something for me to do, a life I could live here that I could never live in Salt Lake. Life had changed so radically for me, and I didn't know if I could live in Salt Lake that way. But someday I'll have to go back. I know that now, and I don't worry about it. For the time being I'll stay in Snowflake and forget all the other."

She sighed, tipped her head back, and stared at the sky for a moment. "You know," she continued, raking through her hair with her fingers, "when you move to a new place, even though you have to move from the old, it's always a frightening experience because you will be with strangers. You never know how they'll treat you. I prayed I would find someone." She chewed gently on her lower lip. "My first night here I was so lonely, I had an empty spot in me this wide." She stretched her arms far apart to demonstrate. "In the morning I was ready to pack my bags and go back to Salt Lake and forget all about Snowflake. I went out on the porch to see whether it was really worth it to unpack those last few boxes." She straightened up, pressed her palms down on her thighs, and kept her arms stiff. "Then the three of you came." She looked at each of us. "I guess you are the friends I prayed for. And after I talked with you, I knew the running was over. I knew I would stay."

BB grinned sheepishly and snatched at and missed a tiny white butterfly that fluttered by. "We can be about the best friends a guy can have," he stated.

"And a girl?" Miss Willie raised her eyebrows.

"Oh, and a girl too," he added, suddenly flustered.

"There might be a few folks in Snowflake that won't say everything good about us," Jefferson explained. "We don't do everything real good, but like BB said, we can be real good friends. You'll give us a chance, won't you?"

She looked into our eyes. The smile had disappeared from her face, but the pretty gentleness was still there. "You've given me a chance. Without knowing anything about me, you've accepted me. I shall do the same for you."

That afternoon the three of us met down on the church lawn under the elm trees and did our regular thinking.

"Do you think we'll get Miss Willie for English?" Jefferson mused, lying back on the grass.

"I hear Miss Paine gets most of us sophomores," I lamented. "She likes to break the new kids in. I guess she figures that once a kid's gone through her routine, anybody can handle him."

"Miss Willie said she'd be teaching one class of sophomores," BB said excitedly. "Maybe we'll luck out and get that class."

"I don't think so," Jefferson sighed. "Aunt Betty told me the high school's waiting for us. They're going to reform us good. We'll get Paine. You can count on it. The meaner the kids, the more Miss Paine wants them. It's a challenge for her. That's why she teaches. She likes to see them crack."

There was a dismal pause, each of us contemplating our terrible fate. Then BB asked, "Do you think Miss Willie likes us?"

Jefferson shrugged. "Well, sure. At least I think so. She's nice to us. She said we were her friends."

"Well, I don't mean that, not exactly. Do you think she *likes* us? You know, really likes us?" BB twisted and picked at the grass until there was a bare spot in front of him. "I mean, do you think she likes us, not just as kids but . . . well, you know, as . . . you know, like . . ."

"We're younger than her, " Jefferson pointed out.

"But I like her. Don't you suppose she could like us?"

"I don't know if that could work out," I said, the disappointment obvious. "I wish it could, but . . ."

"You know," Jefferson observed, "there really isn't anybody here in Snowflake that's good enough for Miss Willie, at least nobody her own age. Nobody stays around much."

"There's Clyde Clancey," BB said.

"Yeah, but he smells like a butchered steer," I pointed out. "He spends so much time down at the packing house, he wouldn't know a girl from a side of beef. Besides, he's forty years old and almost bald. Let's save him for Miss Paine. She can read him Shakespeare while he's sawing on a bone."

"There's Silas Flake."

"BB," I moaned, "Silas Flake didn't finish grade school. He thinks that because he can ride a horse and slap a brand on a calf's rump, he's an authority on everything, but he's as dense as a bale of last year's straw. Every time he opens his mouth, the world's polluted with ignorance, and he talks like he learned English from the Union Pacific Hobo Academy."

"Miss Willie deserves something better than those two," Jefferson said.

"What about Frank Martin? He's pretty rich."

"Frank Martin," I muttered. "There are slobs and there are bigger slobs, and then there's Frank Martin. I don't even think his mother likes him. Miss Willie would have to want his money pretty bad to marry that horse's ear. Miss Paine would be too good for him."

We went through the entire town of Snowflake and considered every eligible bachelor. There weren't many of them, but after we'd examined each one, it wasn't hard to understand why they were still bachelors. The prospect of marrying one of them was enough to induce a girl to join a nunnery.

"Well, I guess we're the best there is," BB observed humbly. "There's not much to choose from. Maybe we are a little younger than Miss Willie, but we'll grow. I mean, we're not going to be sophomores all our lives. Besides, remember what she said about us the other day? She thought we was seniors, and a senior is old enough to get married. Bill Hunt got married last year, and he was a senior. If he can do it, we can."

"There are always a few returned missionaries coming home," I pointed out. "Some of them might give Miss Willie a good match."

"I still think she better settle for one of us," BB insisted. "At least we're here and available. You know that counts for something. There might be lots of good guys around, but they're not around here. It's not like we can ship Miss Willie off to where the men are. Those RM's might come off their missions and then be off someplace. They might marry another girl without giving Miss Willie a chance. It's best if she stays with a sure thing, and we're the only sure thing right now."

Well, we had come to a consensus: Miss Willie was ours by reason of elimination. We had eliminated everyone else.

# Chapter Four

---

THE DAY AFTER LABOR DAY, Jefferson, BB, and I congregated at BB's wearing stiff, crackling Levi's and shirts still creased with package wrinkles. Our hair was slicked down, and we were all saturated with cologne or after-shave.

"Well, this is it," I announced morosely, looking at BB and Jefferson. "Do you think we're ready for high school?"

Jefferson rubbed his neck under his stiff, starchy collar. "Today would sure be a good day to get sick."

"We could always head down to the wash and hide out," BB suggested.

I shook my head and looked down the street where I could see the tin roof of the old library building on the edge of campus. "We can't go to the wash every day. They'll keep waiting for us." I picked up a rock and hurled it across the street at a garbage can. "We might as well get it over with." The other two nodded. "Can you remember when we used to hate going to school because of the teachers?"

Jefferson nodded ruefully. "I've heard my share of bad things about Miss Paine, but this is one time I wouldn't mind having her walk me to class for a day or so. She'd keep the seniors away better than a good dog."

"I'll take my chances with the seniors," BB muttered.

Glumly we started toward school. "Just don't get smart with anybody," I counseled the other two. "Seniors can overlook a lot of things, but a smart-mouthed sophomore isn't one of them."

"And stay together," BB added. "Maybe they'll leave us alone when they see we're a gang."

Stepping onto the high-school campus that first day was like entering a war zone. I'd never had the shakes so bad. My mouth was dry, my palms wet. I could feel my heart thump nervously in my chest, and my stomach was doing a hundred careless tricks on my morning's breakfast. My eyes kept darting about searching each tree, bush, corner, and door. Every time I saw another human being, I got this terrible urge to turn and run.

As we passed the library a sparrow fluttered from the shrubs next to the steps, and the three of us jumped three steps backward and almost bit our tongues in half.

BB forced out a sick groan that was intended as a laugh, but there was no humor in the sound. "Just a bird," he said.

Jefferson and I nodded.

It was still early, barely 8:15. Most of the kids on campus were just jumpy sophomores like ourselves, creeping around and headed for the cafeteria to pick up class schedules. The juniors and seniors didn't have to show up till nine. Unless they wanted to! Consequently, after being on campus five minutes without seeing any upperclassmen, we tried to shake off our fears and snatch at the elusive hope that we might be safe. Then we saw Rusty Bluth with his new pants soaked. None of us laughed. Our hopes vanished, and the old fears returned.

"The cafeteria's over there," I rasped, pointing to a building across the street from the principal's office and searching the school grounds for the tenth time.

Jefferson swallowed and ran his hand across his forehead. "It looks clear," he observed, his voice shaking.

Gingerly we shuffled across the lawn in front of the administration building and crept onto the street. We would have held hands had it not looked so strange.

I had never realized a Snowflake street was so wide until we crossed the street that day. It seemed we walked forever, all the time exposed and vulnerable. Then we were on the sidewalk, with the cafeteria doors only fifty feet away. We sighed. But our relief was short-lived. The morning's eerie silence was shattered as a car screeched to a stop by the curb. A numbing chill raced up my back.

"Hey, you three!" a voice called. We froze without turning around. "We got something for you. Get over here!"

All three of us stared at the door, ten good steps from where we stood. Sanctuary was behind those doors. Once inside, not even the boldest senior would dare approach us. We debated for a split second; then we heard car doors slam, and we bolted forward.

I reached the door first, gripped the handle, and reared back. The door pulled open a few inches, only to be slammed closed again as BB and Jefferson crashed into it. Three pairs of hands clawed at the door and finally ripped it open, and the three of us squeezed through, almost tearing the door off its hinges.

BB was the last through the door. Drunk with the triumph of his narrow escape, he turned and called out just before the door slammed, "Tough luck, suckers!" He sucked in a breath of air, gave a hysterical laugh, and faced Jefferson and me. "I guess I told them," he bragged.

We gaped at him in horror. "Why'd you yell that?" I groaned. "It was bad enough that we ran."

"We made it, didn't we?"

Jefferson nodded, suddenly furious. "Yeah, we made it in here. But in a few minutes we gotta go back out there."

The smile on BB's face melted into an expression of agony. He pressed his head between his hands and moaned.

"Well," I muttered, "so much for our chances of surviving the first day."

Despondently, we proceeded from the foyer into the cafeteria. At a table in front of us, handing out sophomore class schedules, sat Miss Paine. "Miss Paine!" we all gasped.

"She don't know us, does she?" BB asked as we stepped into line.

"She couldn't," Jefferson whispered.

"Maybe she's heard of us," I said, "but I doubt she knows our faces. We're safe."

With our hands dug deep in our pockets and our heads hanging low to maintain our anonymity, we presented ourselves in front of Miss Paine. Miss Paine was occupied momentarily, and I began to think our identity was going to remain a secret. Not even glancing at us or asking our names, she cleared her throat loudly and handed us each a packet with his name written in bold black letters at the top and underlined twice in red.

"I hope you boys can handle being treated as adults," she said, frowning. She pursed her lips. "We did have you separated." Picking up a pencil, she began drumming impatiently on the tabletop. "But Miss Willie pleaded your defense. She said she'd like to try you—together." She raised a threatening finger and added, "Miss Willie is new around here and doesn't know our students very well. If there is one bit of horseplay from any of you, you'll be changed. Immediately! I'll have you then, as originally scheduled."

"We got Miss Willie?" BB gasped. "For sophomore English?"

Miss Paine nodded, her cold, dark eyes boring into us, but we didn't notice. In fact, the unexpected good news elated us and erased from our minds the threat of the seniors lurking outside. Grinning, we backed to the door in a trance. Overcome with joy, we raced across campus, laughing, joking, shoving, feeling ecstatic.

We didn't notice the four seniors trailing us until it was too late. Our first intimation of trouble was a loud whisper behind us just as we stepped into South Hall. "You get the fat one and we'll get the skinny one. We'll leave Johnson till last."

Though BB wasn't exactly fat, he was stocky and had that fatso look, which he kept until he was almost a senior. Jefferson wasn't skinny unless he stood next to BB. The descriptions didn't exactly fit, but instinct warned us of imminent danger.

BB glanced back and called quickly, "They're onto us again. Run!"

Mrs. Call's door, halfway down the hall, was the only door open. We knew if we could make it that far, we were safe again. We broke into a dead sprint. We might have reached Mrs. Call's room, but before we had taken ten steps we were surrounded. Seniors must have crawled out of the walls, all of them wearing a hungry look, just waiting for a sophomoric morsel to fall into their grasp.

"Excuse me," Jefferson mumbled, trying to push through the wall of seniors. He was shoved back against BB and me.

"What's your rush?" one of the seniors asked. "You guys are always in such a hurry. Slow down and enjoy yourselves. We'd like to get to know you better."

BB gulped and found a shred of courage he should have left hidden. "We don't have to take nothing from you guys," he muttered.

Had he fallen at their feet, fawned, groveled, and begged, he might have survived with just a little harassment; however, humility had never been one of the virtues BB had cultivated.

"What do you mean you don't have to take nothing from us?" one of the seniors demanded.

"I mean just get out of my way. We got things to do, and if you know what's good—"

Before BB could finish, a host of senior hands grabbed him and dragged him to the floor, where he was soon twisted and turned into submission. As soon as we saw that the seniors' efforts were concentrated on BB, Jefferson and I sneaked down the hall to Mrs. Call's room. From there we stared open-mouthed, witnessing BB's ordeal.

Stretched and incapacitated, BB was lugged down the hall to the drinking fountain, where, amid enthusiastic shouts, he was firmly planted until poor Rusty Bluth's pants looked dry in comparison. He was then wrestled to the floor, and two senior artists proceeded to paint on him the mustache and black eyes they thought he needed. Then he was stuffed headfirst into a garbage can and rolled into the girls' rest room. There was a chorus of shrill screams, then a loud banging as BB tried to extricate himself from the garbage can. Suddenly the door crashed open and BB stumbled into the hall, red-faced, wide-eyed, and disheveled.

It really wasn't a very auspicious beginning, but Jefferson and I hoped that BB had suffered for all of us. The rest of the morning we attended our classes with the first bit of genuine humility we had ever experienced.

Fourth hour we stepped into Mr. Bott's science classroom. There were almost as many rumors in circulation about Mr. Bott as there were about Miss Paine. "Bosko" Bott, as he was known behind his back, had a reputation of being a hard-nosed, no-nonsense despot. Living just down the street from BB, he was more than familiar with our past and was of the opinion that stiff discipline and a strong, unyielding hand were all that was needed to cure us of our foolishness. We entered his biology class with a great deal of trepidation, hoping that the rumors about him were grossly exaggerated.

As was our custom, the three of us slinked to the back of the room, took corner desks, and ducked behind the students in front of us, hoping we could go unnoticed, at least for a time.

When Mr. Bott came in, he gazed out across the class without seeing the three of us. He picked up his roll sheet and began calling out students' names. BB's name was third on the list. "Bartholomew Bradley Bunderson," Mr. Bott called out.

"Here," BB answered, muffling his response with his hand and keeping his head down so Mr. Bott couldn't see him.

Mr. Bott searched the crowded room. "Are you new, Bartholomew?" he asked, still looking for the student in question.

"No," BB replied without lifting his head.

Still baffled, Mr. Bott continued to search the faces. "Do you go by Bartholomew, Bradley, Brad, or . . . Would you raise your hand please so that I can see where you are sitting and can become familiar with your face."

A lone hand went up behind Mindy Moore, but no face followed.

Mr. Bott cleared his throat. "I'd like to see your face."

BB peeked over Mindy's shoulder, his face shining with embarrassment. Several snickers erupted throughout the class.

Mr. Bott's mouth sagged momentarily. He glanced down at his roll sheet. "Bartholomew . . . Bradley . . . Bunderson," he said slowly, pronouncing each name carefully. "B . . . B," he added. He stared down at the blushing BB. "I believe I recognize the face now; I didn't associate it with such a distinguished name, however."

Mr. Bott continued moving down the roll sheet. When he came to my name he called out, "Daniel John . . ." He took a deep breath. "D . . . J."

I raised my hand and head. He nodded. "And I suppose the corpse next to yours," he said, indicating Jefferson, who still had his head down in hiding, "is none other than Jefferson Judd."

Jefferson's head came up slowly and he nodded.

The class continued without incident, and when the bell rang, BB, Jefferson, and I raced for the door.

"Gentlemen," Mr. Bott called after us, "could I keep you for a minute? You'll still have time for lunch."

Grudgingly we stayed while the rest of the class filed out ahead of us. Mr. Bott motioned for us to come up to his desk. Reluctantly we did so.

"Gentlemen," he began, "we're going to have a good year." We stared indifferently, not in the mood to argue. "I'm convinced you boys have potential. You have creative minds—although at times you channel your creativity in forbidden parts. This year in science we will mine that creativity. Even if I have to squeeze it out of you." He filled his lungs with air, more for effect than to breathe. "Therefore, when you come to class, leave your junior-high foolishness at the door. Better yet, at home. You shall start fresh in here. Remember," he added with a humorless smile, "we're going to mine your creativity. Don't disappoint me."

A moment later we were in the hall. "What's he jumping all over us the first day for?" Jefferson complained. "We didn't do anything."

"Sounds like he's been waiting for us," I said.

"They've probably all been waiting for us," Jefferson grumbled.

"Dad says Mr. Bott isn't such a bad guy," I remarked. "He says he just has a strange way of going about things."

"Well, that was sure a strange way," Jefferson snipped.

"I don't like Bosko," BB muttered. "And he don't like us. He bragged that he could bring us around. I heard him tell Willard Francis that. All that potential and creative junk is just Bosko bunk. If he's not careful I'll channel my creativity right down his throat."

We came out of the building and started across the lawn toward the cafeteria. As we passed the flagpole, Phil Taylor and Tuck Wildes, two seniors, detained us.

"Still in a hurry," Phil remarked. "You guys rush everyplace."

Tuck and Phil were not as big as any one of us, so we were not immediately intimidated. In fact, since there were three of us and only two of them, we were about to brush right past them. Phil, the smaller of the two, looked at BB and said, "I guess you can go. You got yours this morning."

"These are my friends," BB insisted boldly. "We don't split up."

Tuck shrugged and said, "Fine. We can give you another dose."

BB licked his lips and swallowed hard, his courage suddenly gone. "That's all right," he whimpered. "I was just on my way to lunch." Without so much as a backward glance, he abandoned Jefferson and me.

Phil and Tuck watched him go and then pulled two ragged skirts from behind them. "You two like hiding behind skirts," Phil said casually. "We thought you might like hiding inside one for a change. They really do fit your personality." He handed the skirts to us.

"We ain't putting them old things on," Jefferson sputtered indignantly.

"You don't scare us," I added with bravado. Then I whispered to Jefferson, "We can handle these two."

Tuck and Phil smiled. "I think you'll want to put them on, because if you don't, we have a . . . shall we say a surprise for you, one that will make BB's look fun."

"You and who else?" I challenged, stepping forward.

The two turned and looked across the lawn where a group of twenty or thirty senior boys were milling around, looking our way. Several of them waved at us. Slowly we took the skirts and pulled them over our pants, feeling hot blood creep into our cheeks.

"Roll your pant legs up," Phil commanded.

We were about to lodge a protest, but then we glanced at that crowd of hungry seniors. Grudgingly we did as we were told.

"Now, girls," Phil instructed, "this area around the flagpole needs to be patrolled. We would like you two to patrol it, parading back and forth here, counting time and stepping high. Make sure nobody makes off with the flagpole. Any questions?" We shook our heads. "Step lively, girls. And by the way," he added in a whisper, "if anybody asks you what you're doing, remember this whole thing is your idea. No one forced you."

We began our humiliating vigil. All noon we paced back and forth, counting time, while the seniors across the lawn hooted and howled with delight. Occasionally one would shout, "Look at them legs," or "Those sweeties are the best-looking girls in the whole sophomore class." Several times some of the bolder ones crept over and pulled at our skirts or pinched our cheeks.

At one point Jefferson stopped marching. Phil strolled over and said in a low voice, "Judd, if this isn't wild enough for you, we do have something else." Jefferson choked back his rebellion and began marching again.

Halfway through the noon hour Mr. Reynolds, the principal, noticed our maneuvers and came out to investigate. As he walked toward us, he peered over his horn-rimmed glasses with his bald head cocked to one side, as though he were trying to ascertain if our presence was real or merely an illusion.

"Are you boys all right?" he asked, eyeing our costumes.

I glanced at Jefferson, and from the corner of my eye I could see the marauding seniors. I stood at attention and nodded.

"Who's making you do this?" he questioned, pulling off his glasses and looking toward the seniors.

Jefferson hiked up his skirt and scratched his stomach. "No one, sir. It's just an obligation we have. Duty to our school and country, you might say."

Mr. Reynolds coughed. "Do you do this kind of thing often?" he asked skeptically, glancing at our skirts and hairy white legs.

"Only when we feel real patriotic," I replied, careful not to look toward the seniors and cast any suspicions.

Replacing his glasses and pulling on his ear, Mr. Reynolds said, "Why don't you boys call off your patriotism for today and—"

"Oh, no," Jefferson protested. "Duty's not done."

Mr. Reynolds stared for a moment at us and then at the seniors lounging on the other side of the lawn, seemingly oblivious to our presence. "I didn't realize seniors could inspire such a fervent out-pouring of patriotism among the underclassmen," he remarked. Jefferson and I didn't comment. Finally he shrugged and returned to his office, and Jefferson and I resumed our humiliating vigil.

As soon as the bell rang, we stripped off our skirts and ran for South Hall, hoping to lose ourselves in the student throng and escape our public disgrace. But there was no escape for us. The rest of the day we were the objects of ridicule. Everyone had either seen us or heard about us, and hardly a person passed in the hall without reminding us of our ordeal with either a comment or a snicker.

When seventh hour finally arrived and the three of us dragged ourselves into Miss Willie's class, we were frustrated and angry.

"I was just thinking," BB whispered as we took our accustomed back, rear-corner seats, where we could slump into a position of bored observation. "What's going to happen when Miss Willie finds out we ain't the brains we told her we was? We made it sound like we knew all there was to know about English. She'll be asking us to teach the class for her."

"You're the one with the big mouth," I grumbled.

"Well, you guys went along with it. You thought it was a pretty good idea at the time."

"We didn't ask you to lay it on so thick."

The bell rang and ended our discussion, but we remained rest-less. The only thing that made the class at all bearable was Miss Willie.

I didn't hear a word she said that afternoon, because as soon as she started in on English, I turned off the sound. But I kept the pic-ture turned on the whole time. I couldn't take my eyes off her.

She was wearing a pleated white skirt and a light blue blouse that looked as smooth as silk and highlighted the soft, smooth pink in her cheeks. Completely gone was that fleeting boyish impression I had received while she was in her patched jeans and tennis shoes. She was all girl, and I marveled that I had ever thought otherwise.

Her whole face sparkled with beauty, the kind that grows on you and gets better with time. Her brown eyes darted gaily about the room, and every time they stopped on me, my heart fluttered and I could hardly breathe.

Walking back and forth in front of the class, she took short steps, putting her toes down first and letting her whole body sway with gentle grace. It wasn't anything put on; her every movement was as natural as her beauty. And when she stood at the front of the class, she knit her fingers together in a pose of dainty shyness.

I didn't realize how small she was until I saw her that first day in class. She couldn't have weighed much more than a hundred pounds, and though she didn't look frightened or intimidated by her new surroundings, I felt an overpowering urge to protect her. And yet, all the while, I never had the impression that Miss Willie was something a guy could touch. She seemed too good for that. She was like a delicate china doll, encased in crystal to preserve her magical beauty and appeal.

But the class was still English, and I knew that sooner or later I would have to stop staring and begin the odious grammarian trek. But this first day, I postponed the future and feasted.

When the bell rang, shattering my pleasant dreams, BB, Jefferson, and I made a dash for the door and freedom. Miss Willie, anticipating our intentions, raised her hand and asked us to stay.

For the second time that day we were detained after class. As the other kids filed from the room, the three of us cowered in the far corner, glad to stay longer with Miss Willie but completely leery of any after-school conference with a teacher, regardless of how pretty she was. Every time we had ever stayed after class, it had been to receive a reprimand.

Miss Willie straightened a few papers while the other students left the room. "Why don't you three come up to these front seats," she said.

Slowly we dragged ourselves from our desks and crept to the front of the room, trying to remember if we had caused any disturbance seventh hour. Miss Willie stared at us for a moment and then her face slowly lit up with the familiar warm smile. We all breathed a sigh of relief.

"How was your first day of school?" she asked, leaning back in her chair and clasping her hands together. We shrugged and looked at the floor. We began to fidget. The last thing we wanted was for Miss Willie to learn that we were not the supermen she thought we were.

"I guess seniors are always like that," she said sympathetically. "The worst is over, though. Once they've had their fun, they settle down and are really pretty good people."

We nodded and felt our cheeks color. Miss Willie cleared her throat. "I asked you to stay because I want to make a request of each of you." We looked up as she pursed her lips. "Beginning in a new school is always a challenge. Even though I've taught before, I'm still a little nervous and unsure of myself."

"Oh, you done real good," BB said. "You don't have nothing to worry about. You got all the teachers around here beat."

Miss Willie looked down at her desk, and a faint, fleeting smile touched her lips. "Thank you, BB. When Miss Paine was going over my class schedule," she continued, "I told her about three young men who had been so kind to me. She had a slightly different impression of them. She shared it with me. She went over their past history." She sighed. "But I couldn't believe all those things. I couldn't believe that those three young men, who had helped me move in, given me a tour of their town, and done so many other nice things, could be any less than very special. I had to believe that young men who were that spontaneous with kindness were without doubt gentlemen of the highest order."

I hadn't ever before heard anyone praise Jefferson, BB, or me like that. I glanced at Jefferson and BB. They were red and shifting around in their desks as much as I was.

"I made a special request to have all of them in my sophomore English class. Miss Paine tried to discourage me, but I insisted."

We all stared at the floor without speaking.

"I guess before I asked to have you in my class I should have spoken with you to see if it was all right. If you are in my class, there might be those who think I'm playing favorites. I try not to have favorites, but I'm not sure a teacher can always prevent that. So we are all going to have to work to show no favoritism. In class I will have to treat you like any other student, and you will have to treat me like any other teacher. That means you might have to work harder than any other student in the class, because if you don't, there will be those who'll say I'm not being fair. Now, I know that's a lot to ask of young men, but I know you're capable of that and more. If you would rather not accept that kind of a challenge, though, we should make the change now. We'll still be good friends. Your not being in my class will never affect our friendship."

"What did Miss Paine say about us?" BB asked.

"Oh, different things. But that doesn't matter. We will always be friends. That's why I'm telling you this. This is something I could tell only very dear friends."

"She's a mean one," BB mumbled. "I hope I don't ever get her for a teacher. I'd drop out of school."

"Oh, BB," Miss Willie said, smiling. "She's not mean."

"She does a real good job of pretending, then." He shook his head. "She'd like to fry us for lunch. That's why everybody hates her. There ain't a kid in this school that likes her, at least no normal kids. Some of the freako-brainos like her okay, but that's because they ain't normal. They've spent too many nights reading her books and correcting each other's English. That's why I hate English so bad, because of witches like Miss Paine."

"Why, BB, I thought you liked English, that it was your favorite subject."

BB looked at the floor. "Oh, I do like English," he stammered. "I really like English. I just can't stand English teachers. They're all such ornery old bags, always correcting you and making you be so proper and acting like you didn't even know how to talk your own language and making you feel just like a . . ."

"I'm an English teacher," Miss Willie said. "Is that what I'm like?"

Jefferson and I shook our heads as we watched BB squirm and choke with his big blundering foot in his mouth. "Well, I didn't exactly mean it that way, Miss Willie. Maybe other places English teachers are more human. But here in Snowflake they're a bunch of animals, and pretty poor ones at that."

Miss Willie laughed. "I can see we need to change your impressions of English teachers."

"You didn't believe what Miss Paine said about us, did you?" BB asked. "I mean, she's pretty prejudiced and all, since we don't read her dumb books and talk like an uppity moron."

"I'll believe only what I see. So far all I've seen has been good."

BB looked at me and Jefferson looked at BB and I looked at them and they looked back at me. "Do you really want us in your class?" BB asked.

Miss Willie smiled. "I would love to have you in my class."

BB ducked his head and mumbled, "There's something you better know then. We don't know English like we said we did. I said English was my favorite subject. Well, it ain't. The only way I ever passed in junior high was that DJ helped me. He don't have such a hard time. I know math and algebra pretty good, but all them verbs and nouns and stuff really get me turned around."

Jefferson and I nodded. "We didn't mean nothing by it," Jefferson added. "We just thought . . . well, we just thought you might . . ."

Jefferson looked at me to rescue him. "Well, we just thought that since you were an English teacher and all," I stammered, groping for the correct explanation, "that you would probably . . . well, you know how English teachers are, don't you? They think everybody's got to speak just so, or at least they think everybody should, and if they don't, they wrinkle their nose and put their hands on their hips and glare and get all upset. We didn't want you to do that because . . . well, because . . ." I had come to a dead end.

"Because you looked so nice and all," BB blurted out, "and we wanted you to like us."

Miss Willie put her head back and started to laugh. It was a laugh that started in her eyes and quickly spread all over her. It wasn't a loud laugh. It was a girlish giggle, sounding as close to happy music as anything I'd heard. And it was contagious because we knew she wasn't laughing at us. Her laugh was a genuine expression of joy, and soon we were all laughing, caught up in the same singular joy. It felt good, a soothing balm after such a hectic day.

Finally Miss Willie stopped, wiped a tear from her eye, and said, "We will be friends—regardless. However," she added, raising a finger, "knowing English and knowing it well can be helpful. If you're willing, I would like to show you that English can not only be understood by anyone but it can also be enjoyable." She took a deep breath. "I hated English until . . . well, until I went to college. Do you know what my worst subject was in high school? English! I have failed only one class in my life—Sophomore English."

She sat back and stared at each one of us, then said, "There are a lot of people in Snowflake who have some strange ideas about three young men. I would like to prove them wrong. It won't happen overnight. Perhaps it won't happen in a year. But someday the people of Snowflake are going to remember three young men not because they terrorized a town, but because they were by far the best young men in the town. And I'm convinced that they can learn English as well as any old stern-faced English teacher."

# Chapter Five

---

MISS WILLIE CLAIMED that the first week of class was just a review. I'll admit that a few of her terms were vaguely familiar, meaning that at some time during the course of our educational vagary a teacher had droned in the background while we drew pictures on the desk, planned after-school escapades, or shot spit wads. Our minds had not been fertile ground then. Very little related to English had taken root, and now we were lost.

We did attempt a mediocre fight, though. We sat with our heads up and our eyes pried open. There was a semblance of interest etched on our faces. But it was all a facade. Only snatches here and there ever penetrated. We had tried to be candid with Miss Willie and dispel all illusions, but merely saying we were dumb was not the same as permitting her to peer into our minds and experience the abject ignorance herself. We weren't sure any English teacher was capable of comprehending that kind of mental deficiency; therefore, we were drowning in our own ignorance, unwilling to call for help.

After the first week, Miss Willie announced our first quiz. Just a review, she added to reassure us. But a quiz by any other name would be just as ruinous. After that quiz, there would be no more bluffing.

That evening following the quiz, we met at the church lawn and held a conference. "How did you do?" Jefferson asked BB and me as we dropped onto the lawn and snatched at blades of grass.

"Oh, I aced it for sure," BB grumbled, chomping on his grass and staring into space. "I hate English," he snapped. "I speak it all the time and I get understood. Nobody's got to tell me how to talk right. I know. But you put me in an English class, and it's like I'm learning a whole new language. If I stay in there very long, I forget the English I already know."

"Maybe if we listened better," I suggested. English was not as hard for me, and though I hadn't done really well on the quiz, I knew I hadn't failed.

"I listened. I listened till my eyeballs crossed. My brains are permanently scrambled. English just ain't for me. Who cares how I talk? People understand me. I don't need to tell people I'm using a verb or a noun or whatever else there is."

"Miss Willie's nice and everything," Jefferson mumbled, "but we gave her a real bad job. We laid it on way too thick. I don't mind being a little good, but she thinks—shoot! She thinks we're tops." He grinned. "You know, it was kinda nice while it lasted. She almost got me believing it."

"I think I liked us the old way," BB said. "That way nobody worried one way or the other. It didn't matter what we was like. We was just a bunch of mess-offs to everybody else."

"Do you suppose Miss Willie really thinks we're that good?" I asked. "You know, nobody else does."

"She said so," BB replied with surprise. "Why would she say it if she didn't think it?"

"Maybe to make us feel good."

"You think Miss Willie would tell a whopper like that just to make us feel good?"

I shrugged my shoulders. "But if she isn't lying . . ." I let the question linger.

"Do you think she's in . . . well, you know. Maybe she is in . . . I mean, maybe she likes us so much that she just can't see straight. Kinda like a guy's mom."

"Do you think a girl like Miss Willie would . . . you know, like someone like us?"

The next day, when we received our quizzes back, our worst fears changed to realities. I barely made a C, Jefferson had a weak D, and BB dropped clear off the scale. Even Chet Brunson scored higher than BB, and Chet didn't have much more intelligence than a good homegrown turnip.

Our hopes were shattered. We had tried. At least we had worked harder than we had ever done before, and where did it get us? Right at the bottom of the pile, where we had always been. What was the sense in working so hard if we were going to end up in the same place regardless? Why struggle to be last?

After seeing our quizzes and concluding that we really weren't budding scholars, we gave up the fight. BB slept quietly, Jefferson drew a caricature of BB with his head down and a buzzard perched on his shoulder, and I pulled out a western novel, hid it inside my grammar book, and read.

As soon as the last bell rang, we stampeded for the door before Miss Willie had a chance to open her mouth. We had an important football scrimmage that afternoon, and we didn't want to be late. And we definitely wanted to escape that stifling English atmosphere.

The three of us were struggling to pin down starting spots on the JV team, so English was soon forgotten. Though we were not exceptional in the classroom, we did manage to hold our own on the football field. When the scrimmage was over, the coach announced that Jefferson would be starting as quarterback, BB as guard, and I as end.

Elated, we strolled off the field with our helmets under our arms. We were so pleased with the coach's announcement that we didn't even notice Miss Willie coming out of the bleachers to intercept us on the track. "Congratulations!" she beamed proudly. "Now I know where you channel your talents. What a threesome!"

We stopped and grinned sheepishly. "Did you see much of the game?" Jefferson asked.

"All of it, I think."

"Did you like it?" I asked.

"Very much. Football is one of my favorite sports. In fact, when I'm feeling very unladylike, I do a little scrimmaging myself. I do have to be careful who I play with."

BB had a football, and Miss Willie lifted it from his arms. Nodding to me, she said, "Go out for a pass, DJ."

I stared at her skirt and down at her nylons and high heels. She gripped the ball and prepared to throw. I hesitated. "Go on," she said, "I've never played for the pros, but on a good day I can throw a ball."

BB and Jefferson were grinning and waving me away. Halfheartedly I trotted to the other side of the track, fifteen feet away, and waited with my hands at my side.

Miss Willie sighed, put her left hand on her hip, and let the right hand holding the ball drop to her side. "Come on, DJ, I can throw better than that. At least give me a chance to prove myself."

Feeling terribly awkward playing with a female quarterback, I trotted ten yards onto the field and then cut to my right, glancing over my shoulder.

Miss Williie took two shaky steps on her heels, cocked her right arm back, and then fired the ball through the air—hitting me right on the numbers! I was so surprised that I dropped the ball.

BB and Jefferson let loose with a cheer, and I ducked my head and scrambled for the fumbled ball. Picking it up, I reared back to throw, but Miss Willie waved her hands and laughed, "Throw it to Jefferson." She tugged at her skirt and pointed down at her shoes and explained, "Throwing is one thing, but I'd surely hate to make a diving catch dressed like this."

"Oh, I can throw better than that," I assured her.

"I hope so, because you sure can't catch," BB guffawed.

"Give me another chance," I called to Miss Willie as I threw the ball to Jefferson.

Miss Willie took the ball and waved me to the left. I sprinted off across the field, and she cocked her arm and then fired the ball. Once again it hit me right on the numbers. But this time I caught it.

With the ball tucked under my arm, I trotted back to the others.

"Hey, you're not bad," I admitted. Miss Willie bounced lightly on the balls of her feet, put her hands on her hips, and smiled with pleasure. "You didn't learn to throw like that from Shakespeare," I said.

"Oh," she replied, cocking her head to one side, "don't be so sure. Old Bill was really a very talented man. Have you read all of Shakespeare?" I shook my head. "For all you know he played for the England Patriots before going to the Globe and making a name for himself in the theater."

"Oh, sure," Jefferson said, laughing. "I suppose he wrote about his football days too."

"Why, of course," Miss Willie said with all seriousness. "He described his football life in his play *Much Ado About Nothing*." She placed her forefinger under her chin and pondered for a moment. "Or was it *A Comedy of Errors?*" Suddenly she laughed and snatched the ball from me and sent BB out for a short pass.

"Where did you learn to play?" I asked as BB came running back with the ball.

She took a deep breath and relieved BB of the ball. "My brother played end for the University of Utah. When we were growing up, he didn't always have a quarterback, so I got volunteered for the job. I hated it at first, but he bribed me with a few dimes and nickels along the way. Now that I think about it, I'm sure he was more interested in making a football player out of me than helping him with his pass receptions. I couldn't have been very good, but I'm glad I learned. Don't tell anyone," she added furtively, "but I used to play quarterback for the neighborhood team. I was the only girl on the team."

"Touch or tackle?" BB gasped.

"Neither," Miss Willie whispered. "I never played unless my brother was on my team. And he threatened to break the neck of anyone who so much as touched me."

"Wasn't that unfair to the other team?" I asked.

Miss Willie shrugged. "Oh, I suppose it was. But it wasn't a written rule. In fact, it was never verbalized. Everyone just knew that I was off limits. If someone got a little careless . . . well, the next play my brother was stomping all over him. My brother was a big boy. He didn't take after me."

"Shoot! You'll have to play for us," Jefferson said. "We need a good back-up quarterback."

"What do you mean back-up?" I teased. "She's better than you."

"Oh, Jefferson's safe. I play only if my big brother is around to protect me. Besides, I'm a little fragile now." She breathed deeply and wrapped her arms around herself in an attempt to ward off the evening's growing chill. "After watching you three play, I can see you're out of my class. You take football seriously, don't you."

We all stood there grinning and kicking the cinders on the track and feeling terribly embarrassed. Finally Miss Willie remarked, "I hope we are still friends. I hope our friendship doesn't ever depend on how high you score in English."

"I hope so too," BB muttered, "or else we'd be worst enemies right now."

She laughed.

Guiltily we stared at the ground and thumped our helmets against our legs. "I know my test don't show it, but I did try, Miss Willie. I really did try, harder than I ever tried before. Even harder than I tried out on that football field today. Honest. I just don't have it in English."

She smiled and nodded. "I know. I appreciate your trying. I don't suppose it will ever be really easy. Learning seldom is, but if you want to—I mean learn English—I'd like to help you, not just in class, either. I don't want you to think that you can't come for help."

"I'm afraid there's not much hope for us," Jefferson answered. "Like BB said, we just don't have it, but we do appreciate you thinking we did. Not many have done that."

Miss Willie sighed. "I don't just think you have potential. You do. Now you might need some extra help finding it, but it's there. Anytime you need help, anytime, I'll be ready."

I'm not sure what provoked us, but that night the three of us accepted Miss Willie's invitation.

The sun was just sinking into a pile of clouds to the west, splashing the early fall sky with rich oranges and golds. With our grammar books tucked under our arms, we tromped up Miss Willie's front steps and tapped lightly on her door. Inside a radio was playing "A Hard Day's Night" by the Beatles. We glanced at each other and shrugged our shoulders, wondering if that was really Miss Willie in there.

Soon the door opened and Miss Willie greeted us with a surprised smile. Obviously she was not expecting us. She had on a pair of patched Levi's and a man's button shirt, which was about six sizes too big for her. The tails hung down around her knees, it seemed, and the sleeves had been rolled up about fifty times, but they still hung down to her elbows. She looked almost like a little girl playing dress-up in her dad's clothes. She was padding around barefoot and seemed just a little embarrassed for us to find her so casual.

"We come to learn some English," BB announced.

"Tonight?" she asked, a little taken back.

"If it's all right," Jefferson said.

Miss Willie touched her lips with her finger and then smiled. "I guess the sooner the better." She stepped back and motioned with her hand for us to come in. "I've fixed the place up a little since you were here last," she explained. "It still isn't the way I want it, but it's improving."

When we had helped Miss Willie move in, I had found her rented house rather drab and bare. It was supposed to be furnished, but it didn't have much. In the living room were an old green sofa, a brown overstuffed chair, a coffee table with a deep gouge running the length of it, and two yellow lamps with battered shades. The kitchen wasn't a lot better. The only furniture, besides the sink and the appliances, was a chipped white table and three odd chairs, none of which matched the table.

A week earlier I had been anything but impressed by Miss Willie's house, but she had fixed it up. In the living room she had built a bookshelf out of bricks and boards, and it was bulging with everything from Shakespeare to *Mormon Doctrine*. The sofa and the overstuffed chair were now covered with two Indian blankets, and the lamp shades had been remodeled. The kitchen table was draped with a white lace cloth, and a vase full of red and yellow flowers sat in the middle.

Miss Willie had decorated the walls with pictures and posters, and about the room were little knickknacks and dried flower arrangements, most of which she had made herself. For example, when we had given her the tour of the town, she had found an old branch, dry and gray from months in the sun. She had taken it home, and now it sat on the coffee table, covered artistically with dried weeds, colorful rocks, and yellow stalks of barley. What had just days before been an ordinary piece of wood, something to be kicked around, left to rot, or thrown into the fire as kindling, was now a minor work of art.

"Was that you listening to 'Hard Day's Night?'" Jefferson asked as she led us in to the kitchen table.

"I was listening to the radio. I'm really not sure what's been playing."

"And here I thought you'd be in here quoting Shakespeare," Jefferson quipped.

"Oh, didn't you hear me?" Miss Willie teased. "I'll have to shout it out the window the next time."

She stared down at the kitchen table and the three chairs. "It looks like we have a problem," she stated. "There's a wooden box in the backyard. I guess we'll have to use that."

Jefferson, after a lot of pushing and shoving and arguing, finally ended up with the box, and we were soon sitting around the table with our books open in front of us.

"We want to learn English from the beginning," Jefferson declared. "We've got to find out once and for all if we can make it in English."

Miss Willie raised her eyebrows and asked, "From the beginning?"

"Maybe you'd better start before that," BB suggested. "Maybe if we start on some kindergarten stuff, I'll be able to handle it."

"If not," I snickered, "we can try baby talk and work up."

Miss Willie looked around at our books, paper, and pencils. "Is this all you brought?" she asked, almost sternly.

We looked around, trying to think of what we might have forgotten. "Is there somthing else?" BB squeaked.

Miss Willie sighed. "No wonder you've never learned or liked English. Bare books and blank notepads would scare anyone off. Do you like popcorn?"

"Popcorn?" we all asked.

"Surely Uncle Roy's store sells popcorn," Miss Willie said. "It has everything else."

"We love popcorn," BB said, perplexed. "But what does popcorn have to do with English?"

"Popcorn and fudge and cookies and apples and cream pies and ice cream—they're the foundation of English. At least they make English more palatable," Miss Willie added with a grin, as she pushed her chair back. "You three read the first six pages of the first chapter. Maybe you won't understand all of it, but go over it while I'm popping the corn, and then I'll help you with it."

Miss Willie grabbed a pan from the cupboard, poured in some oil, sprinkled in the popcorn, and shook the pan over the stove. While the music of popping corn filled the room and the tantalizing aroma made our heads light, we began our study of English.

When the popcorn was buttered, salted, and sitting in the middle of the table in a huge glass bowl, we started at the beginning. Miss Willie, perched on one of the chairs with her legs tucked underneath her and her elbows leaning on the tabletop, began to tutor.

For the first fifteen minutes, I couldn't concentrate on English. I was too enraptured with the realization that we were really spending an evening with Miss Willie. I just wanted to stare at her pretty face and listen to her musical voice. I didn't care what she talked about, even nouns and verbs. I just wanted to listen. Everything she did, from subconsciously drawing pictures on the tabletop with her long fingernails to shaking her curls when she laughed or emphasized an important concept, fascinated me. That first evening I was so sick with love that I was sure I would melt off my chair and onto the floor.

We didn't get far that first session, just nouns, but we covered them completely. Miss Willie had more patience and popcorn than

I ever thought possible in a person. BB came up with some of the dumbest questions, and after having something explained fifty times, he still didn't seem to understand. He became flustered and upset, but Miss Willie always calmed him down with a quiet, "Have some more popcorn, BB. It will come."

There was only once when Miss Willie became angry. That was when BB made a mistake, a real dumb mistake, and Jefferson and I burst out laughing. Miss Willie stared at us, and there was nothing nice about the way she looked. Her eyes were dark with rebuke, and our laughter dried up quick. She cleared her throat and said steadily, "We will have one rule, and we'll never violate it. No one will ever laugh at someone else. Nor will we laugh at or ridicule ourselves. This is one time when we will all be able to make mistakes without worrying about being foolish. We will come here and we will laugh and we will have fun, but not at someone else's expense."

When all the old maids had been crunched and eaten and all that was left in the popcorn bowl was a buttery film, we closed our books and prepared to go. Before we headed for the door, BB became very serious. Staring down at his hands, he said, "Miss Willie, before we go I gotta know something."

"What is it?" Miss Willie asked, leaning forward with her forearms on the table.

"You know the other day you said we was friends, good friends." She nodded. "You said friends could tell each other things, things they can't tell just anyone." She nodded again. "Well, I want to know something. I want you to tell me something. And I want you to be honest. I want you to be straight, even if you think it might hurt me. And them," he added, pointing to Jefferson and me. "Can we do it?" he said after a short pause. "Can we learn English, or are we just wasting our time here and eating all your popcorn?"

"When we run out of popcorn, we'll get something else," Miss Willie said.

BB shook his head. "That's not what's worrying me, Miss Willie. We've got to know. We've had a good time here. We've had fun, more fun than we've had for a long time. I could do this every night, but it's no good unless we can learn something. Do you think we can? We can still be friends, and we'll promise not to mess around in your class." He smiled. "I'll even try not to sleep."

Miss Willie pressed her palms onto the table and spread her fingers wide. She studied them for a moment, and then with the forefinger of her right hand she began tracing the outline of her left hand. "There are some things that aren't generally said between friends," Miss Willie began slowly and seriously without looking up. "They aren't said because between friends they are just understood. Verbalization is not necessary to convey those feelings. Those things are just known." She looked up at us. "I believe in you," she said with a whisper. "I've believed in you from the very first day. If I didn't believe in you, I'm not sure it would be worthwhile staying in Snowflake. You can. I know you can."

"You're not just giving it to us soft?" BB questioned. Miss Willie shook her head definitively. "But the others . . . I mean no one else has . . ."

"Perhaps no one else has been this kind of friend."

Once we left Miss Willie's that night, we didn't speak until we reached Jefferson's yard and were getting ready to split up and head home. BB spoke. He wasn't speaking to Jefferson and me as much as he was just making a statement, a commitment, but it was a commitment all of us felt.

"She's got more faith in us than we got in ourselves," he said. "Maybe she's wrong, but I'm not going to let her down. I'm going to try." He was quiet for a moment and then he said, "You know, this afternoon when we was playing football, you threw me a pass, Jefferson. It was that long bomb. Barnard and Mann were covering me and it didn't look like there was any way I'd haul it in, but I got this gut feeling out there that I was going to get it. As soon as it left your hand I just knew that ball was mine. I caught it. Against the odds." He coughed but it was just a stall. "I got that same gut feeling when Miss Willie was talking tonight. The whole thing looks like a long, wild shot, but I got this old gut feeling that we're going to make it. Not because of us. Because of Miss Willie."

To our surprise, the next day in class Miss Willie went over everything we'd covered the night before. She even asked some of the same questions. Without realizing what he was doing, BB raised his hand after one of Miss Willie's questions and blurted out an answer. Anything intelligent coming from BB in an English class was such an unexpected shock that the class was dumbfounded, assuming that his remark was either a bad joke or blatantly incorrect.

To everyone's surprise Miss Willie smiled and said, "That's exactly right, BB."

I stifled a laugh with the back of my hand as everyone in the class looked at each other and shrugged.

That night we were back at Miss Willie's. This time she was expecting us. The popcorn bowl was on the table, filled to overflowing, and the old box, the fourth chair, was transformed. Miss Willie had scrubbed it down, tacked a puffy pink pillow on top and painted on the side the distinguished words "The Scholar's Throne," and the three of us fought for the illustrious privilege of sitting there.

Miss Willie set a simple pattern during these evening sessions. She discussed in detail with us those things she was going to cover in class the next few days; consequently, we never went to class feeling completely lost. Suddenly English was not the mystery that it had been.

However, we didn't go to Miss Willie's just for English. Miss Willie was the real pull. And we didn't always discuss English. Sometimes we studied math or biology, and on those nights Miss Willie was not the tutor. Jefferson was the expert in biology; BB, in math. And there were times when school was the furthest thing from our minds. On those occasions we talked about football, old cars, jackrabbits, and even old Bill Shakespeare. After listening to Miss Willie, we began to suspect that even Shakespeare was human, maybe even an all-right guy.

Even as much as we enjoyed going to Miss Willie's, none of us would have ever dreamed of going there alone. We had discovered her and made her acquaintance together; it seemed only natural that our relationship would continue in the same way. Oh, we were all smitten by her, totally captivated by her charm, but ours was a shared love, and I'm sure it would have withered and died without the companionship of all three of us.

I suppose one of the highlights of those evenings was food. Miss Willie always had something for us to eat. She never forgot. Sometimes it was only an apple that we split four ways, but those were the best apples we ever ate.

One evening Miss Willie was waiting for us with two banana cream pies.

"You remembered!" Jefferson almost shouted when he saw them.

"Banana cream!" I drooled.

"Let's dive in right now," BB said, hungrily licking his lips and rubbing his hands together. "Forget the English tonight."

Miss Willie casually slid the pies off the table and set them in the refrigerator. Ignoring our drooping mouths and dripping tongues, she sat down at the table and remarked matter-of-factly, "I left them out just so you'd get a peek. Now, English. Later, pie."

"But, Miss Willie," BB groaned, "can't we just have a little piece just to see if it's worth staying for?"

"If you have your doubts, you may go," she replied.

"Can't I just dip my finger in?"

"Absolutely not," she answered sternly. "It will be even better after a little English."

Never had we found it so difficult to concentrate. Our gaze was forever drifting from our grammar books to the closed refrigerator door. Finally our hungry looks were too much for Miss Willie. She snapped her book closed, groaned in frustration, and stepped to the refrigerator.

"We might as well eat pie," she muttered, "because we certainly aren't making phenomenal strides in grammar. Besides, you're making *me* hungry with those starved looks. One of you will have the honor of slicing the pie," she said, setting a pie on the table and returning to the cupboard for a knife.

As soon as the pie was on the table, all three of us lunged for it, vying for the privilege of sinking a knife into it. Miss Willie, hearing our struggle, turned to see the three of us tugging on the pie tin relentlessly. "Don't tear it to pieces!" she gasped.

BB, determined to maintain possession of the pie, retained his tenacious grip and gave one final pull while Jefferson and I let go as soon as Miss Willie called to us. The pie suddenly went sliding across the table out of BB's hands and sailed off the edge, where it flew through the air and crashed into the refrigerator and finally landed face down on the floor, splattering whipped cream and banana filling all over the kitchen.

Suddenly I felt as if a giant hand was squeezing my stomach into a little, hard ball. I couldn't breathe as I gaped at the demolished pie, and I was sure my heart had stopped beating—permanently.

For ten agonizing seconds no one spoke. The horror of the moment was oppressive. I didn't dare glance at Miss Willie. My gaze was riveted to the floor, and from the corner of my eye I could see Miss Willie's bare feet splattered with fragments of pie.

"Well, you three really are hard on pies," Miss Willie finally commented, breaking the silence. I had a quick glimpse of her face and thought I detected the faint traces of a smile. "That's one way to get rid of a pie. Not very creative, however. I think it's been done before. At least you didn't need to turn the lights off this time," she added, bending over and wiping the whipped cream from her foot. "If you didn't want it, BB," she remarked, shrugging her shoulders, "all you had to do was tell me."

"I didn't . . . mean . . . ," BB stuttered, his face white, his lips beginning to move soundlessly. He gulped and held his head in his hands. "I don't know . . . what to say."

"If you think it's that easy to get out of eating one of my pies, you're wrong. That's why I always make two."

"I'm sorry," BB moaned.

"Sorry? How can you be sorry? You haven't even tasted it. You might like it. That's the problem, BB. You jump to conclusions too fast. You might have liked that first pie—before you threw it all over the floor."

All of us stared, dumbfounded, utterly amazed that Miss Willie wasn't screaming, tearing her hair, and throwing us out of her house. She actually seemed amused.

"You're not mad?" BB asked.

"Yes, I'm probably mad," Miss Willie replied. "But," she added with a calming smile, "I'm not angry. Madness is generally hereditary, so you're not responsible. But," she said, raising a finger and jabbing it toward the pie, "you *are* responsible for that. So while you three clean up the splattered pie, something I believe you're experienced in, I'll slice the other pie, something *I'm* experienced in. And this time if you don't want any pie, just tell me. We'll feed it to that black-and-white stray dog."

There's no way to compare cherry and banana cream pies, so we didn't ever know who made the best pie, Sister Hatch or Miss Willie, but when we were finished with Miss Willie's banana cream, there wasn't so much as a flake of crispy crust left in the pie tin. And as we licked our fingers, we each cast a furtive glance toward the garbage pail, wondering if there was anything salvageable and wishing we hadn't disposed of the first pie so quickly.

BB did feel terrible about his accident. He wanted to redeem himself, so he offered to bring something the next evening.

He was proud as he marched up to Miss Willie's door with a pan of fresh-baked brownies. They were sunken in the middle, but they looked good enough for the likes of Jefferson and me. We coaxed him for a taste, but he guarded them all evening, insisting that everyone wait until the end of our lesson so that we would have something to look forward to.

"They better be good," Jefferson mumbled as BB cradled the pan of brownies in his lap.

"They are," he assured us.

"They probably are," I agreed, looking at Miss Willie. "BB's mom makes good brownies. The best I've ever tasted."

"Oh, Mom didn't make these," BB said. "She wasn't around. I whipped up this batch myself."

"*You* did?" Jefferson grimaced.

BB nodded. "Don't worry, I followed Mom's directions. I did add a couple of things."

"Like?" I asked.

"I put in three cups of pecans instead of one. I love pecans in brownies."

"And?" Jefferson prodded.

"I threw in a little coconut. Love coconut, too. And I stirred in some marshmallows and something else, but I forgot what. I was going to put in some gumdrops and chocolate chips, but Mom was fresh out."

"Good for your mom," Jefferson muttered.

Finally the big moment arrived and we closed our books as BB set his treasure on the table. Miss Willie handed him a knife and he began to saw. As soon as his knife sliced into the middle of the pan, a dark ooze, laced with milky goo, seemed to bubble up from beneath the crispy crust on top.

"What's that?" Jefferson croaked, pulling a face.

BB stared for a moment. "I didn't put filling in it. That stuff looks like chocolate marshmallow filling. I wonder where it come from."

I glanced over at Miss Willie, who had her hand pressed over her mouth.

BB dug a piece out of the middle, but everything except the crust dripped back into the pan. "What is this?" BB called out, totally confused. "Mom's don't ever look like this. Who wants the first piece?" he asked, holding the crust on the end of the knife. There were no takers. He thrust the loathsome thing toward Miss Willie. She backed up and held her hands up; then the giggle she had been struggling to squelch erupted, and she was shaking with laughter.

"What's wrong?" BB asked, just a little hurt.

"I'm sorry, BB," she finally managed to say. "I just couldn't help it." She wiped the smile lines from her face and took a deep breath.

"Did you cook them in your oven or your fridge?" Jefferson asked dryly.

"In the oven," BB snapped.

"They do look a little raw in the middle," Miss Willie observed. "What size of pan were you supposed to use? That pan does look a little small."

"I didn't check. I didn't know it mattered, just as long as the dough fit."

"What temperature was the oven?"

"Shoot, I don't know. I just turned it on full blast because I was in a hurry, and when the top looked good and done I took them out."

"Well," remarked Jefferson, "I speak not to try BB's treat. And the next time, BB, why don't you just pick something up at the store. Uncle Roy might not sell burritos, but he's got lots of things better than those brownies."

We did eat part of the brownies before the night was over. Around the edge of the pan, about an inch strip, the dough had cooked fairly well. The brownies weren't anything to cheer about, but we were hungry and it was part of our tradition to have something to eat.

Before I took a bite, however, I looked at BB and asked, "Did you remember to shell the pecans and coconut and take the marshmallows out of the plastic bag?"

Miss Willie smiled and said, "All right, BB's learned his lesson. DJ, let's see what you can come up with the next time."

"I'll whip up something good tomorrow," I promised.

"Not tomorrow," Miss Willie said. "It's Mutual."

"Mutual!" we groaned. "Who cares about Mutual? We'd rather come here."

Miss Willie shook her head. "I need to be at Mutual."

"Why?" Jefferson demanded.

"I'm the new Laurel leader. Don't you three go to Mutual?"

"Not since the pie episode," Jefferson mumbled.

"I'm not sure how welcome we'd be," I added.

"Oh, I'm sure everyone has forgiven you that. Besides, there's a party tomorrow. The fall social."

"What's for refreshments?" BB asked. "Pies?"

"I don't know if I'm ready for another dance," I said.

"I know darn well I'm not," Jefferson muttered.

"Would you go for me?" Miss Willie asked. "I'd feel a lot better knowing you were there."

"What difference does it make to you?" BB asked. "We're not in your class."

"Because I think that's where you should be."

"Nobody wants us there," Jefferson said sullenly. "DJ heard the bishop and Brother Hill and Sister Hollingsworth talking."

"I'd want you there."

We didn't make any promises, but we showed up the next night at the Mutual party. When we walked into the cultural hall, Sue Willis turned to Rita Flake and commented loud enough for us to hear, "Somebody better guard the refreshment table. The gang's here."

"Somebody better guard the main switch, too," Rita added. "I wonder what they got planned for tonight."

The three of us blushed, and BB glowered over at the two girls. "Willis, why don't you just go out and walk your dog."

"I don't have a dog," Sue retorted.

"Oh," BB replied, feigning surprise. Pointing at Rita, he added with malicious delight, "I thought for sure she belonged to you. I guess it's the other way around. Can't ever tell with these Snowflake girls."

Before the girls could reply, we pushed passed them and wandered self-consciously about the hall.

"Come on," Jefferson said after just a few minutes. "I can do without this. Let's get out of here."

We were turning to go when Miss Willie found us. "I was hoping you'd come," she greeted us.

"You're probably the only one," I mumbled. "No one else has welcomed us with open arms. We were about to cut out."

"You won't, will you?" She gave us a pleading stare, and I wondered what she really saw in us, but I knew she wasn't kidding. I knew she wanted us to stay, and I also knew we would.

The party wasn't much—normal for a Snowflake Mutual party. We made ice cream and played some dumb, first-grader games. We didn't talk to Miss Willie much. She was with her girls most of the time, but we didn't pull anything. Not once, all night. We didn't have fun, but for some reason we were glad we had gone.

The next day we took a quiz in English. We were all apprehensive, knowing that if we failed now there was no hope for us, regardless of what Miss Willie said.

When the quizzes were handed back, I didn't dare look at mine for a while. Then I peeked under the corner at the score. Eighty-five percent! I snatched the paper off my desk and stared at it. Jefferson jabbed me in the back. "Eighty-one," he whispered.

We both turned around and looked at BB. He was sitting stiff in his desk, looking straight ahead like he was in a trance. His quiz was in front of him.

The bell rang, and the rest of the class filed out. BB didn't move.

"You okay, BB?" I asked. Miss Willie was watching us.

"I beat Chet Brunson," BB whispered.

I glanced over at Jefferson and shrugged. He shook his head.

"Seventy-four," BB mumbled.

"Seventy-four!" Jefferson and I jumped to our feet and rushed over to see BB's quiz with our own eyes.

"Seventy-four," BB repeated. "I think I'm going to faint."

Miss Willie had come up behind us. She saw the shock on BB's face and tried to console him. "BB, seventy-four really isn't that bad." I could see worry churning in her eyes. "You don't have anything to be ashamed of. In fact, you were probably just a little above the class average."

"Seventy-four," he said again.

"Don't worry about anyone else. You can do better. This is only a beginning. Seventy-four isn't bad."

"Bad!" BB yelped, bolting from his desk and jumping in the air with his quiz clenched in his right fist high above his head. "Do you realize that I actually blew the top off my highest English score? I don't even think I've scored in the 70s, even with DJ's help. I've never been in the 60s since first grade."

BB was beaming all over. "We ought to celebrate. We ought to rip off one of Old Man Harrison's melons if he still has any and have a real . . ." He stopped and stared at Miss Willie, then at Jefferson and me. Suddenly he became serious. "Well," he muttered, "I guess we don't have to celebrate quite like that."

That night when we went to Miss Willie's to study, there was a huge melon in the middle of the table. As soon as we walked in, our eyes were drawn to it. Miss Willie saw our stares. "One of Brother Harrison's," she commented.

"You rip it off?" BB asked incredulously.

Miss Willie replied, "I offered to buy one from him. He refused."

"So you ripped it off?" BB asked again.

"He refused to sell it. He gave it to me. There are better ways to get a melon than in the middle of the night sneaking into somebody's garden."

"Does it taste as good that way, though?" Jefferson asked.

Miss Willie squinted at Jefferson and pressed her lips together. "Much better. And you're even able to sleep that night, without tossing and turning."

This was the first year in our educational careers that we hadn't been sent to the office before the end of the first two weeks of school. Maybe we were maturing, outgrowing our mischievousness. Maybe we had just been ripe for rescue and Miss Willie had come along. Whatever the reasons, we had made some reforms. However, we did have a ways to go.

The fourth week of school Miss Paulsen, who taught geography, came to class five minutes late. She was a big woman, both in height and width, but she wasn't a bad person. We didn't have anything against her, other than that she was a little boring, but BB had been dying to play a trick on her.

Miss Paulsen's desk was an intriguing mystery, and not for just the three of us. She kept about fifty or sixty odd-sized books there, piled haphazardly about the desk in three crooked stacks that leaned in three different directions. On one corner of the desk were six wire baskets for tests and assignments, stacked one on top of the other. On the opposite corner was a huge globe, Miss Paulsen's personal property, her prize. She didn't even let the students touch it. Scattered throughout this conglomeration of books, wire baskets, and globe were cans of colored pencils and pens, a clock, two staplers, and three vases containing the remnants of wilted flowers from previous years. How she ever found anything amid these heaps of confusion no one ventured to guess. But the real mystery, at least for us kids, was how she managed to keep all her junk on top of the desk, where even the slightest sneeze from the back corner of the room seemed to send a threatening tremor throughout the whole mess; and each time Miss Paulsen pulled one of the books from its precarious resting place, the desk's entire contents shuddered and swayed ominously. Members of the class held their breath, just waiting to see if this was the day that

Miss Paulsen's world was going to crumble to the ground. So far it had remained delicately intact.

However, on this particular day, the day she arrived late, BB had doctored up her desk. She came in and grabbed her roll book from the confusing mess, as she always did, but BB had carefully placed a corner of the roll book beneath one of the rickety stacks of books. There were so many other things strewn about the desk that Miss Paulsen didn't notice. As she pulled the roll book free, the first stack of books teetered and then collapsed in a heap, sliding and crashing to the floor.

Miss Paulsen lunged for them, but she bumped another stack, which crashed into the six wire baskets; these flew off the desk and clattered to the floor, sending tests and assignments flying everywhere. While she was grabbing for the wire baskets, her elbow bumped the third stack of books, which in turn slammed into the precious globe. When Miss Paulsen saw her globe toppling to the floor, she made one last frantic lunge, sweeping pencils, pens, staplers, vases, and wilted flowers onto the floor. Her outstretched hands brushed the globe, but it was beyond her grasp. It banged to the floor, bounced once, and then rolled into the first row of student desks.

There poor Miss Paulsen lay, her bulk sprawled on her desk, her arms outstretched, and her hands groping for her prize. The entire class, having anticipated just such a scene, exploded into laughter. Even after she managed to push herself to her feet, straighten herself up, and shout for silence, the hooting and howling continued. All was bedlam.

BB might have escaped suspicion and his deed might have been attributed to fate, but he flaunted his purported innocence by burying his head in a book while writing furiously. Miss Paulsen took one look at the studious BB and shouted above the laughter, "BB Bunderson, get down to Mr. Reynolds's office right now. And you can tell him I'd just as soon you never returned."

"Me?" BB stammered. "Why me?"

"Out!" she screamed.

"It was just a little joke, Miss Paulsen."

She jabbed a finger toward the door, and BB left.

That evening at Miss Willie's we were rather quiet, especially BB. Miss Willie greeted us as usual, and we began a diligent study of English. Too diligent. Usually we drifted from the subject after the first thirty minutes, but this night, it was all English, not because of Miss Willie, either. We figured that as long as we concentrated on English, Miss Willie wouldn't chance upon BB's blunder.

At the end of an hour Miss Willie pushed the books to the middle of the table and knit her fingers together with her hands out in front of her on the table. "How was geography today?" she asked quietly, looking down at her hands.

We all caught our breath and braced ourselves. BB shifted uneasily in his chair and pulled at the hair on the back of his neck. None of us spoke. I'm not sure any of us breathed. We weren't afraid Miss Willie would do something horrible to us—we knew we were safe there. But the only thing we were not safe from was her disappointment. That haunted us.

"How was geography?" she asked once more.

"I didn't mean nothing by it," BB mumbled with his head down. "It was just kind of a joke. I tried to tell her that."

"A joke for whom, you or Miss Paulsen?"

BB shrugged. "Did she tell you?" he asked.

"I think she told everyone."

"Were you embarrassed that you knew me?"

"BB, I'll never be embarrassed that I know you. But I was disappointed, disappointed because I know you're capable of so much more than that. Would you have ever done that to me?"

"Shoot, Miss Willie," BB said, sitting up. "You know I wouldn't. Honest."

"I know," she said quietly. "I want Miss Paulsen to know that you wouldn't ever do anything like that to her, never again."

"I'm trying, Miss Willie." He bit down on his lip. "I really am trying. We all are. I'd promise never to do anything like that again, but shoot, some of my tricks just come out before I can even stop them. I can't promise to never do something like that again, but I'll sure try. Honest."

# Chapter Six

MUCH TO OUR CHAGRIN, we were not the only students attracted to Miss Willie. And yet, we did feel entitled to exclusive rights. After all, we were the first to discover her. Therefore, any attention she gave to others we viewed with jealous vexation. It wasn't enough to be in her only sophomore English class and have her as our private evening tutor. We begrudged everyone the moments they were able to spend with her, especially the students in her Spanish class.

During the first few weeks of school, we heard countless comments about Miss Willie's Spanish classes. It was "Miss Willie showed us this," and "Miss Willie did that," and "Tomorrow in Miss Willie's class we're going to do this." Spanish with her was more than the challenge of another language. It was an exotic adventure into another culture, other people, other places. Anyone not taking her class was missing out.

We had never had the slightest inclination to learn Spanish. Our struggle with English was more than enough to satisfy our academic curiosity. In the beginning we feigned indifference, but soon our flagrant fraud was too much for even us.

One Saturday afternoon as we sat on the porch at my place, I commented as subtly as I knew how, "You know, if a guy was to leave the country, it would sure be nice to know another language."

"You going someplace?" BB asked.

Jefferson, perceiving my train of thought, agreed. "You know, you're right. I've been thinking the same thing myself. You know, we might get called on a mission to . . . well, someplace like Mexico, and knowing, say, Mexican, might be real handy. Mexican is a good language to know."

"And if you go to college," I continued, "knowing a language would really help."

"Are you going to college?" BB asked incredulously. "I thought you said as soon as high school was over you was going to split and never set foot inside a school."

"Well, I'm just supposing," I defended myself, irritated by BB's density of mind. "And besides, a guy can change his mind, can't he? I mean, shoot, when you get mature you wise up to a few things. I've been thinking that college might not be so bad. Who wants to be illiterate?"

"Do they talk Mexican at college?" BB inquired. "If they do, us guys sure don't have a chance. Mexicans would beat us out every time. Without even trying."

"What do you suppose would be a good language to learn?" Jefferson asked, excitement in his voice.

I shrugged. "I don't know. You'd want to be real picky."

"Well, around here," BB mumbled, "there's only one language to choose from. Mexican. It's that or nothing, so you sure better hope they talk Mexican at college."

"You know," mused Jefferson, "Mexican would probably be a good choice. Being so close to the border and all, we really should know Mexican."

"That's what I think," I agreed.

"What border?" BB asked.

"The Mexican border," I said. "It's the only one around."

"But that's three hundred miles from here," BB pointed out, puzzled.

"Yeah," I said, annoyed that BB couldn't understand without our having to draw him a picture, "but we're closer to the Mexican border than the Canadian border. It's smarter to learn Mexican than Canadian."

"If we took Mexican, we could be in Miss Willie's class," BB said, suddenly brightening up, having made a unique discovery.

"Well," I said, "that sure wouldn't be the reason I'd take the class. I mean, I'd want to learn."

"Me too," Jefferson agreed.

"Not me," BB argued. "The only reason I'd take it would be to be in Miss Willie's class. I wouldn't take it from Miss Paine or someone else. You can be dang sure of that."

"Miss Paine doesn't even teach it," I said.

"My mom says she could if she wanted to," BB argued. "She lived in Panama for four years when she was growing up, and Mom says they speak Mexican down there. In fact, she says Miss Paine speaks Mexican real good."

"Well, what if she does?" Jefferson commented. "We're not taking it from her."

Jefferson and I never admitted our real reasons for wanting into Spanish. Instead, we talked of all the highbrow advantages of being fluent in a foreign language. BB just drooled and pondered life with Miss Willie.

Once we decided to get into Spanish, there remained just one obstacle to hurdle. There was only one person who could arrange a class change for a sophomore. Since the high school was not large enough to hire a full-time counselor, Miss Paine worked part-time in that capacity. If we wanted to adjust our schedules, we had to confront Miss Paine.

The fear of facing Miss Paine almost discouraged us, but our romantic yearnings were so powerful that they soon won out, and the three of us prepared ourselves for the daring assault. We discussed our stratagem and decided that it would be best not to approach Miss Paine en masse. We didn't want her to throw up her defenses as soon as she saw our approach. I volunteered to blaze the way. If I survived, the others were going to follow a day or so later.

I went to her class several minutes before the first bell so that I would have ample time to present my case, but not so much time that Miss Paine would be able to eat me up.

"Hello, Daniel," Miss Paine greeted me as I shuffled in and stood awkwardly before her desk. I nodded a greeting but was too flustered and nervous to speak. "Won't you sit down?"

"I'll only be a minute," I rasped. "I just wanted to check with you about a class change."

"How can I help you?" She seemed almost nice. I was afraid to proceed with my request. I didn't want to upset her after finding her in such a good mood. I was sure she didn't have very many of them. "Well," I began, thinking of the prepared remarks the three of us had finally settled on, "I've been thinking about my future and all. You see, I haven't always been real dedicated." Miss Paine nodded. "I haven't taken school very serious. But I'm planning to start. Right now, if you'll let me. I might even go to college or to Mexico on a mission. I figure that I should start thinking about learning another language. Don't you think it would be plenty smart to learn another language?"

"I think that's an excellent idea."

"And since we're so close to the border and all, I thought Mexican would probably be my best bet. Don't you think Mexican would be a good language to know? I mean, English is all right too, but this would be just in case I ran into trouble and had to talk to some Mexicans. There are a lot of them around."

Miss Paine's gaze bore into me, and I felt my stomach melt right into my shoes. She pushed back in her chair. "So you would like to learn Spanish?" She emphasized *Spanish*.

"Yeah."

"You have a genuine desire to learn Spanish?" I nodded. "Learning a language can be difficult. It's not an easy task. One must apply himself and do the best he possibly can." I nodded mutely, staring in wide-eyed terror. My mouth was dry, my heart was thumping wildly in my chest, and I was sweating like a work plug. "Many students find English difficult. Do you find English difficult?"

"Well, things are clearing up some."

"I can assure you that learning another language can be even more taxing mentally than, let's say, an English class. I don't mean to discourage you, but I do want to make certain you know what you are getting in to. Are you sure you want to learn Spanish?"

"I sure do."

"You would be several weeks behind. How would you catch up?"

I gulped. We hadn't thought of that. "That wouldn't be a problem for me," I blurted out.

"Oh," she said, obviously amused. "Have you had Spanish before?"

"Well, not exactly, but I know some Mex . . . I mean Spanish."

"For example."

I almost swallowed my tongue. "Well," I stammered, "I know *tortilla, adios, bueno, como está,* and, well, some words I'd rather not say to you . . . or to anyone else."

She pursed her lips. "Obviously your background is quite extensive." She paused, and I caught the trace of a smile at the corners of her mouth. "Do you think you could get along with Miss Willie?"

I smiled broadly. "I sure do. Why, she's the main . . . I mean, I know her real well, and we're good friends."

"Would you be as anxious to learn Spanish if someone else were teaching the class?"

"Huh?"

"Would you be as anxious to learn Spanish if someone else—let's say Miss Paine, for example—were teaching the class?"

"You're not teaching the class, are you?" I tried to make the question sound like a question rather than a groan.

"I'm just supposing. Would you still want to learn Spanish?"

I licked my lips and stared down at Miss Paine's desk so I wouldn't have to expose myself to those penetrating brown eyes. I wanted to stuff my hands into my pockets and prevent the tremendous squirm that was exploding within me, but I knew how Miss Paine felt about boys who stuffed their hands into their pockets. "I sure want to learn Spanish," I replied simply.

"Very well, we'll arrange it."

My whole body sighed. "Thank you," I mumbled as I started for the door, afraid I would faint if I stayed in the room another minute.

"Mr. Johnson," she called out. I stopped. "I've heard some good reports about you." I stared blankly, trying hard to detect a trace of sarcasm in her voice. "I believe you are capable of learning Spanish, and I think Miss Willie can handle you. If I didn't, I wouldn't even consider this request." She paused to let her words sink in. "If I make the change, I demand that you behave. I'll accept nothing less." I began creeping toward the door. "Oh, by the way, Daniel."

"Huh?"

"Mr. Judd and Mr. Bunderson? Is their appointment later?"

"Huh?"

"Are your two friends coming in later?"

I hesitated and then nodded sheepishly. A smile drifted across her lips. "Why don't you have them come in today and save my time—and their agony."

Early in the morning, four weeks into the first term, BB and Jefferson and I entered Miss Willie's classroom to ask permission to enroll in her Spanish class. We tromped self-consciously into her room and stood at attention in front of her desk.

"Hello," she greeted us with her usual vivacious smile. "Coming in for an early start on English?"

We cleared our throats and each of us looked to the other two to broach the subject of a class change. The other two remained mute, so rather than appear as the bumbling fools we probably were, I began to speak haltingly. "Ah, Miss Willie, we ah, had something we wanted to ah, well, ah, ask you about."

"Yes."

I looked at BB and Jefferson and they ducked their heads in their characteristically cowardly way. I pushed onward, my ears and neck red with embarrassment. "You know, we've been thinking about going on our missions. Not right away, but you know, someday we'll go on a mission maybe. Well, a lot of the guys get sent to foreign countries now, and, well, we thought if we were going to be missionaries it would sure be nice to learn a language, especially if we get sent to . . . well, to some place like . . ."

"Like Mexico," BB offered. "You know we sure would like to learn a little Mexican so we'd know what the people were talking. No sense in going all that way unless you could talk with the people. Mexican is what we figure we need."

"He means Spanish," I corrected, "but he's right. We do want to be prepared."

Miss Willie nodded her head sagely. "What makes you think you will get sent to Mexico?"

BB replied, "Well, where else would they send us? I mean, we're so close to the border here. It would be easy just to ship us down there and they wouldn't have to worry about running us all over the world. We'd be right there. And besides, my family is kinda Mexican. I hear they like to know where your family's from. Sometimes they send you there. You know, so you can teach your relatives."

"Your family is Mexican, BB?" Miss Willie asked.

"Just kinda. No big deal. You see, I have a cousin that's Mexican."

"Just one cousin that's Mexican? How did you ever manage that?"

"My aunt adopted a Mexican kid. I mean, he was straight from across the border. He didn't even know English. He didn't know much Spanish either because he was just a baby, but he was a pure-blooded Mexican."

Miss Willie looked at Jefferson and me. "Do you two have a Mexican heritage as well?"

Jefferson shifted his weight and said, "Our family rode the train from Nogales to Hermosillo. We were there three days, so you might say we lived in the country."

"I just love the people," I said, having no better credentials to offer.

The room was silent for a long time; then Miss Willie asked, "Do you think you could catch up?"

"To what?" BB wanted to know.

"To the rest of the class. After all, you're four weeks behind. That would put you at a disadvantage. Do you think you could do it?"

Jefferson and I nodded. BB asked, "You wouldn't flunk us, would you?"

"I won't play favorites. I'll help you, but I won't give you anything you don't deserve." We stared. She smiled and added, "Like I've said before, you don't have to be in my class for us to be friends, but if you are in my class, I will insist that you work, that you learn, because when you go on your missions, I don't want any Mexican gentleman or lady wondering to himself or herself who the phony was who taught you Spanish. I want them to be duly impressed. You see, your Spanish will be a reflection on me."

That was how we commenced our Spanish lessons, back at the bottom of the pile. Everyone else was ahead of us.

Though we had been exposed to a little Spanish growing up in Snowflake, where migrant workers passed through occasionally, our knowledge was limited at best. It didn't take us many days to realize that we had accepted much more than we had anticipated. From the start we were so baffled that we were unable to do anything except gape in total perplexity as each class period passed us by.

After discovering what the class entailed, we had second thoughts. Four days after enrolling in the class, while we were on our way to school, BB suggested, "Let's just not worry about Spanish. We got enough to worry about with English. We're in her class now and we can have the fun and all. She ain't going to flunk us. I can live with a D-minus. It won't be the first time. My mom already thinks I'm a brain for just getting into the class."

"I'm not sure that would be fair to Miss Willie," I said. Jefferson nodded. "After all, she let us into the class. She let us in because we said we'd learn."

"Oh, brother," BB moaned. "If we keep this up, we'll have to drop out of football and become full-time students."

"You can always drop out of Spanish," Jefferson suggested.

"I don't want to drop out of Spanish," BB snapped. "I just got in the class. I like being in Miss Willie's class. I just don't see the sense in learning Spanish."

Miss Willie was the one who finally rescued us, helping us evenings with Spanish as well as English. It was slow, tedious progress, but we grudgingly persisted.

One evening when we were having a particularly taxing struggle with Spanish verbs, Miss Willie pushed the books into the middle of the table as she usually did when she wanted to talk and said, "Do you want to forget about Spanish?"

"Yeah, I'm pretty burned-out tonight," Jefferson confessed.

"No, I mean for good."

"You mean drop out of your class?" I asked.

She nodded. Her suggestion was greeted by silence. "Some things you have to want very badly. You don't get them just because you say you want them. You have to want them so badly that you are willing to do whatever is necessary to obtain them. Learning a language is like that."

"You don't think we want to bad enough?" I asked.

"I don't know," she answered. "I don't know if that's even the point. I don't care if you learn Spanish."

"You don't?" BB said, smiling.

She shook her head. "But," she added, raising a forefinger, "I don't like anyone to give up on something just because it's hard, especially if it's something he wants. Sometimes you need to finish a thing just to prove to yourself you can do it, that you're willing to pay the price. By doing the impossible, or even the improbable, you gain confidence. Oftentimes that rugged confidence is more valuable than the task itself."

She paused for a moment, then went on. "When I was in junior high, I hated to run. In PE, each semester we had to run the 600-yard dash. A good time for the girls was 1:50. That was a very good time. The record was 1:46. One day after coming in almost last, I decided—it was a crazy idea at first—but I decided I was going to run that 600-yard dash in 1:45, just to prove I could do it.

"I exercised and ran, and before the year was out I ran the 600-

yard dash in 1:43. It almost killed me. I was sick. My muscles ached. My lungs were on fire. But I had done it! There was a sense of satisfaction there, a feeling of victory that I'd never experienced before. You know, I never ran that race again, but I proved something to myself, and it filled me with confidence."

Miss Willie picked up a pencil and began doodling on a notepad. "I had never had outstanding grades in school, but I wanted to go to college. Mom was a widow and really didn't have the means to send me, so I knew the only way I could go to college was with a scholarship. To get a scholarship, my grades had to be good, much better than they were. I remember thinking to myself, 'If I can run the 600-yard dash in record time, I can bring my grades up.' My junior and senior years I had straight A's. It seemed impossible, but I did it. I kept thinking back on that 600-yard dash. That run gave me confidence that I fall back on even today."

For several minutes Miss Willie was quiet. "Learning Spanish can be your challenge," she continued. "If you really want to, you can do it."

"That's a lot of work just to prove we can do something," BB muttered. "Besides, English has been a pretty good challenge for us. And if it's just a test we want, why don't we do something like run a four-minute mile or hike across America?"

Miss Willie shrugged. "You can do anything. But don't sell yourselves short."

I took a deep breath. "I can't see that this Spanish is getting us anyplace."

Jefferson nodded. "Can't you just let us forget the whole thing?"

"And we'll start right now looking for something to do that will build our confidence," BB volunteered.

"I'm not holding you to anything. If you feel good about putting Spanish aside, then do it. But don't ask me to make the decision for you. You chose to take Spanish. Now you must choose whether or not to pursue it." She looked at each of us.

"Will you think we're quitters?" BB wondered.

"Will *you* think you're quitters?"

BB thought for a moment and then reached for the Spanish

book and opened it. "It would sure be a lot easier climbing Mount Everest or something, but I sure ain't going to be no quitter. Run them verbs past me again."

One of the things that helped us over the rough places in Spanish was our standing joke about going on a mission. After all, we had pushed our way into Spanish under that pretense. We joked as though Miss Willie's class were a crash course to prepare us for this imaginary mission call that was to come any day. We almost began to believe the call was imminent. If a member of the bishopric interviewed one of us or just stopped to visit in the hall at church, the other two would whisper, "He's probably going to get his call now."

"Yeah, and with his luck he'll probably get sent to the Eskimo Alaskan Mission."

"Is there such a mission?"

"When the bishop's finished with him there will be. We'll probably all get sent there."

"Do Eskimos speak Spanish?"

"How would I know? They probably talk Eskimoan. They better start learning Spanish, though, because if I get sent there, I ain't about to learn another language."

"Yeah, we'll have to teach the Eskimos Spanish first, and if they make it through the language lessons, we'll throw in a little gospel."

"What if they're as slow as we are?"

"Then our grandkids will have to finish the job for us."

When one of us became despondent, the others would encourage with mock seriousness, "This will sure help you on your mission," or "You better go over that one more time. How are the Mexicans going to understand you if you talk like you got mush in your mouth?" or "What kind of a missionary would say it that way? You'll give them a headache just listening to you."

Miss Willie listened to our bantering without comment until one evening she said with her usual intuition, "What's so funny about a mission? Why don't you want to go?"

"Who said we weren't going?" I asked. Her question made us

uneasy. We hadn't exactly said we weren't going, and yet none of us had really committed ourselves to a mission.

"*Are* you planning to go on a mission?" Miss Willie asked.

The three of us shrugged sheepishly. "Well, it's hard to tell right now," Jefferson said. "You know we still have a few years."

"No sense rushing things," BB added. "Besides, we *are* preparing for a mission. You know, learning Spanish."

Miss Willie got a far-off look in her eyes and remarked almost as though she were talking to herself and yet wanting us to overhear, "If I were looking for a young man to marry, the first thing I would want to know would be if he had served an honorable mission."

We squirmed. But she had our attention. "Why's that?" I asked.

"Because I would know so much about him. I would know that he was dedicated, spiritual, unselfish, hard-working. So many other things. Those are the kinds of things I'd look for in a young man."

"Couldn't you be all those things without going on a mission?" Jefferson asked.

"Maybe," she conceded, "but a mission makes so many things obvious. Personally, I wouldn't marry anyone else. And there are lots of other girls who feel the same way about good missionaries. So you see, when you joke about missionaries, you're joking about the young men I admire most."

"Is that what's wrong with the guys in Salt Lake, none of them are returned missionaries?" BB asked.

"There are lots of returned missionaries in Salt Lake," Miss Willie answered.

"Then what's wrong with them guys?"

"Now, what is that supposed to mean? What makes you think anything is wrong with them?" She knit her brow and squinted at BB.

"Are they normal?"

"Why, of course they're normal! Why?"

"They're not all blind or retarded or something?"

"BB, whatever are you talking about?"

"I was just wondering," he said bashfully. "The fact that you're still single doesn't say much for those guys in Salt Lake. They couldn't be all normal."

"BB," Miss Willie scolded, her face suddenly glowing with embarrassment.

"It's just something I wondered about."

"Well, you can stop wondering and start on your Spanish."

We were all quiet for a moment, making a pretense of study but doing little more than staring at our open books. Then Jefferson asked, "Do you have a missionary, Miss Willie?"

Miss Willie opened her eyes wide. "Do I have *a* missionary?" she asked, trying to sound indignant. She laughed suddenly and pushed back in her chair. "Why, I'll have you know that I have not only one but three." She cleared her throat and then added in a lower tone, "At least they are future missionaries. I hope." She winked at us and we all grinned.

"Come on, Miss Willie," Jefferson coaxed, "that isn't what I mean. Do you have a missionary now?"

"You're prying," she said, pointing a pencil at Jefferson.

"We're just curious."

Miss Willie's cheeks colored and she opened a book. "No, I don't. Now, back to Spanish."

"Did you ever have one?" Jefferson persisted.

Gradually the smile on Miss Willie's face faded completely and was replaced by that lonely, far-off gaze. It was as though the question punctured her exuberance and deflated her spirit. I glanced at Jefferson, and I could tell he wished he had not asked the question.

For the longest time no one spoke. We lacked the social graces to cover up a blunder. All we could do was sit in suffering silence and hope Miss Willie would rescue us. Finally she did.

She heaved a sigh and attempted a smile, but no joy was reflected there, only sadness. "Yes, I had a missionary once."

"You don't have to tell us anything," Jefferson reminded her, trying to cover up for his question.

Miss Willie laughed weakly, then stared down at the table and began talking. "It seems so long ago now, but it's been only a few months. There was a returned missionary in Salt Lake, one I was very fond of."

"Just fond?" BB asked, his curiosity overpowering his silence.

Miss Willie laughed again, this time with genuine humor in her voice. "No, I was more than fond of him. We had talked of getting married. He was planning to start law school this fall. But before we got married I wanted to go on a mission."

"You a missionary?" BB gasped, sitting up in his chair.

Miss Willie looked at him and said, "Girls go on missions. All the time."

"Some girls," BB argued. "Not all of them."

"Well, I was one of the some who wanted to go."

BB scratched his head and said, "You just don't seem the type."

"And what may I ask is wrong with me?" Miss Willie demanded, putting her hands on her hips and glaring at BB. She was on the verge of laughter, but she held it in check with feigned austerity.

"Nothing's wrong with you," BB said, "that's why I wondered." He grinned over at Jefferson and me.

"Mr. Bunderson," Miss Willie chided, "you have a very warped opinion of missionaries, sisters and elders."

He shrugged. "I guess so, because I sure didn't think you looked like lady missionary material."

I glanced over at Miss Willie. Her cheeks were a ripe crimson.

"Well, I was going to be a missionary. You don't think I'd ask you to do something I wouldn't do myself, do you?"

"I won't think it anymore," BB assured her.

"So you were going to go on a mission while your missionary went to law school?" I asked. She nodded. "Is he still in law school?"

"He started this fall."

"But you didn't go on a mission," I pointed out.

Once again the sadness returned, but this time she didn't stop talking.

"No, I didn't go. When I went for my physical, I discovered ... well, I discovered that I wasn't as healthy as I had hoped, as I had thought."

"Shoot! You look great to me," BB blurted out.

"Well," she sighed, "that's what I'd thought too, but I was mistaken."

"And so you wanted to get out of Salt Lake while your RM went to law school," Jefferson said, having drawn a unique conclusion.

"Oh, I suppose that was part of it. I didn't want to be so close to something that would never be. It was best for both of us."

"You mean you're not marrying the guy?" BB asked.

Miss Willie shook her head.

"What's wrong with the guy?" BB persisted.

"Nothing is wrong with him. It just wasn't the right thing. Sometimes two people can want something very badly but it's still not the right thing."

"Did he do something to you?" Jefferson asked.

"No," she whispered. "It wasn't anything either one of us could have prevented. It was just there, and we both knew it wasn't going to go away."

"When you first came," BB pointed out, "you said you were . . . well, that you were running, trying to get away. Were you running from that? You know, him?"

Miss Willie pressed her lips together and closed her eyes for a moment. She shook her head slowly.

"You don't have to say," Jefferson whispered. "We'll understand."

"At least you know how I feel about missionaries," she finally said, the cheeriness back in her voice. "So when you speak of missionaries, remember they're special. At least *I* think they are."

The three of us sat in silence, each contemplating Miss Willie's revelation. The thought suddenly occurred to us that if we were to be any better than Silas Flake, Clyde Clancey, Frank Martin, and the other notorious bachelors in Snowflake, then we would have to at least commit ourselves to a mission.

BB rubbed his chin. "Actually, I've always wanted to go on a mission. Always."

Jefferson and I glanced at each other and then at BB. "You haven't said much about it," I said. "Has it been a secret?"

"Well, that's just because . . . that's . . . I . . . it's a private thing."

"And I guess you've always wanted to go to Mexico too?" I remarked sarcastically. "Wanted to go back to the old country and look up more of your family?"

"I haven't exactly thought about where, but I'd sure go to Mexico if I got sent."

"Especially if you had the right girl suggest it," I observed.

"Huh?"

Jefferson nodded knowingly, not wanting BB to get an unfair advantage. "I guess I'm going too," he said. "I haven't thought about it all my life like BB, but I'm going. That's for sure."

"Would you two hold down the noise," I barked, not to be outdone. "If I don't get these verbs down, I'll never be ready for my mission."

# Chapter Seven

ONE FRIDAY EVENING as we were rushing to the theater to see a western for the fourth time, we noticed that Miss Willie's light was on. Returning two hours later, we found the same light still burning. None of us said anything that first time, but as the weeks passed and that lonely light burned each Friday and Saturday night, we felt the unmistakable stirrings of guilt.

There wasn't much social life available for anyone in Snowflake, but for the single woman there was absolutely nothing. Unless, of course, she chose to watch ball games, stroll deserted streets, catch an occasional movie, or count stray dogs.

The first part of November, during one of our discussions on the church lawn, I broached the subject that had haunted all of us.

"Do you suppose Miss Willie has any fun here?"

"You don't mean in Snowflake?" Jefferson asked.

I nodded.

"Nobody else does," BB interjected. "I don't see why she would."

"That's just what I mean. You see, we have things we can do. We have somebody to do them with, but what about Miss Willie? What can she do? And who does she have to do it with?"

"Sometimes she goes to those parties and dances at the church," Jefferson remarked.

"You mean the ones the old maids and bachelors go to?" BB asked.

Jefferson nodded.

I shuddered. "Do you know who else goes to those?" I demanded. "Clyde Clancey, Silas Flake, Rupert Turley, Barney Willis, Thomas Peterson. Just to name a few."

"Why does she hang around that crowd? One of those old guys will try to marry her. Can't she do better than that?"

"Who else is there?"

"Us," Jefferson said. "I mean, we're young but we're not bald and belly heavy."

"That's what I mean. We're the only real . . . you know, good friends she has. Unless we want to turn her out to pasture with those . . . *bachelors.*" I said the word like it was a curse.

"What can we do?" Jefferson asked.

"Well, I don't know how much more she can stand."

"Do you think we ought to ask her to the movies?" BB inquired. "Or we could take her rabbit hunting tonight."

"Somehow I can't picture Miss Willie shooting rabbits. She doesn't have the stomach for it. She reads too much of that Shakespeare to be much of a rabbit poacher."

"Well, if Shakespeare's what she likes, we better leave her to it because I sure don't want to spend my Friday nights reading Shakespeare. Even for Miss Willie."

"The Harvest Ball's coming up," I suggested, trying to sound casual.

The Harvest Ball was the big fall affair, one notch above the homecoming dance. However, it wasn't something the three of us had ever seriously considered. We would have preferred an evening with John Wayne in the Alamo or El Dorado.

"You mean a dance?" BB choked.

I nodded.

"Shoot! That's worse than spending a night with Shakespeare."

"You going?" Jefferson asked.

"Well, I haven't decided." I paused and snatched at a blade of grass that was beginning to yellow from the fall cold. "I'll bet Miss Willie would sure like to go. I hear that people from big cities really go for things like dances. Any English teacher would like a good dance."

The other two looked at me and nodded slowly but dubiously.

"Someone ought to take her," I suggested.

"There are probably lots of guys that would like to take her."

"The trouble is there's no one that Miss Willie would like to go with," I said. "Have you seen Rupert Turley hanging around her after church? He's as square as a brick and probably only half as exciting. She'd rather stay home than go with a clod like him. But if someone else doesn't hurry and ask her, old Rupert is going to bully his way onto the scene, and Miss Willie is too nice to turn him down."

We contemplated, going over Snowflake's eligible bachelors one more time to see if we had overlooked any promising prospects. Our review of the potential candidates only discouraged us.

"Well, like you said, Jefferson," I pointed out, "she's got us."

"You don't mean *us!* Us take her to the Harvest Ball? I don't turn sixteen till January."

"Me neither," BB chimed in, panic in his voice.

"I won't be sixteen till December," I said, "but that's not the point. We're not really going on a date. I mean, we're not going to marry her. I mean, we would just be trying to help her out a bit."

"I wouldn't know the first thing about going on a date," Jefferson confessed. "Getting into her Spanish class and going to her place for help is one thing, but a date? That's out of my class."

BB nodded in agreement.

"So we let Rupert and Clyde fight over her," I growled. "Well, I think we ought to do something."

"You going to ask her?" Jefferson said.

"I figured that maybe it was all of our jobs, not just mine."

"You mean we all ask her and let her decide which one she wants to take?" BB asked.

"No," I snapped.

"Aunt Betty and Uncle Roy won't let me date, so I'm out," Jefferson said. "I have to be sixteen."

"Same here," BB said.

I could feel they were nervous and didn't want to be part of this. "It isn't a date," I insisted. "Not to the Harvest Ball. Everyone's going to be there anyway."

That was true. In some of the bigger cities the rock bands had pushed the parents and other old folks out the back door and left the kids to rule the dimly lit dance floors. But in 1966, Snowflake was pretty conservative. Rock bands were considered musical freaks, the only acceptable attire to a dance was a person's Sunday-go-to-meeting clothes, and though the lights were dimmed, it was always easy to recognize the faces on the opposite end of the floor. And the really big dances, like the Harvest Ball, were still community affairs. Nobody paid much attention to who came with whom, because anybody over fourteen who could walk showed up, and once the dance got cranked up nice, a guy could dance with anybody he bumped into.

"You guys are letting Miss Willie down."

"But we're not old enough."

"Alone we're not," I reasoned, "but together we're forty-five. That's plenty old."

"Together?" Jefferson and BB asked in unison.

"Yeah, we'll all take her!"

"All of us?" Jefferson rasped.

"It's us or Rupert."

I finally managed to prick their consciences, and they admitted that we did have an obligation, and since we were about the best that Snowflake had to offer, BB and Jefferson decided to throw in with me.

We debated how to ask her. Jefferson thought it would be easiest to phone her and that way we wouldn't have to face her in case she turned us down. None of us would volunteer to act as voice, so that idea died. BB suggested sending her a card with an invitation, but we weren't sure how she would reply, and sending an invitation in Snowflake, especially to someone like Miss Willie, whom we saw regularly, seemed terribly ostentatious.

"Why don't we just go over there like men and ask her?" I suggested.

"Together?" the other two gasped. "You mean just stand there and ask her? What if she says no? We'll feel real dumb."

"She won't tell us no. How could she?"

That evening the three of us marched reluctantly up Miss Willie's walk. No one had volunteered ahead of time to be the spokesman, so when the other two cowered behind me like scared pups, I knew I had been appointed. I had wanted all of us to stand there in a line and have the proposal come out naturally, but I could see that that was wishful thinking.

"Hello," Miss Willie greeted us as she opened the door and motioned for us to come in.

"Actually, we're in a hurry and don't have time to stay," I explained, refusing to move a step forward. Jefferson and BB were poking me in the back, prodding me so our misery could be laid to rest. "We were wondering if you knew what the Harvest Ball is."

"Isn't that the Thanksgiving dance?"

I nodded. "It's a special dance. One of the big ones. Everyone goes to it, the whole town. It's not like one of those dances we have after the football games, just for kids. This is a big dance. Lots of decorations and things."

"It sounds nice."

"You don't have to have a date but some people do."

She smiled.

"Do you think you'll go?"

Miss Willie laughed. "Well, I'm not sure. I would like to drop by and see the decorations."

"They have refreshments, too," BB called out from behind me.

"Well, maybe I'll get some refreshments while I'm there."

"So you'll go?"

"Probably. I don't want to miss one of the best dances in Snowflake."

"Well, that's great. Just great." I smiled broadly. "That's all we wanted to know. Good-bye, Miss Willie," I said, waving and walking backward down her front steps, tromping on BB's and Jefferson's toes.

Smiling triumphantly, I turned to the other two and asked, "How was that? She's going. I really asked her. Nothing to it."

BB patted me on the back and congratulated me, but Jefferson shook his head slowly and said, "I don't think she got the message."

"Huh?"

"I really don't think she realizes that we asked her to the dance."

"But she said she was going."

"But not with us."

"Maybe she has a date."

"Maybe we better go back and do it right."

I hesitated, but the other two insisted, and a few minutes later we were ringing Miss Willie's bell again.

The door opened a second time and Miss Willie stared out at us. "Yes?" she asked, cocking her head to the side in puzzled fashion.

"We forgot to ask you something," I blurted out. "We'll take you."

"Take me where?"

"To the Harvest Ball."

"To the Harvest Ball?"

"Yeah," BB called out. "We're going to be your date to the dance. We didn't figure anyone else would ask you except for Rupert or Clyde, so we thought we'd kinda help you out."

I felt like sinking into my shoes. "He doesn't mean that. I mean, he means it, but not the way he said it. What BB means," I explained, "is that we really wanted you to have a date, and we didn't know for sure if you had one, so if you don't have one we'll take you. It wouldn't exactly be a normal date because we'd all take you."

"The three of you?" she inquired, smiling slightly.

We all nodded. "It's us or Rupert Turley," BB added.

Miss Willie tried to stifle a laugh, but it burst out anyway. "Now how can I refuse? I feel flattered to have the three most eligible gentlemen in town want to escort me to the Harvest Ball. Of course I'll go. What time will you stop by for me?"

We stared at each other, having forgotten that minor detail; in fact, we had not worked out any details, thinking that just asking her to the dance would suffice. "Well, it's next Friday," I said, pursing my lips. "I believe it starts at eight-thirty. But we can't drive yet so we'll just have to walk, but it's only two blocks to the school. We can make it unless it rains or something."

"And we can go down to the Frost-top for something to eat after it's over," BB volunteered.

"It sounds . . . interesting," Miss Willie said. "I'll be looking forward to my first Harvest Ball in Snowflake."

If Snowflake was backward, our naïveté and our lack of social graces made us barbarians of the lowest order. Our understanding of anything formal or proper was shallow to nonexistent. Etiquette was not part of our meager vocabulary. We were learning Spanish, not French. We didn't know the pronunciation of the word, much less its meaning.

Formal to us was a pair of slacks, button shirt, and no tennis shoes, although under some circumstances we might have allowed for the tennis shoes. On this particular night we went semiformal—we left our tennis shoes home but wore our white athletic socks.

Fortunately, we had arrived at that stage in life when we were beginning to realize the benefits of a regular shower, but we weren't ones to indulge liberally. We had showered in PE the morning of the dance, so we didn't see any need to repeat the process that night. After all, how dirty can you get between 10:00 A.M. and 8:30 P.M.?

The three of us congregated at Jefferson's house and checked our funds to see if we had enough for something to eat at the Frost-top. That concluded our preparations for the evening. Certain that we had done everything possible to make this a memorable evening for Miss Willie, we left Jefferson's place and crossed the street to Miss Willie's.

I don't know what we had expected at Miss Willie's, but it wasn't what we got. She came to the door in a long dress. It was the nicest dress I had seen her in, and yet I didn't notice its color or fit. Her hair was different, but I didn't know why exactly. She was pretty, probably dazzling, but of course she was always beautiful, so the three of us just assumed everything was normal. Her beauty was wasted on us. There were no remarks of admiration, just a blurted, "Well, you ready to go?" We were too naive to realize that her appearance and ours were terribly incongruous.

Miss Willie had us come in and sit down. She went into the kitchen and came back with three little square boxes and handed us each one.

"What's this?" Jefferson asked.

"Open it," she laughed.

"Flowers!" we said in unison.

"Which one of us pins it on you?" BB asked, his brow knit together in puzzled pain.

"They're 'buttoneers,' I think," Jefferson whispered. "The guy's supposed to wear them."

"The guy?" BB choked. Miss Willie nodded. "I always thought the girl was supposed to wear the flowers."

"Oh, she does—if someone brings her one. Generally she doesn't buy the flowers for herself too." The hint was far from subtle, but it escaped us. Had she wanted to drive the point home, she would have needed a sledgehammer.

The three of us fumbled with our flowers for a while until our fingers were sore and the flowers almost torn to pieces; then Miss Willie offered to help, saving our fingers as well as our flowers.

When we reached the cafeteria, where all of Snowflake's dances were held, the three of us charged through the door, pushing and shoving each other like we were going to a cockfight. Miss Willie brought up the rear. Once inside we discovered to our horror that the dance was not free. It cost two dollars a person or three dollars a couple. Since no arrangements had been made concerning a foursome, we paid the two-dollar price, which took almost all our dinner money, meaning we would have to settle for drinks after the dance instead of a round of hamburgers and fries.

Inside, we jabbed our fists into our pockets and promenaded around the floor once with Miss Willie tagging along. When we had discovered who was at the dance and decided what kind of dance this was going to be, we found the refreshment table and did everything we could to eat up two dollars' worth of punch and cookies so that our dance tickets would not be a complete waste.

Miss Willie nibbled on an occasional cookie and listened in si-

lence while Jefferson and BB and I snickered and criticized every
girl we saw.

"How did Mae Ellen get a date to this?"

"Her old man probably hired the guy. He looks like he's from
out of town. Probably does this kind of thing for a living."

"What a way to make a living!"

"Yeah. He ought to hire himself out as a dog walker at a pet
show. He'd have lots of practice."

"Ruth came with her brother."

"No one else would ask her."

"Look at Tanya's hair."

"Looks like she dried it with a blowtorch and combed it with a
rake."

"Have you seen Ruby dance?"

"Yeah. She looks like a duck."

"Actually, I think a duck is a little more graceful."

The girls were not the only ones who were the targets of our
whispered abuse. "Looks like Rupert poured himself into his suit
for the big dance."

"I hope his seams hold out."

"Did he come with anybody?"

"I think he came with Sarah Haws, but she ditched him as soon
as she saw him head for the refreshments."

"He'll never even know it as long as he's at the trough."

"Don't tell me Silas showed up."

"Alone?"

"I think he brought one of his cows but they wouldn't let him
bring her in."

"Yeah, they were afraid Rupert would dance with her."

"Hey, Danny's wearing a suit."

"A suit to a dance?"

"He's really trying to play cool."

As we giggled and poked fun—I suppose in a crude attempt to
impress Miss Willie with our sophomoric sophistication—we
didn't notice the stony change that came over her. Halfway
through the dance, after we had bloated ourselves with punch and

cookies, she asked, "Is anyone going to dance? This is a dance, you know." There was a crisp edge to her voice, but in our punch-drunken state, we didn't detect it. We slid down in our chairs, poked each other, and laughed raucously.

"We don't know too much about dancing, Miss Willie," BB answered. "Besides, dancing is dumb, if you ask me."

"Yeah," I agreed. "I'd feel like a fool prancing around out there like that spastic idiot Danny Carson."

"I hate to dance," Jefferson added. "You couldn't get me out there with a team of horses."

Miss Willie nodded, then stood and asked to go home. We grabbed one last cup of punch, filled our pockets with cookies, and filed out of the cafeteria into the crisp November air, feeling rather proud of ourselves for having survived our first dance.

"Do you want a drink down at the Frost-top?" Jefferson asked.

"No, thank you," she answered.

"We were going to buy something to eat, but we didn't know they were going to rob us at the door. We don't have enough money for eats now."

"Thank you, but I think I would rather go home."

"We're paying," I said. "You don't have to worry about the money."

"I wasn't thinking about the money."

We started home. It was then that we realized just how quiet Miss Willie had been all evening. We began to sense for the first time that something was wrong. Our joking stopped, and the four of us walked the two blocks in silence.

As we took her to the front door, BB spouted off, "Did you have a good time?"

She waited a moment before responding. "It was an experience I probably won't forget."

"Yeah, I didn't have such a bad time either. It was kinda funny watching some of them guys try to dance, especially Rupert and Silas. And the punch and cookies was good. Not two bucks good, but what can you expect at a dance?"

Miss Willie was about to go inside, but she reconsidered,

turned, and faced us. The porch light shone on her face, and we saw the wan smile she wore. "I appreciate your asking me to the dance. It was thoughtful."

"But you didn't have a good time?" Jefferson inquired suspiciously.

She stared at each of us and shook her head slowly. "I had hoped I would. I really did. Maybe my expectations were too high. I thought this could be a special evening. In spite of the circumstance, I believed we could have a good time."

"We haven't had too much experience," I said in our defense. "We're just . . . well, we need some more experience."

"I guess a little experience wouldn't do any of you harm," she said, "but I think it was more than just experience." She looked down at her hands and then at us. "I guess I thought I was going with three gentlemen. I ended up with three boys."

Even from the very first day Miss Willie had never referred to us as boys; to her we had never been anything but young men. Needless to say, in spite of the cold, our cheeks burned. We fidgeted awkwardly on the front steps, sensing the collapse of our little world.

"We didn't mean to make you feel bad," Jefferson whispered, bowing his head. "We really did try. I guess we just don't know much about girls and dances."

I'm sure Miss Willie knew she had devastated us, because she sighed deeply and pondered for a moment. "There are lots of boys around," she said. "It's easy to be a boy. It takes effort to be a gentleman. Weren't you the ones who made fun of Rupert Turley?" We nodded. "Rupert, for all he's not, is still quite a gentleman. I appreciate that in him. He would never think of rushing through a door ahead of me or making me tag along behind him while he checked everyone out on the dance floor. Nor would he sit through an entire dance munching cookies and slurping punch."

We were silent for a while and then Jefferson said, "We were pretty bad, I guess. I mean as dates go."

"You were pretty rough and unpolished."

"Worse than they are in Salt Lake?" BB wanted to know.

"A place doesn't really make a person. There are boys in Salt

Lake just as there are boys here. But you are capable of being gentlemen. You were not this evening. That surprised me."

We were quiet for several minutes. "Do you think we could do it right?" Jefferson wondered. "I mean, show you that we can be gentlemen."

"How?"

"Well, we could maybe take you . . ." He looked over at me for help.

"How about the Christmas dance?" I said.

"Yeah," Jefferson agreed. "That's the biggest dance of the year, except for the Junior Prom."

"Could you handle a dance that big?"

"We'd show you we could be gentlemen," I said, almost pleading, feeling that we had to redeem ourselves in some way.

"I don't know about these two," BB confessed, "but I don't know if I could handle it. I'm not sure what a gentleman does. Going to another dance would just make you madder at us."

"Maybe you could give us some pointers," Jefferson suggested.

Miss Willie shook her head and started to laugh. "I'm not sure I would know what to teach you."

"You're a girl. You could at least tell us what a girl thinks."

She closed her eyes for a moment. "When you take a girl to a dance," she began, most of the reprimand gone from her voice, "you should dance with her—at least once. Now, it didn't hurt too much with me tonight, but someday you're going to meet a very special girl, one you'll want to keep, and if you treat her like that, you'll never see her again."

"But we don't know how to dance," BB protested. "We can't even do that fast stuff where you just go out there and shake a little bit. And we sure can't do that trotting around like the old fogies do."

"You can learn." She took a deep breath. "Another thing, when you take a girl someplace, make the occasion special. Make it something she'll want to remember. Treat her like a lady, not just one of the gang, not just a tagalong. The only way you can do that is by thinking that girls *are* special. *All* girls."

"Even Mae Ellen?" BB snickered.

Miss Willie stared at him. "Even Mae Ellen. Once you treat Mae Ellen like a lady—and she is a lady—then it will be easy with all the others."

"I'd feel real stupid treating Mae Ellen like a lady."

"That's because you've never thought of her as anything but a dingy girl who deserved nothing but your scorn."

"The girls would laugh at us."

"No true lady will ever make fun of you for being a true gentleman."

"But why be nice to Mae Ellen?" I asked. "We're not going to have anything to do with her. We're not ever going to ask her out."

"Unless it's to a dog—"

"BB," Miss Willie warned. She waited for a moment and then said, "Maybe you won't now, but Mae Ellen will change. All girls change, especially sophomore girls."

"She hasn't changed none the last few years," BB grumbled. "She's pretty set in her ugliness."

"When I was a junior in high school," she said, "I was what some people would call a little plump."

"You?" we all gasped with surprise. "You were fat?"

"I didn't say fat. I said plump. Just enough to make me feel self-conscious."

BB whistled. "I can't even picture you being hefty. You're too . . . just right, I guess. I mean, you're almost small now."

Miss Willie shook her head. "I assure you that there was a time when I had to concentrate on being even remotely small. Now I worry about blowing away into nothing."

"You'll have to eat more," Jefferson suggested.

"I do eat," Miss Willie said. "I try to stuff myself. I have to force myself to eat. But as you can see," she smiled, pointing at herself, "my efforts have gone unrewarded."

"BB's sure been rewarded for his efforts," I said, jabbing BB in the stomach. "Eating works for him. You'll have to let him give you some pointers."

The smile on Miss Willie's face melted into seriousness, and she gazed into the night with an ominous, far-distant look, one reminiscent of another day, and strangely I remembered the morning we had sat in the football bleachers and listened to her. Tonight I detected the same sadness in her gaze. It was that fleeting, foreboding fear that crept into her eyes and made us realize that under all her gaiety and charm Miss Willie was haunted by something still unknown to us.

"I don't think eating will ever be the answer now," she remarked, almost to herself. She forced a smile to her lips and returned from her ponderings to us. "But none of that can be changed. And who started all this gloom anyway? We were talking about . . . What were we talking about?"

"When you were fat," BB blurted out. "I mean, when you were plump."

"Oh, yes! Well, I was rather shy and had never had a date. I was the co-chairman of the prom committee. I had worked hard to get ready for a dance I didn't ever think I would attend. It was hard working on something I knew I wouldn't enjoy. But I resigned myself to my fate, as I had done many times before.

"There was a boy named Ronald Peterson. I suppose Ronald could have gone with almost any girl in the school. He was in my ward, and we were good friends. We had spent a lot of time talking together, and although I had never said so, he knew I wanted to go to the prom. He asked me. No one coerced him. He did it on his own. To be nice. To be a gentleman. He knew how much the prom meant to me."

Miss Willie looked into the night, remembering. "We never fell in love. We were good friends, but I knew this wasn't a dream romance in the bud. We never had another date, but that night I had one of the best times in my life. He made it extra special for me, doing more for me than a lot of boys did for their regular girl friends. I will never forget Ronald Peterson. He was a gentleman. He was the first real gentleman I ever knew. Maybe the only one.

"It's not a crime to be nice to a girl, even to a girl you don't plan to date or marry. It doesn't ruin your character. On the contrary, it builds character."

"I can't imagine you being ugly," BB commented.

"I would dare wager that what you now consider homely will, after a few years of maturity, become very beautiful. Beauty grows.

True beauty is much more than a superficial covering. So much of beauty is within the person."

The three of us sat there rubbing the palms of our hands up and down our thighs in nervous agitation. "Are you going to give us another chance?" Jefferson asked. "Maybe we can be as good as Ronald Peterson."

"On one condition."

"What's that?"

"That you become polished gentlemen."

"How polished?"

"How do we do that?"

"We could start you on some gentleman classes."

"Gentleman classes?" we cried.

"Just something to knock off the rough edges. Wouldn't you like to go to a dance and know what you were supposed to be doing without having to look around to see what everybody else does? Wouldn't you like to take a girl someplace and know how you were supposed to treat her without having to ask *her?*"

"I'm not very good at manners and things," BB admitted.

"I won't argue with you there, but if you can learn English and Spanish, you can certainly learn something about treating a girl special. Someday you will meet a young lady and you will give anything to know how to treat her."

"Do we have to be as good as Ronald Peterson?" BB wanted to know.

"At least. I want a trio of gentlemen."

"When do the classes start?" Jefferson asked.

"Next Friday. Here."

## Chapter Eight

BECAUSE WE DIDN'T KNOW HOW PAINFUL this proposed transformation from unpolished sophomore to legitimate gentleman would be, it was with a great deal of apprehension that the three of us found ourselves fidgeting Friday evening on Miss Willie's front steps.

When she came to the door, she took one look at our Levi's, tennis shoes, sweatshirts, and mussed hair and asked, "Do you remember what tonight is?"

Thinking that we had taken care of everything by physically showing up, I replied, "Yeah, you're going to teach us some manners. Something about being a gentleman." I then started for the door.

Miss Willie held up her hand. "Well, let's start learning right now. If you're here to learn to be gentlemen, why, may I ask, have you come dressed for a dogfight?"

"Huh?"

"When you play football," she said patiently, "do you go in a Sunday suit?"

We shook our heads.

"Why?"

We looked at each other and shrugged our shoulders. "Maybe because we'd get killed the first time somebody plowed into us," BB ventured. "Besides, my mom would break my neck if she saw me playing football in my suit."

"Well, when you play gentlemen, you dress like gentlemen." She received blank stares. "I have seen all of you at church wearing suits, ties, and polished shoes—well, almost polished. That is gentlemen's attire for the Christmas dance."

"But the dance isn't tonight," Jefferson said, utterly confused. "Tonight's just practice."

"Your attire will put you in the spirit of the occasion. Besides, the brownies are still in the oven."

"Brownies?" BB drooled.

"You didn't think I was going to starve you?" she said. "After watching you at the Harvest Ball, I knew the only way I could get and keep your attention would be with plenty of food. Be back in fifteen minutes." She thought and then added, "Make it thirty. That way you'll have time to polish your shoes."

To this day I don't know what provoked us to do what we did. It was almost impossible to get us into a suit for a few hours on Sunday, but all three of us went home and returned dressed in our Sunday best. Of course, we moaned and groaned about stiff collars and pinching shoes and threatened to abandon our lofty quest for manners and social poise, but beneath our grumbled protests was the smug satisfaction that Miss Willie thought we were important enough to put on a suit just for practice. I suppose we would have done anything for her, and before our training was over we almost did.

When we returned, we did feel different. We were different. Of course, we were just rough shells of anything remotely refined. Beneath our suits there was no substance to our pretentious chivalry, but at least we were deceivingly dressed. That was more than we had ever before attempted to be.

When Miss Willie opened the door the second time, her eyes widened, she took a step backward, and her face brightened with a smile. The way she lavished us with compliments, one would have thought we were the finished products rather than the raw materials. All protests and grumblings ceased as we basked in her generous admiration.

"We're going to start at the beginning," Miss Willie announced after we were inside and seated. "We'll do the simple things tonight and progress to the more difficult. First we'll start with the coat." She took her coat from the hall closet and handed it to BB. He took it, stared at it, and asked, "What do we do with the coat?"

"That's my coat. I'm your girl, and I would like to put it on."

BB shrugged, handed it back, and said, "Why'd you give it to me then?"

"No, I want you to put it on."

Miss Willie turned her back to BB while he struggled to push one of his arms into the sleeve of the coat. "No, on her," I whispered, kicking him in the leg.

"Oh," he mumbled, pulling his arm out and draping the coat across Miss Willie's shoulders.

"BB," she coached, "the idea is to get the coat on me so that it will function as a coat, not a tarp. Also, you want to make it as easy for me to find the sleeves as you possibly can. Don't make me guess. Don't hang it up too high or down too low. And don't throw it over me like you were trying to cover a corpse."

With those few instructions, BB stumbled through the coat routine. It took him ten or fifteen times before Miss Willie let him go, but by then he was doing it like he was at least related to a gentleman.

It was easier for Jefferson and me after watching all of BB's mistakes, but Miss Willie still made us practice over and over again until I could have done it in my sleep.

"Now we'll try the door," Miss Willie said as she hung up her coat. "We'll use the door going into the kitchen. That way we won't freeze to death out on the front steps."

I didn't realize going through a door with a girl could be so complicated, but when we tried it with Miss Willie as an extra appendage, we found that it took real concentration. Miss Willie walked us through the operation until we could open the door, help her through, and come up behind her without tromping on her heels or knocking her on her face.

Learning to offer a girl an arm was our next lesson. That was the part where we really felt awkward because none of us had ever had anyone hanging on his arm. It didn't seem at all natural. But Miss Willie insisted. At first we were so stiff and tense that Miss Willie said she felt as though she were walking with a board fence, but we loosened up and soon felt rather proud to be parading around with her attached to our arms.

We practiced walking up and down stairs and getting in and out of a car. Miss Willie also indoctrinated us on appropriate conversation techniques. We were instructed not to show off, not to brag, not to be rowdy or boisterous, and not to embarrass our girl by anything we said or did. Her instructions were a shocking revelation to us because doing all of those things came natural with us.

After our verbal instructions, Miss Willie had us sit down, munch brownies, and play gentlemen. Playing gentlemen with the likes of BB and Jefferson was a challenge. With Miss Willie's gentlemanly restrictions placed upon us, we turned into mutes. All we could do was sit with our hands in our laps and gawk at each other, afraid to open our mouths for fear that what would come out would be a brag, an embarrassment, an indication of ignorance, or something uncouth.

Miss Willie coaxed, flattered, coached, and persisted until we could carry on a conversation well enough to pass as very shy gentlemen, which was far better than passing as our loud, knavish selves.

At the conclusion of the evening, Miss Willie announced, "Next week we'll start on dinner."

"You mean a real dinner?" Jefferson asked, licking his lips.

"A real dinner. However, no one eats anything unless he has the best of dinner manners."

"You mean we have to eat with a napkin and the right fork and all that other stuff?" BB moaned.

"Exactly."

"We'll starve."

"Although learning proper eating procedures might prove to be painful, it will not be fatal. I think you'll learn quite rapidly, especially if your dinner is at stake."

"Do we have to come dressed up?" Jefferson asked.

"Won't you be dressed up when you take your girl to dinner?"

"Well, generally. I mean, when I'm at home, Aunt Betty always makes me change my clothes so I won't spill on my tie and suit."

"Well, I think it's time you learned to eat a meal without spilling all over yourself. We'll be eating at the table with knives and forks. Not at a trough."

"I'd rather change," Jefferson mumbled.

"What are you going to do when you go out to dinner, change into some coveralls? We're not going to be eating with shovels. I'll show you. After next Friday, eating out, even in a suit, will be a pleasure, not a frightful ordeal."

The next Friday evening the three of us marched over to Miss Willie's in our suits and ties. She had told us we couldn't eat anything before coming, so we were starved when we arrived, ready to eat everything in sight.

As we crowded about the table with our tongues hanging out in hungry anticipation, Miss Willie remarked, "The first thing you do at a dinner is help your date sit down."

"I always thought that was kinda dumb," BB complained, eager to get started on the food. "She can sit down all right without me shoving the chair under her."

Miss Willie sighed. "BB, she can do a lot of things without your help, but this makes it easier for her. Provided you don't just shove the chair under her. Remember, you're not trying to knock her over or break her legs. Later on you'll want to dance with her, and you won't want her limping about the floor. Of course, if you would prefer to dig right in without waiting, you might consider asking a Saint Bernard."

Before any of us sat down, we had to help Miss Willie about ten times apiece. We knocked up her legs pretty bad and stomped on her foot a couple of times, but we soon settled down and did it right. Smoothly even.

When we were finally seated and each of us had a salad sitting in front of him, we were about to grab for the nearest utensil and begin shoveling. "You will notice," Miss Willie pointed out, "that you have two forks by your plate."

"Oh, good, we get to use both hands," BB joked. Miss Willie pretended not to be amused, but the corners of her mouth were playing with the first traces of a smile.

"You'll notice that you have a napkin next to your plate. What do you suppose we do with it?"

"Clean our hands and face with it and wipe up any messes."

Miss Willie cleared her throat. "That is a crude way of saying what is partially true. However, it is not a mop. What do we do with it in the meantime?"

"In the movies they stuff it down their front like a bib," Jefferson volunteered.

"There are a lot of things we see in the movies that we will not reenact at the dinner table. Place the napkin in your lap. Then take the outside fork and begin to eat your salad."

The meal was a slow one. Even though we were starving, we ate as though we had all the time in the world, and Miss Willie walked us through each dish. The food was on the cool side before we got to it, but toward the end of the meal I got to thinking that if this was all there was to being a gentleman, then we might have a chance.

I'm not sure any of us had ever gone through an entire meal without knocking over a drink or slopping something down our front or into our laps, but we did with Miss Willie. That was probably our biggest accomplishment of the evening.

"Are we ready now for the big date?" I asked, extremely proud of our progress.

"There's one more thing you lack. That's tomorrow's surprise."

Saturday night, two weeks before the Christmas dance, we began our last lesson in chivalry. When we stepped into Miss Willie's living room, the sofa and chairs were pushed back, the coffee table was missing, and the lamps were crowded into a corner. In the kitchen doorway was a record player.

"You been cleaning today?" Jefferson asked.

Miss Willie looked around the room, nodded, and said, "But that's not the reason the room is arranged like this. This is for our dance."

"Dance!" we gasped, taking an involuntary step backward.

"We wanted to be gentlemen, not dancers," Jefferson said.

"If you're going to a dance, don't you think it would be nice to know how to dance?"

"Yeah, but we've never danced before," I argued. "We just can't dance. They used to try to teach us in junior high, and sometimes they pull a fast one at Mutual. You know, they line the boys up on one side and the girls on the other, and whoever you're facing is the one you're stuck with. They run us through some of those cattle stomps, but nothing ever penetrates too good. We're a bunch of clumsy bulls to start with, and we aren't any better off after they've herded us around that dance floor. That's the truth, Miss Willie. I'm not being modest at all. We can learn to eat and take a girl through a door, but dancing . . . well, that's another thing."

"We've got two weeks before the big night. We're going to start at the very beginning and go slow. When we're finished, dancing is going to be easier than playing football." She smiled. "If you can play football, you can surely dance a waltz or a fox-trot."

We tried to protest, but Miss Willie ignored our objections, sat us down, and started with the waltz. She walked through the basic step while we watched. "See how easy that is," she beamed. "All it is is a box. You pretend you're stepping on the corners of a box."

"That's a dance?" Jefferson asked. "I mean, do people really just go out and walk around in a square?"

"Well, there are some other things later on, but that's the basic step. Now get up on your feet. Line up in a row and let's do it together."

It really was quite easy. We looked like a trio of stomping bull elephants at first, planting each foot like we were squashing mice in tall grass, but Miss Willie gave us a few pointers, and soon we could go around that imaginary square with a modicum of grace.

Little by little she showed us other steps. She made each step seem so easy that we were actually dancing before we fully realized it. Even when she put the music on we didn't get flustered like we had in junior high and at Mutual dances. Then the music had unnerved us; now it seemed natural and necessary.

Then Miss Willie dropped a bombshell: "Now that you have the hang of it, grab a partner."

"A partner?" we croaked, backing up a little and staring suspiciously at each other.

"Of course. You didn't think you would waltz by yourselves, did you?"

"Well, no," I stammered, "but we didn't plan on dancing with each other, either. I mean, that just isn't normal. They might do some of that in Salt Lake and other big cities, but in Snowflake that's not normal."

"That's worse than not normal," BB said.

"What if somebody saw us?" Jefferson added.

Miss Willie grinned. "I'm not asking you to do anything but practice your dancing. If we had girls here, you could dance with them. I could call some girls."

"No!" we exclaimed.

"Then you'll have to make do with what we have here. Once you learn to dance with each other, dancing with a girl is going to be heaven."

Gingerly we moved closer to each other. BB took Jefferson's hand and then threw it aside with revulsion. "You mean I have to touch him?" he grimaced. "I hate touching boys' hands."

"Well, the girl has to touch it."

"Yeah, but she's, well, you know."

"I'll dance with you, BB, and you other two dance together. We'll trade off every few minutes so you don't gag all over each other."

The infamous junior high and Mutual dances we had detested so vehemently were not nearly so abhorrent as dancing with each other. We made certain that we were always at arm's length. But still we were too close.

We did learn to dance, though. I suppose that knowing our partner was no more graceful than we ourselves helped kill our inhibitions. We were eventually able to learn what had always terrified us when we had been paired with girls. We didn't learn in a day. Several evenings we traded our grammar books for dance partners. After a while we knew the fox-trot, the waltz, and the swing. We were even able to recognize which dance went with which music.

Several days before the Christmas dance, the three of us made our way to Miss Willie's place for our final dancing session. When we stepped into her living room, we found ourselves in what seemed at the time a room crowded to the ceiling with girls. Actually, there were only five of them, but they outnumbered us and were a year older.

We were petrified, aghast at the prospect of spending just five minutes in that room. But we were trapped. Miss Willie had closed the door behind us before we could effect an escape. With our retreat cut off, all we could do was stand and stare. We did manage, however, to keep our hands out of our pockets, and we didn't turn into the pushing, poking, pinching fools we generally devolved into whenever we met girls. Miss Willie had taught us that much.

Miss Willie taught the Laurels in our ward. At times during our social skills lessons she had remarked how her girls often complained of never having the chance to meet any real gentlemen. "You see, gentlemen are scarce," she had preached. "Always in demand. You will never regret having known proper behavior. Your male friends might snicker now, but the day will come when they will observe you with secret envy."

Little did we know that Miss Willie had been priming us for this very moment. All along she had been planning to turn us loose on her Mutual class. Or was it the other way around? Perhaps we were the Laurels' service project for the month—like visiting the sick or caring for the less fortunate.

"I believe you're all acquainted with each other," Miss Willie said as she came from behind us with a smile on her face. Unfortunately, we had grown up with these same girls, and they had developed a rather odious impression of us. Sue Willis had once called us "the most horrible boys in the world." Becky Thomas had said we would never amount to anything because we were such "incorrigible creeps." We didn't know what the *incorrigible* meant, and Becky probably didn't either, but we knew that *creeps* was not a term of endearment. Rita Flake had insisted that if we were just half the slobs we appeared to be, we had more than enough "slobbery" for all the boys in Snowflake. I can't remember any specific innuendos made by Pattie Hancock or Cindy Call, but they never gave us any reason to believe they were admirers of ours. It was in this den of feminine hostility that we found ourselves.

"In Mutual," Miss Willie began, attempting to allay our fears and make us all forget that we were casual enemies, "you young ladies have been learning some dance etiquette. I have asked BB, DJ, and Jefferson, who are surprisingly talented, to help you practice." The girls glared at us and grimaced. I don't know who they were expecting, but it was obvious we were not tailored to their dreams. "Now I realize this is not a real dance. We don't have a big crowd nor do we have a lot of room, but I do think we have room for three couples. There is a refreshment table in the kitchen. I want you all to visit there at least once during the evening. You boys will have to make two trips so each girl will have her turn. But I don't think you'll mind that at all."

With that short introduction, Miss Willie stepped back, turned up the music, and left us to ourselves. I hadn't gone to many dances before that night, and most of the ones I had gone to were church dances where the boys congregated on one side of the hall and the girls congregated on the other. The only time any dancing took place was when the teachers did it themselves or when the bishop and his counselors herded the boys across the hall and forcibly paired them up with the waiting girls. The only way for a dance to last any length of time was to lock all the doors and have enough refreshments on hand to keep the boys relatively content and passive.

As the music started, I sensed this was going to be another one of those youth dances—minus the bishopric. I can remember standing there hoping Bishop Williams would crash through the front door and ride herd on us because I wasn't sure I was capable of making a move on my own. I also remember staring at Becky Thomas and detecting a sneer of contempt on her face. It was as though she was thinking, "Haven't changed a bit. Once a creep, always a creep. And to think we let Sister Willie talk us into this!" My pride was wounded, almost fatally. I remembered all the things I was supposed to do; I just couldn't begin the motions.

For the first minute we stared at each other, each second dragging ponderously by. Then Jefferson, conjuring courage I didn't know he had, gulped twice, stepped across the room, and asked Rita Flake to dance. He did it like he'd been doing it all his life, just like a son of royalty. He confessed afterward that it was all a frantic attempt to salvage his mutilated pride, but his motivation was of no consequence. The fact that he did it at all was paramount.

Oh, did he shock those girls! They were expecting this horrible, creepy boy to make an utter fool of himself, but Jefferson Judd was actually charming. At least as charming as anything they had ever seen in a boy.

When BB followed suit, actually appearing graceful, I knew we had it made. I was the last, and by the time I had Sue Willis on the floor and into position, the dance had ended. But we were triumphant. Dizzy with victory, I turned to Sue and, with the poise of a blooded gentleman, commented casually about dancing in general. Nothing profound, but for Daniel Johnson, one of the terrible threesome, it was impressive—if not awesome.

The next dance was a waltz, our favorite. Oh, how we glided about that room, never once tromping on feet or colliding with another couple. Like Miss Willie had told us the night of our first practice, "If you can dance with each other, you'll be able to dance with anyone." How true that was! Dancing with Sue was almost fun.

It took us a few minutes and a mild headache to shake the jitters out, but after that we settled down and actually had a good time. I would have never admitted it that night, but years later I did admit that that was the first time I had really enjoyed a dance—not merely endured it but actually had fun, something tantamount to going to a movie or playing a game of football.

We were even able to carry on a conversation without sounding like "incorrigible creeps." Oh, we didn't say anything earth-shattering. Words of wisdom and wit didn't drop from our lips nor were we engrossingly entertaining, but we were far better than any partner these girls had ever had at one of the circuses the ward called a youth dance.

After two hours, when Miss Willie announced that the girls had to go home, the three of us had actually taught the girls a thing or two. Pleased with our evening's performance, we walked the girls to the door, thanked them for the evening, and told them good night with a style that would have impressed the most critical adherents of proper social behavior. Never in our lives up till then had we been flattered and congratulated as we were by those girls. I suppose much of the complimenting was due to simple shock. The girls had braced themselves to dance with a trio of freaks, and we had surprised them. However, I do like to think that some of the praise was the result of sincere appreciation.

As we helped Miss Willie put her house back together, clean the dishes, and put away the remaining refreshments, we quietly bragged of our evening's glories.

Miss Willie commented, "Now, wasn't that better than sitting in a corner stuffing your faces with food and laughing at every girl who passed?"

In our euphoric state, all we could do was shrug our shoulders, push the sofa back into position, and pull the coffee table from the corner.

"Well, I think you're ready for the big dance." She smiled at us.

Remembering Miss Willie's boutonnieres, the three of us paid a solemn visit to the floral shop. When Mrs. Roberts asked us what we wanted, Jefferson responded, "We want the best corsage you got. The best you can make."

"Well, there are some with carnations or roses or . . ."

"We just want the very best."

"Well, that would probably be an orchid, actually a combination of orchids, and it is rather expensive. Just under fifteen dollars. Most of the young people going to—"

"We'll take the orchids. We have the money."

"Three?"

"Just one. We only got one girl."

"The three of you have just one girl?"

We all nodded.

"She must be a very special girl."

We nodded again.

The night of the dance we must have each spent four hours getting ready. Miss Willie hadn't preached any hygiene, but this night we were definitely not content to let a morning PE shower suffice for our Christmas dance bath. Our suits had been to the cleaners, our shirts were pressed, and our shoes were polished. Everything was immaculate.

At eight o'clock we were standing on Miss Willie's doorstep with the fifteen-dollar corsage guarded by the three of us.

Miss Willie came to the door in a long pink formal with a skirt that lightly brushed the floor, covering her feet. As she walked, she seemed to glide smoothly, suspended in air, as though her feet never touched the ground. The dress made her seem sleek and elegant with its long silky sleeves and its soft, graceful fit. It was a part of her, naturally assuming her movements and charm, and magnifying but never detracting from the real beauty—Miss Willie.

Her hair was pulled up on top of her head, forming an enchanting crown of curls, so different from the way we had ever seen her before. The way the hair was pulled away from her face and neck made her seem taller and more slender, her face narrower, her neck delicately thin.

Her skin had a creamy ivory hue, even more so than usual, and her cheeks were touched with a pleasant pink shadow that brought her face vibrantly alive. Her eyes, framed and accentuated by long lashes and perfectly drawn eyebrows, sparkled as we entered, and emanating from her whole person was an enticing, faint fragrance of perfume.

Dangling from her ears, with subdued scintillating splendor, were two tiny pink and silver earrings. They were so small that one was not overtly conscious of them; and yet, without their quiet glitter, the perfect picture, which was Miss Willie, might have seemed oddly incomplete.

When I saw her standing there, as close to anything queenly as I had ever experienced, my whole insides seemed to melt in awe, incapable of absorbing all the beauty at a single glance. We fell in love with her all over again. Even today when I remember Miss Willie, I think of her as she appeared that night.

Stepping into the room, BB handed her the corsage box and announced, "We figured you might want one of these, and since the girl doesn't usually go out and buy one for herself, we did it for you."

She opened the box and looked inside. Her eyes got big and her hand went to her mouth. For a long time she didn't say anything, but we could tell she liked it. Finally she looked up and said with that enchanting smile that had captivated us from that first day, "It's lovely. I've received a lot of flowers in my life, but never one so beautiful as this. I don't know what to say. It's so lovely. I hardly dare touch it, much less wear it."

We stood there, feeling very proud of ourselves, our faces beaming our pride. Had the evening ended right then, we would not have complained. We felt so good.

Slowly she picked the flower from the box and held it up for all of us to see; then she smiled and handed it to me. "No, it's for you," I stammered, thinking there was a mistake.

"Someone has to pin it on me," she said, her eyes twinkling.

I licked my lips and glanced over at BB and Jefferson. Their faces were pinched with panic because they knew that if I had to do it now, their turn was rapidly approaching.

"I've never pinned a flower on a real girl. Ever." I gulped.

"That's why you'd better learn. If you're going to go to dances and buy beautiful flowers, you have to learn to pin them on your girl."

"But, Miss Willie, I . . ."

"Come on. It's not hard. I'll help you."

I took the flower and stepped close to Miss Willie. My heart was pounding, my hands were shaking, and I could hardly see. I just knew that my long bath was all a waste, because I was sweating like a mule. I was so terrified to be that close to Miss Willie that I didn't dare touch her. What a dilemma I was in! I don't know how I managed it. Miss Willie did coach me along, but even then my fingertips were pricked raw before I was able to get the corsage into place. I stepped back and sighed, thankful the ordeal was over.

When I was finished, the flower was removed and passed to BB and then to Jefferson. Before we were finished, I thought the flower would wilt and fall apart.

The evening was so much better than the Harvest Ball we had made Miss Willie endure. We took her to dinner at the Silver Creek Ranch House, the nicest place in town. Then we went to the dance.

We danced until I'm sure Miss Willie was exhausted. The only reason she survived at all is that we traded off with BB's mom, my sister Sharon, and Jefferson's Aunt Betty. And even Miss Willie's Laurels. In fact, we were so proud of our newly acquired talents that there were probably few people we didn't dance with. Had Silas brought his cow, we would have probably danced with her.

When we took Miss Willie home, she stood in the doorway and thanked us for the evening and told us how proud she was of each of us.

"Would you really call us gentlemen?" Jefferson wanted to know.

"Without a doubt!"

"As good as Ronald Peterson?" BB pressed.

A warm smile touched her lips. "You know, I used to wonder if I'd ever find another gentleman like Ronald Peterson. I was beginning to think he was one of a kind. But tonight I found three just like him."

# Chapter Nine

In FEBRUARY, TOWARD THE END of one of Miss Willie's meager paychecks, when she was struggling to budget an empty purse against the imminent demands of a minor crisis, she sought our aid. Her '54 Ford had never functioned well, always giving the distinct impression that it was about to collapse into a sputtering, hissing heap of bolts and scrap metal.

Because Miss Willie and the Ford had gone through so much together, she was reluctant to speak ill of it. She insisted that it was a good car—perhaps a little temperamental, but still a good car. She was realistic enough to concede that the car did have its minor problems, but she sincerely believed that with a little encouragement even those could be eliminated, or at least circumvented.

On the other hand, we were convinced that her Ford functioned strictly on faith—the kind that moves mountains. Nothing else could explain how the car still managed to rattle and squeak down the road. Miss Willie was the only person who had that kind of faith, but even she was experiencing some doubts.

She had a seminar in Phoenix and sensed that the notorious car needed something more than a softly spoken word and a gentle pat on the fender in order to make the grueling trip down the mountain and back again.

Knowing that BB's dad owned a garage and was a mechanic and that BB was mechanically inclined as well, she asked him for advice one Sunday as we were all walking home after Sunday School.

"What do you think my car needs?" she asked.

"Do you want the truth?" She nodded. "That car needs the last rites and then it should be hauled to the nearest junkyard, where it should have been taken about ten years ago."

"BB, I know it is not the best car in the world, but—"

"If there's another worse, I'd like to see it."

"There must be something that can be done, something constructive. I can't afford a new car."

"Well, you believe in prayer. It would take a whopper, but maybe something like that would pull it through for the trip."

"That would be like raising the dead," Jefferson chuckled.

"BB, I have to make that trip. My car is all I have right now. Can't you do something?"

"Miss Willie, I just don't know. The old bomb's shot."

"Would it help to put some water in the carburetor?"

BB stopped walking and turned to her. "You haven't been working on that car yourself, have you?" She shook her head. "I was just wondering, because if you've been working on that car, that just might be the problem. No, Miss Willie, I don't believe water in the carburetor will do the trick."

"Would it help to change the oil?"

"Probably wouldn't hurt, but it might be a waste of five quarts of oil. Miss Willie, I'm not an expert on dancing or English or things like that, but I've learned a couple of things about cars, and your car just isn't any good. It was probably a lemon when you bought it, and the only thing that has happened between then and now is that it's gone rotten."

"Well, I guess I'll just have to take it the way it is then," she said morosely.

BB pulled on his ear and said, "Maybe a tune-up would put a

little life into it. It would have to be a good one, and I sure wouldn't make any promises about the finished product."

"How much does that cost?"

"Thirty or forty dollars, depending on where you go and what the car needs."

"I only have fifteen dollars right now." She thought for a moment and asked, "Do you do work like that? If I bought the parts and things, could you tune the car up?"

"Well, I could probably get the parts from Dad's garage at a discount. We could probably get everything for ten or fifteen dollars."

"Would you do the work for me?" Miss Willie ventured shyly.

BB took a deep breath, tugged on his ear again, and said, "I could but I won't."

"You won't?" she asked incredulously.

"No, but I'll help you. As long as you're set on keeping that bucket of bolts . . ."

"Help me? Help me do what?"

"I'll teach you what to do. Then you can do your own work. You know, be your own mechanic."

"Me? I'm no mechanic. I have a hard enough time turning the key on and putting the car in gear. I've never even looked under the hood. I don't even go to self-service gas stations because I don't know how to put the gas in, and you want me to tune up my car?"

"Well, another time we can teach you how to put the gas in, but right now we better work on getting your car running so you can make it to Phoenix and back."

"BB, it's out of the question. I can't learn that."

"Oh, you underestimate BB's teaching ability," I said, anxious to see if BB could persuade her.

"Yeah," Jefferson piped in. "We might be boneheads in English and Spanish, but we know a wrench from a screwdriver. We'll teach you anything you want to know. Even DJ and I know a thing or two about cars."

"But I don't want to know anything like that."

"All right, we'll teach you all you don't want to know, but when you're finished with that little Ford, you'll have it humming good."

"Maybe you could teach me later on. You do it this time and I'll watch. The next time I'll . . . well, I can hold a wrench for you or something."

"Nope. If you want to be a mechanic, you have to start now. You can't let someone else do the work."

"BB, I can't work on my car. I'm a girl."

BB looked down at his hands and began tracing the lines in his right hand with his left forefinger. He was suddenly serious, something that didn't happen often. "You know, Miss Willie, I didn't ever think I could learn to dance. That was sissy stuff, but I kinda like to dance now. I didn't ever think I'd ever learn to speak English. I still don't do it very good, but I haven't used *ain't* for weeks. I learned those things because you taught me, even though I didn't think I could. I didn't want to, but I'm glad now that I did."

"You really can't expect me to play mechanic," Miss Willie pleaded. "Learning to dance and speak English properly are one thing, but—"

"You mean you really didn't mean it when you said a person could do anything he wanted to do?" Jefferson asked, entering the discussion firmly on BB's side.

"Yes, I meant it, but I wasn't thinking of fixing cars."

We were all quiet for a moment. The three of us stared down at the sidewalk, waiting for Miss Willie to say something. What had started as nothing more than a playful suggestion had evolved into something that was suddenly important to us. We had always believed in Miss Willie. Now we wanted to know if Miss Willie believed in Miss Willie. Right then we didn't need the pithy platitudes. We didn't need the arrogance of adulthood, that state of superiority that refuses to stoop to the mundane. We needed the humility of youth.

I suppose in a real sense our request was a test. We hadn't meant it to be, but that's how it ended up. I know all of us secretly hoped that Miss Willie wouldn't disappoint us.

She laughed. "Come on, BB, you can't be serious." BB didn't reply. "DJ, tell him," she said to me. I shrugged my shoulders. "What's the sense of my learning to fix my own car when I can take it to a garage?"

"That's the point," BB countered, "you can't take it to a garage.

You're broke. You can save thirty or forty dollars by doing it yourself. You're afraid of your own car, aren't you."

She nodded.

"That's just the way we felt about dancing," BB went on. "Now, we're still not the world's greatest dancers, but at least we're not afraid to go out on a dance floor anymore." Miss Willie eyed us menacingly, knowing that we were winning the argument with her own arguments. "You can do it, Miss Willie." She pursed her lips and sighed. "Forget about the parts. I'll get the parts, and tomorrow after school we'll meet here and give you your first lesson—free. If you only knew how simple it is, you'd be embarrassed to give us this much hassle."

"We'll even toss in the soda pop," Jefferson said. "Everyone knows you can't be a mechanic without soda pop."

"All right," she said, smiling, "I guess if you're going to throw in the soda pop, I can't refuse. Just remember I'm a girl."

At a time when women's rights was a faint whisper of protest and it was unthinkable for a girl to stoop to the greasy mechanics of auto repair, Miss Willie took a giant step in the direction of equality. True, we had to do some shoving and pulling to get her moving, but once she was involved and committed—even though she lacked a male's penchant for cars—she moved forward with determination.

The next afternoon BB, Jefferson, and I, along with the oil, filters, plugs, points, and tools, met at Miss Willie's. She was waiting for us in the driveway by her car. BB took one look at the skirt she was wearing and said, "Miss Willie, do you remember what today is?"

She nodded without enthusiasm. "It's the day I practice being a mechanic."

"Then why did you come dressed for a grand ball?"

"What?"

"If you were going to the Christmas dance, would you wear bib overalls?"

She shook her head.

"Why?"

"Because I would like to look nice. But—"

"When a person changes the oil in her car, would she wear a formal and corsage? No, she wears the oldest things she's got because when she's finished, she's not going to be in any condition to wear those clothes for anything but changing the oil."

"This is an old skirt. I use it when I clean the house."

"Changing the oil isn't the same as sweeping the floor. You don't want to be crawling around on the ground in a dress, do you?"

"Crawling on the ground?"

"You didn't think you were just going to turn on a tap and let the oil run out, did you?"

"BB, I said I would learn to work on the car, but—"

"Miss Willie, when you work on your car it's not like throwing a load of sheets in the washer. When you're a mechanic you have to become involved. I mean, this is one time when you literally cover yourself with your work."

"Even wallow in it," Jefferson added.

"Look, I'm not about to—"

"Miss Willie," BB interrupted, "why don't you change your dress, and we'll be getting the tools ready and the car into position."

While Miss Willie changed, BB parked the car along the curb with two wheels on the curb and the other two in the street, leaving enough space underneath for someone to crawl under. He set the tools and parts out and waited.

Miss Willie soon joined us, wearing an old pair of Levi's with a patch in the seat and one over each knee. She wore an old sweatshirt and a pair of ragged tennis shoes. "How's this?" she asked. We all nodded our approval.

"What do I do now?" She stood beside the car, her hands on her hips. BB picked up a wrench, got down in front of the car on his hands and knees, and motioned Miss Willie to follow. Reluctantly she got down on her knees and touched one hand to the pavement, then drew it back quickly, wiping the few grains of dirt and gravel that had stuck to the palm of her hand.

"Don't worry about that little bit of dirt. If you're going to save yourself forty bucks, you have to accept the fact that you're going to get a little dirty." Pointing under the engine, BB said, "Do you see that nut?"

"What nut? That's all I see, nuts and bolts."

BB touched the nut with his wrench. "That nut." Miss Willie nodded. "Okay, all you've got to do is take that off and all the oil drains out."

"Why do I want to let all the oil out?"

"So you can put some new in. You have to change the oil regularly, or the engine wears out. Now, I realize that has probably already happened with your car, so we're doing this mainly to help you. The car's a lost cause. Simple, isn't it?"

Miss Willie shrugged her shoulders and crawled under the car with a grimace on her face. For a moment she fumbled with the nut, trying to get the wrench to stay in place; then she began to tug and jerk on the wrench while the three of us shouted words of praise and encouragement.

"Which way do I pull?" she gasped, chewing on her tongue and squinting to keep dust from her eyes.

"The other way," BB coached. "That's right. See, it's easy. It's just that first turn that's hard, and then that old nut just pops right out of there. Oh, I forgot one thing. We forgot something to catch the oil in."

Unfortunately, we forgot to tell Miss Willie to stop turning the nut. When we finally thought of it, it was too late. The nut popped out, and a black, grimy stream of oil began spattering all over the pavement.

Miss Willie screamed and tried to raise up, but she bumped her head on the engine. Gasping and sputtering, she made a desperate attempt to check the black flood, but oil was everywhere, oozing through her fingers, trickling down her arm, and puddling in the street. BB was shouting directions to her, but in the confusion nothing penetrated. Finally she called out, "I think I stopped it."

BB cleared his throat. "I think it's just dry. You don't have to cover the hole anymore."

Slowly she pulled her finger from the hole and watched the sluggish drip of oil. "What happened? What did I do wrong?"

I was so shocked I couldn't speak. I decided to turn away from the scene of disaster, but BB never lost his poise. "Oh, you didn't do much. That's really not bad for a beginner. You just forgot to put a pan under to catch the oil."

"What pan? Did you say something about a pan?"

"Don't worry about it now. It's no big deal. We're not going to use that oil again anyway. We would've just thrown it away. At least you know what not to do. The next time you'll be prepared."

"What now?"

"Why don't you crawl out of there and we'll go to the next thing."

When Miss Willie came from beneath the car, my mouth dropped open in horror. Her face was splattered with flecks of oil, her right hand and arm were streaked with the black grime, and the back of her shirt was oil-splotched. She looked like a dyed-in-the-black mechanic.

I would have called off the rest of the lesson, having admitted that Miss Willie had proved herself, but the intrepid BB didn't even pause. He pulled a rag from his back pocket, handed it to Miss Willie, and said, "You can use this to clean up with. One thing you need to always keep with you—besides your tools—is something to wipe your hands on. I'll let you use mine this time, but next time you better bring your own."

BB shoved a wrench in Miss Willie's hand, pointed her in another direction, and proceeded with the lesson. She was so bewildered that she was unable to protest at his persistence. He really didn't give her a chance. Afterward he confessed he had been scared. Once she came out from under the car looking as if she'd just wallowed in a grease bath, he knew he had to keep her mind on the car or she would begin servicing him—and good!

Before she could catch her breath again, BB was showing her the oil filter and how to take it off without spilling oil all over, not that a little more oil would have made much difference. Next came the points and plugs and air filter. He did the timing himself, explaining that that was pretty tricky for a beginner.

As the afternoon progressed, she became involved and seemed to mildly enjoy what she was doing, asking questions and making her own amateur observations.

When the job was complete and the hood down, BB stepped back and said in all seriousness, "You know, to do this right we should have you go through it about five or six times. That way you would have it down good, but since the parts and oil are so expensive, we'll just have to wait until the next time you need some work done."

"What about my soda pop?" Miss Willie asked.

"Huh?" BB grunted.

"Jefferson said we couldn't do this right without soda pop. The only thing that kept me going was knowing I had a soda pop coming. Where is it?"

Jefferson nudged Miss Willie and whispered in an attempt to divert her attention, "Ask him to test it. Make him show you that the car works."

Unbeknownst to BB, Jefferson had tampered just a little with the distributor cap, a trick BB himself had taught us.

"Why don't we test it?" Miss Willie suggested.

"Huh?"

"Why don't we test it?"

"What for?"

"Just to see if it works, to see if we did a good job."

"To see if it works? Of course it works. I . . . we tuned it up. I was watching every move."

"So let's hear her hum. You said you'd make her hum. She hasn't hummed for a long time."

Grumbling, BB crawled into the car and began the test drive. The engine moaned but wouldn't turn over. BB grinned as his face turned a dark red. With each try the grin faded until all that remained was a clamped jaw.

"Did this thing work before we started?" he asked.

"Sure," I answered. "You're the one that drove it up on the curb."

"Did you forget something?" Jefferson inquired with a look of concern.

"No, I didn't forget nothing. It's this lousy, no-good car. We should have used the ten dollars to tow it to the dump."

"Could we have done something wrong?" Miss Willie asked anxiously.

"Of course not," he snapped. "Let's look under the hood."

When the hood was up, Jefferson called out, "Maybe you didn't put the distributor cap on tight."

"I put it on tight."

"I'll check it just to make sure," Jefferson said, pretending to check the cap.

"I checked it," BB growled.

"You're right. It's in good shape," Jefferson called out, winking at me.

For twenty minutes BB exhausted himself checking the engine, wires, plugs, nuts, and bolts. Everything except the faulty distributor cap, which Jefferson furtively guarded. When he began checking things the third and fourth time, Jefferson said, "Maybe we should take it down to your dad."

"We're not taking it anyplace. I know what I'm doing."

"Why doesn't it work?" I inquired, struggling to keep a straight face.

"Because it's a pile of junk. But I'll fix it. Don't worry."

"Can you do it before Miss Willie has to go to Phoenix?"

"Don't be smart."

"BB," Jefferson said, biting his lip to squelch a laugh, "Miss Willie knows this car as well as anyone, and now that you've taught her all that you know—"

"What do you mean taught her all I know? All I did was walk her through a simple oil change and tune-up. How much do you think she knows after that?"

"She seemed to be learning fast," I said. "Let's have her check things over and maybe she can find the problem."

"I think BB's right," Miss Willie protested. "I really—"

"Come on, BB, she's being modest. Give her a chance."

"She'll work under the hood while you get in the driver's seat and try to start it," I ordered.

"All right," BB exploded, thrusting a wrench toward Miss Willie and stomping toward the driver's seat. "We'll do it your way. But it's this lousy car. That's the problem. Now, don't mess anything up worse than it is."

While BB was fuming and grumbling, Miss Willie looked under the hood and, with Jefferson's help, found and corrected the problem before BB had settled down behind the wheel. "All right, BB, see if that works."

BB turned the key and the engine moaned twice and then turned over. Jefferson and I cheered and lavished Miss Willie with praise, while BB eyed us suspiciously.

"I want to know what's going on," BB demanded, pulling himself from the car and glaring under the hood.

"Going on?" I asked. "Why, BB, you're the best teacher around. In one lesson you taught Miss Willie, who didn't even dare put gas in her tank, enough to fix her own car. Of course, she was a quick learner, but that was some good teaching on your part."

"A lousy job of mechanicking," Jefferson chimed in, "but a fair job of teaching."

Miss Willie, still not sure what was going on, looked at us in puzzled silence. BB glanced under the hood again and tried to find what he had overlooked. Miss Willie said, "BB, you're a good teacher." Looking at Jefferson and me, she added, "I worry about your choice of assistants. They are definitely suspicious. But I know more now about a car than I ever thought possible. It doesn't even scare me—very much."

BB looked around him and began gathering up tools while Miss Willie sat exhausted on the curb with a satisfied smile on her oil-splotched face. "Tomorrow afternoon," BB called out, "we'll show you how to get gas from a self-service pump and—"

"Tomorrow?" Miss Willie protested.

BB looked at her with surprise. "You didn't think one little lesson like this would finish up the course, did you?" He wagged his finger in her face and said, "Tomorrow we'll show you how to put gas in the car. That alone will save you three or four cents a gallon. When was the last time you rotated the tires?"

"What?"

"That's what I thought. Well, we'll show you how to rotate the tires, and that will do two things. First, you'll know how to rotate the tires, something you need to do every few thousand miles, and second, once you've rotated all the tires, changing a flat will be a cinch. Then if you ever have a flat out on the highway, you'll be able to whip out your spare, take off the flat, throw on the spare, and be on your way in ten minutes. You won't have to play the damsel in distress, waiting on the side of the highway for some gentleman to come along. You know what you said, gentlemen are real scarce. You might have to wait there three or four hours for a real gentleman to happen by."

Miss Willie stood up. "With any luck," she said, "I'll marry a mechanic and he'll do all the work on the car. He won't even let me touch it."

BB grinned. "Miss Willie, when we're done with you, if you marry a mechanic, he'll put you to work in his garage and he'll stay home and wash dishes."

"BB would put you to work in his," Jefferson said. "You already know more than him."

"Great! Just what I wanted to do, work in a garage."

As we were about to leave, BB said, "Miss Willie, thanks a lot."

Miss Willie smiled and replied, "I should be thanking you." She looked down at her dirty hands and clothes. "After all, I'm a completely different person. In fact, I might never be the same again."

BB blushed. "I didn't think you would do it," he continued, looking down at the ground. "Especially after the oil spilled. I thought you were finished then. You're a good sport. And if you want to quit, we'll understand."

She laughed. "Quit?" she said with mock indignation, "and spend all that extra money for gas and oil changes and whatever else? And wait on the side of the highway for a real gentleman to happen by? Not on your life."

We were glad to know that Miss Willie still had a sense of humor. We had begun to wonder whether she would ever speak to us again once she looked in the mirror and saw the havoc we had wreaked. She did admit later that when she saw herself she was shocked, but she couldn't stop laughing, thinking of herself trying to stop the oil flow and BB trying to get the car to start. She spent most of the night soaking in the tub to remove the grease and oil from her hair and from under her fingernails, but she claimed that she was glad she now knew the difference between the radiator and the carburetor.

# Chapter Ten

UP UNTIL MARCH WE HAD BEEN Miss Willie's only competitive male admirers. Oh, she had plenty of admirers, but she remained aloof with all of them. Occasionally she went out with different ones, but no lasting relationship developed.

We were just beginning to feel secure in our knowledge that Miss Willie was exclusively ours. Then Ross Stratton came home from his mission. Earlier, when we had considered Snowflake's prospective bachelors, we had inadvertently overlooked Ross. Perhaps the oversight was a subconscious effort at self-preservation, a wild attempt to further our own romantic ambitions.

But Ross Stratton was not the kind of person you could easily disqualify. The thing that was so disconcerting about Ross was that he was just the kind of guy you wanted to marry your sister, the kind of guy you hoped had married your mother. In all honesty, had we carefully selected a suitable companion for Miss Willie, we could not have found a better candidate than Ross.

Handsome, athletic, hard-working, ambitious, considerate—those were only the beginning of his qualifying credentials. He was the epitome of chivalry, graciousness incarnate. After seeing Ross, we called to mind what Miss Willie had said about missionaries. Now we knew she was right. If we had had any doubts about going on a mission, Ross eliminated them. If a mission could do that for us, we wanted into the program.

Ross was in our ward, so there was no feasible way to keep the two apart. They were destined to meet, and that same strange destiny seemed to presage an auspicious future for them. We were convinced that if we, his competitors, were applauding him and conceding defeat, Miss Willie would be smitten by him, completely helpless to avert the impending romance.

No one in Snowflake observed Ross and Miss Willie more closely than we three, and in our ever-prying eyes everything had romantic overtones. Every time the two passed in the hall at church, we silently interpreted each smile, nod, or casual handshake. Our observations and imaginations became so intense that we soon forgot that we ourselves had once hoped for a stake in Miss Willie's future.

Since the weather was warming up, we often retired to the church lawn and discussed this budding relationship.

"Do you think Miss Willie likes Ross?"

"I don't know about her, but he sure has it bad for her."

"What do you mean?"

"He sure held her hand a long time after church. It was supposed to be just a handshake."

"They don't sit together in sacrament meeting."

"That's because he sits with his family."

"But he was sure staring at her during the meeting."

"Yeah, he looked at least twice."

"He walked her home last Sunday. When that happens you're getting down to business."

"You mean they're getting married?"

"No, but pretty close. He'll probably ask her on a date anytime now. It's bound to happen."

"But they get married right after that."

"Well, he better hurry, because I hear he's going to BYU the first of May."

"He's still got a few weeks, then. A guy can cover a lot of country in a few weeks, especially if he knows he has to hop to it."

"Besides, they can always write. A guy can do some pretty fancy romancing in the mail."

"Oh, those mail jobs aren't any good. Ask any RM. The girl might get excited over a few flowery letters, but after a while the fancy paper and scented ink and all that other junk get real old. She starts looking for somebody that's right there."

"Maybe you're right. Old Ross better get a game plan and stop shaking hands. That won't get him anywhere."

"That's the way all RMs are."

"Maybe we'll have to give him Miss Willie's dating course. That'll open his eyes."

"Do you think he's holding back on account of us?"

"What do you mean?"

"Well, maybe he thinks we've staked a claim. After all, we've gone to two dances with her."

"Or maybe he's slow because he doesn't think there's any competition."

"He better forget that one and quick. The old bachelors are hovering over her like buzzards over a dead steer. They're just waiting for their chance."

"Maybe if we asked her, he'd get to thinking—maybe even get a little jealous—and then he'd get the lead out."

I don't know if we solved anything during our discussions, but we certainly did our share of planning and speculating, always hoping that something would work out for Miss Willie.

Ironically enough, the three of us were still as infatuated with Miss Willie as ever, but that didn't prevent us from cheering for Ross.

One evening, three weeks before the Junior Prom, the three of us were at Miss Willie's studying for a Spanish test. When our studies had finally deteriorated to mere chatter, Miss Willie remarked, "I've been meaning to ask a favor of you three." Our talking ceased and we waited expectantly. "The prom is coming up soon and I was wondering . . ."

"Sure, we'll take you," Jefferson blurted out.

"We've been meaning to ask," I said. "We can drive now and everything. And even date legally."

"We'd still have to go together," BB added.

Miss Willie smiled and said quietly, "Why, thank you. But that isn't exactly what I had in mind."

"It isn't?"

"I think this time you would probably have more fun with someone your own age. Besides, it's no fun to share one girl among three guys."

"That depends on the girl," I said. "We don't mind. We'll all take you."

"Well, actually, someone else has asked me."

"Ross?" the three of us guessed.

She laughed and nodded her head, the pleasure evident. "He asked me a week ago."

"How did he ask you?" BB asked. We had thought that we had observed their every move, but apparently we had missed something.

"He just asked," she explained simply.

"But I mean when. We've been keeping a pretty close—"

I kicked BB under the table.

"Do you see him much?" Jefferson asked.

"Oh, we go out a little."

"You mean you've already had a date with him?" I asked.

"Three or four times maybe."

"Is that counting the times he walks you home from church?" BB wanted to know.

Miss Willie shook her head and laughed.

We were shocked. "How did he do that?" Jefferson gasped. "I mean . . ."

"Do you like him?" I inquired.

"He's nice."

"Do you think you'll marry him?" BB questioned.

"BB, he just asked me to the prom. That does not imply any lasting commitment. Besides, he's going to school soon and won't even be around."

"Will you write to him?" I asked.

"As I was saying," she said, winking but ignoring my question, "I have a request to make. Three girls in my Laurel class don't have dates to the prom. Being juniors and all, they would really like to go. I was wondering if you three would mind—"

"No thanks," BB said, cutting her off and closing his book with a bang. "Dancing with them over here was one thing, but taking them to the prom where everybody can see us is something else. They're older than us."

"I'm older than you. You took me to the Christmas dance."

"Oh, well, that's different."

"Yeah, lots different."

"And they wouldn't want to go with us," Jefferson argued. "They think we're a bunch of creeps."

"What makes you think that?"

"They've always thought we were creeps."

"That was before, when you went out of your way to be obnoxious. Lately have they acted like they thought you were creeps?"

"Well, no, but they probably still think it. A girl doesn't just change overnight."

"Sometimes boys do," she remarked.

"Which three want to go?" I asked, making certain I didn't sound anxious.

"Sue Willis, Becky Thomas, and Rita Flake."

We were silent, each of us pondering the prospects. None of the girls could be classified as a beauty. On the other hand, they weren't bad looking either. I suppose had we never known them and just saw them walking down the street, we might have taken a second look.

"Why do you want to make us do something like that?"

Miss Willie cleared her throat and lightly tapped a forefinger on the tabletop. "I don't want any of you to feel obligated," she said quietly. "I wouldn't want you to go unless you really felt like it. It would be unfair to you and the girls if it were any other way. But I really believe you could have a good time." There was a spark of enthusiasm in her voice now. "You know, Ross and I are having dinner here and you would be welcome to join us. I would like some company."

"We had kinda planned on going with someone else," BB said grudgingly, "someone a lot better than Rita Flake or Becky Thomas or Sue Willis." He rolled up a sheet of paper and blew through it as if it were a horn. "Shoot, we've known those girls all our lives. They wouldn't be any fun."

"You had fun when they came here to dance."

"Well, that's because what we expected was so bad that when it was only half bad it seemed like fun."

"The Junior Prom might be like that."

We shook our heads.

"Well, it was just an idea," Miss Willie finally said when she saw our reaction. She grabbed a pencil and doodled for a moment and then mused, "None of you has ever asked a girl out, have you." We looked up at her. "I mean, you've never called a girl up on the phone, all by yourself, to ask her out."

"We asked you," Jefferson said.

"That was different. *All* of you asked."

"We could do it," I said firmly. "We're not scared or anything like that. That isn't the reason we're holding back. We just don't want to go—with them."

"It would be good practice. It's one lesson you haven't learned."

"It's one lesson I don't want to learn on Rita Flake and company."

"It was just a thought," she sighed. "Let's go over these verbs once more; then we'd better quit for the night."

The next few minutes we went through the motions of studying Spanish verbs, but our minds were occupied elsewhere. None of us had seriously considered asking any girl except Miss Willie; and yet, once the idea was unveiled, we couldn't shake it from our thoughts.

Finally Jefferson asked, "How do you ask a girl? I mean, if you thought you might want to ask her someplace. But don't get any ideas," he added quickly. "I'm just curious."

"Just be yourself. Ask her how she is. Maybe ask her what she's been doing. Just a little conversation to put you both at ease, and then ask her if she would like to go to the prom with you. You can supply the details later. That's all there is to it. It isn't painful. No one has ever died asking a girl on a date. And if you get too nervous, just pretend you're calling for your best friend. Then it will be easy. And you'll be surprised how happy the girls will be. Not to mention the boys."

"What if they turn us down?" BB mumbled. "I mean, if we asked. I'm not going to, but if I did and they turned me down, I'd feel like a real jerk. I don't think I could handle that."

"They are not going to turn you down."

"How do you know?" I asked suspiciously.

"I just know."

"How?" I pressed.

"I know what they think."

"Go on," I said.

We waited for her to continue. "The other night the Laurels were talking about going to the prom. Two of them already have dates. One of the others said that going to a dance can be such a bore because most boys don't know how to dance or how to act. Then another one mentioned how fun it had been over here with you three, being able to dance with boys who really knew what they were doing. Gentlemen, they called you. They were impressed. They didn't say they wanted to go to the prom with you. They merely said they had had fun dancing with you. Now, if they had fun dancing over here, they could have a lot of fun at the prom. I know. I'm a girl. Not one of them would turn you down."

"I don't see why we have to," BB moaned.

"No one has to," Miss Willie rebuked mildly. "In fact, if you don't think you can go and have a good time, don't ask. Go because you can have a good time."

"Oh, all right," Jefferson grumbled. "I'll take Becky."

BB and I hesitated. Then, sensing that if I didn't make a move soon I would be stuck with last choice, I volunteered with equally deficient enthusiasm. "I'll take Rita."

BB eyed Jefferson and me coolly. "I guess that leaves me with Sue," he muttered.

"You sound like this is your funeral," Miss Willie chided. "You'll have a good time, if you'll give yourselves a chance."

"I want to get it over with," Jefferson said, unconvinced. "Can I use your phone?" Miss Willie nodded. "What's her number?"

Miss Willie smiled. "I just happen to have all three of their numbers written on that pad by the phone."

"Did you just happen to tell them to be home tonight?" I asked.

"That, Mr. Johnson, is for the three of you to find out," she replied with feigned sternness.

Jefferson picked up the phone and dialed. He quickly hung up. "I think I dialed the wrong number." He dialed again and hung up. He dialed a third time. The room was quiet. We all heard the sound as the phone rang. Jefferson paled and dropped the phone, almost knocking it to the floor.

"Those numbers can be real tricky," BB said, nudging me in the ribs.

Jefferson ignored the remark. He dialed again, this time dialing with deliberate caution. Once again all of us heard the first ring and then the phone crashed back. BB and I began to snicker.

"All right, one of you guys do it if you're so smart," he challenged, holding the receiver out to us. We stopped laughing and became serious—until he dialed and hung up once more. Then we burst out laughing raucously. "Real funny!" he growled. "Your turn is coming."

"She's not going to jump out of the phone and eat you," I hooted. "If she knew what you were going through, she'd probably call up and ask you, just to put you out of your misery."

"Real funny," he snapped.

"Do you want one of us to hold your hand?" I taunted.

"Real cute."

"We'll be right here giving you moral support," I continued. "We're with you, buddy."

"Maybe he needs a pep talk," BB joined in. "Let's give him a couple of good cheers. Then he'll be able to call all three girls."

"Yeah, that's it, Jefferson. Just pretend that it's a football game. Close your eyes and . . ."

"Do you got your speech memorized?" BB called out.

"Be calm," I mocked. "Just act like you're calling for your best friend."

Flushed, Jefferson glared at us. "All right," he muttered, "I'll do it just like I was calling for a friend."

He began to dial while BB and I watched, waiting for him to dial the last number and hang up. But he didn't!

"Hello, Rita," Jefferson said calmly, "this is Daniel Johnson."

My mouth flopped open and I stared in horror.

"I was just wondering if you would like to go to the Junior Prom with me."

Before I could decide whether he was really talking to someone, he had hung up and was smiling smugly. "Well, that was easy," he gloated. "Nothing to it when you do it that way. Well, DJ, looks like you have your date to the prom. Come on, BB. Let's go home and let DJ go over his manners with Miss Willie so he'll be all ready for the big dance. He can double with Miss Willie and Ross."

By then I was on the phone calling Becky Thomas. Jefferson tried to rush me, but BB came to my aid, catching Jefferson with one of his best football tackles, which sent them both crashing to the floor.

While they scuffled on the floor, I made two phone calls, one to Becky and one to Sue.

"Have you called her?" BB grunted, still wrestling with Jefferson. "I can't hold him much longer."

"You can let him go. I called both of them."

BB loosened his grip and sat up. "What do you mean *them?*"

"It was so easy this way, I thought I'd just make two calls so you wouldn't have to suffer."

"Why'd you do that?"

"You didn't think you were staying home, did you?"

"You mean while I was helping you with Jefferson—"

I grinned and nodded.

Miss Willie, who had been trying to smother her laughter during our entire episode, shrugged and remarked, "Well, how does it feel to be going on your first date, at least with your very own girl?"

We grumbled and groaned and accused Miss Willie of a set-up, but under our blustering indignation we were pleasantly surprised that we had taken the plunge. Or should I say that someone else had pushed us and we had plunged?

During the next three weeks we were too embarrassed even to look the girls in the eyes. I don't know if they ever suspected what we had done, but we knew. Consequently, we avoided all the places we thought they might be. When we went to church, we sat on the back row so that we could sneak in and out before they caught a glimpse of us. The more we avoided them, the greater was our embarrassment until we were almost consumed with it. We were on the verge of paranoia, reluctant to go anywhere and chance meeting them. If it had not been for Miss Willie, we would never have been able to make our final arrangements. But understanding our odd predicament, she agreed to become our go-between. All we had to do was worry about showing up.

Even though we suffered a horrendous case of the jitters, the prom was a success. It was surprising what a formal, a hairdo, a corsage, and the excitement of prom night could do for girls like Rita, Becky, and Sue. I almost didn't recognize them. They were actually pretty. I hadn't experienced that kind of excitement for a girl since I met Miss Willie. I'm not saying that they were any kind of a match for Miss Willie, but they were extremely good substitutes. In fact, we were even able to forget that Ross had taken Miss Willie away from us.

Oh, our romantic inclinations were far from dead. We continued to harbor infatuated hopes, but that night we began to realize that our innocent affair with Miss Willie was taking a sudden turn. Later we would discover that there had been no turn. We were merely catching a glimpse of the vision Miss Willie had had from the very beginning.

But that night we didn't think of all that. It was prom night. We were content, filled with a new excitement, thoroughly immersed in the world of chivalry into which Miss Willie had introduced us.

# Chapter Eleven

THOSE SHORT MONTHS WITH MISS WILLIE had a powerful maturing influence on us. Her untiring efforts gradually produced a meager fruit of change. There were, of course, those who found our reform difficult to understand and almost impossible to accept. Mr. Bott, our biology teacher, seemed to be one of the skeptics.

Under Miss Willie's encouragement, Jefferson had begun toying with the idea of becoming a doctor, so biology became an intriguing challenge for him. BB and I, however, had no such ambitions. We didn't have Jefferson's enthusiasm for the subject, and if we had hidden talents, they were indeed hidden.

Our only hope in biology was Jefferson, who coached us along the path of improvement. What Mr. Bott confused for us in class, Jefferson clarified for us after school. As a result, the second term, we both earned our first B-minus in biology. Jefferson maintained a straight A average from the start, the first time he had done anything that bordered on brilliance.

Our grades, however, didn't reflect our love for Mr. Bott; though we worked in class, we were far from his ideal students.

I'm sure our own attitude toward Mr. Bott was a contributing factor to his skepticism where we were concerned. Ever since that first day, when he had kept us after class and extolled our purported potential and creativity out of one side of his mouth while raising suspicions about our character out of the other, the three of us had engaged in a concerted effort to make life miserable for him.

Miss Willie's influence eventually tamed our behavior in our other classes, but because we had nurtured such a negative impression of Mr. Bott from the outset, her influence had little effect on our behavior in biology.

That first day we had made a firm decision to go criminal. We didn't do anything terribly bad. We just made class disconcerting and unenjoyable. One day Mr. Bott opened his closet to find the class skeleton dressed in his coat, hat, and an old skirt from the home-economics room. Mr. Bott had the habit of stepping into the garbage can at the beginning of class to smash down the accumulation of discarded papers. At the beginning of our class, he stepped into the garbage can only to discover that it was half full of water. Test keys and teacher manuals began to disappear just when tests and assignments were to be corrected. They were not found until the class was over. Then they showed up under piles of papers that had already been searched several times. Lab days became especially chaotic. One day the frogs to be dissected, which were supposed to be dead, were suddenly jumping about the room. Mr. Bott's pet rats found their way into his desk drawer and ate his sack lunch.

It was sabotage, pure and simple, and Mr. Bott knew it. But there was never a culprit to apprehend. He suspected us, eyeing us in helpless frustration, but there was no evidence to link us with the crimes.

"Why is it that you have it in for Mr. Bott?" Miss Willie asked us one evening.

"Why does he have it in for us?" Jefferson came back defensively. "From the very first day he hasn't wanted to give us a chance. He's just been waiting to make 'good boys' out of us. Well, we're just beating him to the punch."

"He told you he thought you had potential."

"Oh, but he didn't mean it," BB fumed. "If he did, why did he give us all that other junk about leaving our tricks at the door? We know his type."

Miss Willie was silent for a moment. "I think Mr. Bott is a good man. I honestly believe he sees potential in you. He just doesn't know how to show it properly."

"You can say that again," I muttered.

"Are you going to condemn him for that?" Miss Willie asked. "Some people just have a hard time conveying to others what they are really like."

"No," Jefferson countered, "Mr. Bott's just a mean old guy, looking for some excuse to jump all over us. That's just the way he is. Why, we've been hearing about him ever since he came to Snowflake. Just ask anybody. They'll tell you what he's like."

Miss Willie smiled knowingly. "When I first came to Snowflake, would the three of you have wanted me to go to the rest of the town to find out what you were like?"

My cheeks and the back of my neck began to flame with a burning blush, and all three of us squirmed uneasily in our chairs.

"It's quite possible Mr. Bott was the only one in Snowflake who spotted your real potential, your capabilities. He's just had a hard time conveying that to you."

"And you don't think he's biased?" I demanded.

Miss Willie shrugged. "Maybe he is biased. But just maybe he's interested in you too. I'm not saying he's perfect. He has his faults, but maybe when he spoke to you the first day, he was voicing confidence in you."

"That would be the day," BB growled.

"Can't you at least give him a chance? Maybe he needs just as much of a chance from you as you are demanding from him."

Though Miss Willie's words pricked our conscience, we weren't quite ready or willing to relinquish our bad impression of Mr. Bott. I suppose subconsciously we knew that once we put aside our own prejudices, we ourselves would have to change, and right then we were rather enjoying tormenting Mr. Bott.

Mr. Bott endured a great deal, probably more than we thought he would, but finally at the beginning of the second semester he stopped us as we were leaving class for lunch. He sat us down in front of his desk and paced before us a few moments. Trying to conceal his anger under an expression of pretentious calm, he asked slowly, "Do you know why I've asked you to stay?"

We shook our heads with obvious indifference and gazed carelessly about the room.

Eyeing us coolly, he said, "Since the beginning of the year, there have been some strange occurrences in this room. Have you noticed?" We shrugged. Mr. Bott was a short, stocky man with a thick neck always wrapped tightly in a white shirt and tie. His head was big and shaped like a block because of the crew cut he wore, and he had thick, black eyebrows that shaded his deep-set eyes. When he was angry or upset, he would clamp his jaw shut so that the muscles in his neck and jaw bulged. He would draw his eyebrows together and glare out through black, squinting eyes. That's how he watched us today. For a long time he stood tense and silent. Slowly he began to relax. He placed his palms on the desk and leaned forward. "I haven't wanted to confront you with this. I've tried to ignore it, but the situation doesn't get any better. What do you have to say for yourselves?" We didn't respond. He pushed away from the desk and ran his tongue over his lips. "These pranks," he began again, "resemble the infantile mentality that characterized your junior-high days. I had hoped you might have changed since then, that high school would help you mature."

"You've never once hoped we'd change," BB muttered contemptuously. "You've—" Jefferson poked him before he could continue.

The muscles in Mr. Bott's neck and face tightened again and his nostrils flared momentarily. "This is the only class that seems to fall apart."

"There are twenty-five other kids in the class," BB remarked.

Mr. Bott nodded. "I wanted to reason with you. Apparently you're not in the mood. All right, but I'll have my eyes on you."

"You've had your eyes on us the whole year, just waiting to grab us for something," BB snapped back, "but we got you figured out."

"You, Mr. Bunderson, are going to the office."

"For what?"

"Insolence."

BB nodded and smiled humorlessly. "Insolence? I don't know what it is, but we've been blamed for everything else. I might as well get blamed for insolence."

BB went to the office and Jefferson and I went to lunch, as unrepentant as ever.

Now Mr. Bott was suspicious of everything we did. Every time we stepped into his class, we felt the warm animosity between us. The whole class became tense as a result of our tacit feuding.

One evening toward the end of the third term we stopped by Miss Willie's to help her move some crates to her backyard. We weren't even thinking of Mr. Bott until she said casually, "I hear you continue to have trouble with Mr. Bott." She was not making an accusation, just an observation. We didn't say anything, avoiding her questioning gaze. We didn't like to discuss Mr. Bott with Miss Willie. He was the one subject she didn't seem to understand. "You know, I've heard a lot of compliments about you three. I've bragged a lot myself."

"Old Bosko Baby doesn't compliment us," BB said grimly.

Miss Willie stared at us without flinching and then said firmly, "No, *Mr. Bott* doesn't compliment you. Of course, he's slow to compliment anyone. That's just his way. But I've bragged to Mr. Bott about you."

We looked at the ground and fidgeted under her stare. "What does he say about your bragging?" I asked.

"He thinks you're going out of your way to disrupt his class." She paused and then asked quietly, "Are you?"

"Did he send you to ask us?" Jefferson challenged.

"No. I just want to know."

"We won't lie. We do," BB said, looking at her. "He has it coming."

"Miss Willie," I said, almost pleading, "it wouldn't matter if someone else was playing those tricks. He'd suspect us anyway. As long as he's going to think it's us, as long as we're getting the blame, then we might as well get the fun of pulling the pranks."

"Is he entirely to blame for his suspicions? Have you given him reason to question your behavior?"

160

"Don't worry," I assured her, "we won't get caught."

"Get caught?" she asked. "Is getting caught the only thing that matters? You're not cheating Mr. Bott; you're cheating yourselves. And I don't think you're judging Mr. Bott fairly. You've had it in for him from the beginning. No wonder he has a less than flattering opinion of you. And maybe it isn't all your fault. I would guess that the blame lies at the feet of Mr. Bott and you. Maybe you'll never change Mr. Bott's opinion of you. Perhaps you'll never change anyone's opinion of you. So what? Does that mean you should destroy the opinion you have of yourselves? Don't ruin what you've accomplished up till now just to spite Mr. Bott. It's not worth it."

"I don't care anymore," Jefferson said defiantly. "I don't care if I flunk his lousy class. I don't care what he thinks of me. I'm going to act just like he thinks I act. I'm going to be a royal pain for Bosko Baby."

None of us had ever seen Miss Willie angry. We had begun to suspect that she was incapable of anger, but there was fire in her eyes that evening. Her cheeks were crimson; her lips, a thin, pale-pink line. "So you're going to let Mr. Bott determine the kind of men you'll be? You're going to let this man, whom none of you esteems in the least, whom none of you admires, you're going to let him decide for you what you're going to be like. Is that it?"

We didn't respond, completely taken back by her fiery outburst.

"Jefferson, you've said you might become a doctor. How are you ever going to become a doctor if you allow every Mr. Bott who comes along to determine how you're going to act? How will you become a doctor if every Mr. Bott is able to mold your life after his own warped and narrow point of view? And there are going to be a host of Mr. Botts. They'll be professors, patients, peers. You can't escape them.

"Who is hurt by what you're doing now? Oh, it might be a slight inconvenience to Mr. Bott, but he's being satisfied. You're playing right into his hands. If, like you say, Mr. Bott does believe you are incorrigible pranksters, fooling all the rest of us, then you're proving him right and the rest of us wrong. Is that what you really want?

With each prank you pull, you honor Mr. Bott's supposedly biased opinion."

Her words cut us deeply. We were wrong and we knew it. Knowing this irritated us, enraged us to think that we had played into the hands of Mr. Bott.

"So we just take it?" I wanted to know.

Miss Willie folded her arms. "DJ, I'm not sure if there's anything to take. I still believe Mr. Bott's prejudice is as much imagined on your part as real, but if there really is something you must endure unfairly from him, then do it. I know that's hard, but sometimes that's all you can do."

She could see we were unconvinced. "When I first came to Snowflake, I was scared. I had been asked to face something that I hadn't thought would threaten for years and years. All of a sudden my dreams, my goals, my hopes crumbled into powder. Suddenly life's only guarantee was the present." She bit down on her lip. "I was afraid," she whispered. "I was devastated. I didn't know if I could go on, always pursued by that dark, foreboding shadow." Her chin quivered ever so slightly. "I wanted to run and never stop. Then I discovered that my hope was not in flight. The threat was destined to remain with me. My only hope was in facing it. Facing it and making peace with myself. I soon realized that that peace was contingent upon no other person or thing. It was not had easily. It came only after I learned to accept the inevitable and, even in the face of that terrible challenge, do the very best I knew how."

She smiled weakly. "Even in the face of Mr. Bott's seeming prejudice, you can be at peace with yourselves. That peace will bring you far more satisfaction than your pranks."

"How do we do it?" BB asked.

"Prove to yourselves that he's wrong. Be such outstanding students, score so high on his tests and quizzes that even he will have to admit he's been wrong about you. And even if you never convince him, you'll have still convinced yourselves. Someday Mr. Bott will walk out of your lives, but you will remain. Make certain you have something worthwhile to live with."

It took two sessions on the church lawn before we convinced

ourselves to try Miss Willie's way, but we finally decided to stop our pranks, ignore Mr. Bott's supposed suspicions, and learn biology better than any of his other students, even if it meant failing every other class on our schedule. Reflecting now on that singular resolve, I suppose our main motivation was Miss Willie. She had challenged us to do it, and there weren't many things we wouldn't have done for her.

We didn't realize the magnitude of our challenge until later, but once we had made our commitment to change, we pressed forward. There were no more quick naps, no more doodling, no more sabotage. We fought the boredom, we fought the suspicions, and we fought the temptation to disrupt. I'm sure our change was perplexing to Mr. Bott, if not irksome. He seemed always on the defensive, just waiting for us to strip away our innocent disguise and catch him unawares.

Jefferson became engrossed in biology. He seemed to accept this new challenge with a religious zeal. His biology book became another appendage. He devoured and digested everything. His grasp of the subject became awesome, almost uncanny, and he insisted that BB and I follow suit.

Our major goal was the final exam over the last fourteen chapters of the book and all the notes from the second semester. A person was considered successful if he scored in the eighties on Mr. Bott's final. Rarely did one score in the nineties. The final was a third of the semester grade.

Jefferson pestered BB and me with questions until we tried to avoid him and not be subjected to his barrage of information and unrelenting interrogation. But he was persistent, and we did learn biology. Almost against our will.

When Mr. Bott handed out our final, I broke out in a sweat, fearing that all the work, all the agonizing study, and all the bragging to Miss Willie was for naught; however, as I started writing the answers, I felt a surge of excitement. I knew! These were the things Jefferson had drilled us on. I couldn't write fast enough. I wanted to get through it before I forgot anything. I looked up and glanced at BB. He smiled and gave me the thumbs-up sign.

Jefferson finished his test ten minutes ahead of everyone else.

BB and I were among the other early finishers. We sat back in our desks, gloating and smiling at each other.

Jefferson, however, didn't wallow in his victory like BB and me. His triumph was an angry, defiant one. The test had been an obsession with him. He had not approached it with the playful ardor and determination BB and I had felt. For him the exam was a revenge of sorts, one he could flaunt before Mr. Bott.

The next day the corrected tests were handed back to the class. All except BB's, Jefferson's, and mine. Mr. Bott announced that he wanted to see us immediately after class.

When everyone else had left, Mr. Bott tossed us our tests, his face frowning. I turned mine over—eighty-eight percent. I gulped. It was all I could do to keep from grinning and dancing around Mr. Bott's desk. I glanced at BB's test. Eighty-four percent. And Jefferson's score was an unbelievable ninety-eight percent. I could not stifle the smug smile pushing at the corners of my mouth.

For several minutes Mr. Bott let us bask in the excitement of the moment; then he asked, "Is this your work, your honest work?" We stared at him, all of us puzzled, not quite comprehending the intimation. "For the past few weeks I have wondered what you were up to. I wasn't expecting this. I can live with rats in my desk drawer or water in the garbage can, but I cannot ignore this. I frown on cheating." He cleared his throat. "Every answer you two missed," he said, looking at BB and me, "were the same. The two Jefferson missed, you two missed also. Does that strike you as odd?"

He pushed his thick, hairy arms into his pockets and jingled his keys. Pressing his lips together, he stared down at his desk. "Do you know what the highest score on this test has been during the last four years, Jefferson?" Jefferson didn't answer. He stared coldly at Mr. Bott. "Ninety-three percent," Mr. Bott whispered. "And you came up with ninety-eight. I'm not sure I could come up with ninety-eight, and I wrote the test."

Looking at BB and me, he said, "And, Mr. Bunderson, the highest score you've had all year is an eighty-one—on a chapter test. Now you manage an eighty-four on the year's most difficult exam. And you, Mr. Johnson, have scored an eighty-three once, and you manage to pull off an eighty-eight. Both you and Mr. Bunderson would have had identical scores but he left some of his questions unanswered."

I was too shocked to reply. I had expected anything but this.

"We studied, Mr. Bott," BB responded hoarsely. "We really did. Honest."

Mr. Bott slowly sucked in air between his teeth. "I'd like to believe that, Mr. Bunderson," he said. "That would make my job a lot easier, and more pleasant. But the facts just don't stack up."

Jefferson stared for a moment; then, grabbing his biology book, he threw it onto Mr. Bott's desk. BB and I caught our breath, waiting for the explosion. "Ask me anything," Jefferson said evenly without blinking. Mr. Bott smiled and pushed the book aside. "Ask me anything," Jefferson repeated, more loudly.

"I just want to know if you were cheating. This does look suspicious," he said, indicating our tests. "I would feel a lot better if I didn't have to pry it out of you."

"Ask me anything," Jefferson said again.

"I'm not sure that would prove anything."

"Anything," Jefferson insisted.

"Anything?" Mr. Bott asked, smiling. "I'd rather not do this," he said. Then he pulled the book toward him, opened it in the middle, and said, "Let's see, this semester we started with chapter . . ."

"I said anything," Jefferson cut in. "Anything in the book. Anything from the notes."

The smile on Mr. Bott's face disappeared and he went to the beginning of the book and began shooting questions at Jefferson. Jefferson didn't falter once. He didn't pause. The answers were always there, not just the simple, superficial kind, but answers with clarifying background and amplification. I knew that Jefferson had studied, but it wasn't until right then that I knew how well. I wanted to stand up and cheer and dance.

Finally Mr. Bott closed the book and looked up. "I guess you have studied a little," he conceded.

"A little?" Jefferson snapped. "And by the way, one of these you marked wrong is correct." He thumbed through the book until he

had the right page and proved his point. "I have ninety-nine percent."

"I've never given a ninety-nine percent," Mr. Bott said with surprise written all over his face.

"You've never given anything," Jefferson came back. "That
ninety-nine percent is mine. I earned it, every last point."

"And your two friends?"

Jefferson thumbed to chapter fourteen. "Start there. Ask them
anything."

BB and I almost sank into the floor. There was no way we could
stand up to an interrogation like Jefferson's. I tried to kick Jefferson
so he would let up, but he didn't. "If you think I helped them during the test, ask them questions."

Mr. Bott shook his head. I was never so relieved in my life. He
forced out a nervous laugh. "I'm impressed," he stammered. "I
never thought that . . . well, I just wasn't expecting this. But I always
told you," he added quickly, "that I knew you had potential. Maybe
this proves it."

None of us replied. We sat in stony silence, waiting for Mr. Bott
to dismiss us.

"Let's go tell Miss Willie," BB suggested when Mr. Bott finally let
us go.

The three of us found her in her room correcting papers. We
burst in bubbling with excitement. "We did it," I announced with a
grin. "We aced Baby Bosko's test. We knocked him right out of his
chair. Especially Jefferson. Bosko even made a mistake on the test
and Jefferson showed him where he was wrong."

Miss Willie beamed with pleasure. "I knew you could do it. I'm
proud of you."

"Don't be," Jefferson confessed grimly. "Not yet. He still has his
coming."

Miss Willie raised her eyebrows and cocked her head to one
side. "What do you mean?"

"I'm going to get him back."

"Didn't you prove your point by beating him on his own
ground?"

"He called me a liar," Jefferson flared. "Not a mess-off, a liar!"

"I didn't hear that," BB mumbled.

"You didn't? Why did he keep us after? Because he thought we cheated. When I asked him to ask me anything in the book, I was telling him we hadn't cheated. What did he do? He asked me questions for ten minutes. He knew after the first two or three questions that I hadn't cheated, but no, that wasn't enough. He had to keep going and going trying to find just one little weak place. He has his coming. That's all I've got to say."

"It might have been an honest mistake, Jefferson," Miss Willie said. "Anyone might have done the same thing."

"Would you have suspected us of cheating?" Jefferson asked.

"I know you. I trust you."

"Well, in a little while Mr. Bott's going to know me better than he does now."

"You're going to condemn him for an honest mistake?"

"It's his fault."

"And if I had made that kind of a mistake with you, would you be just as quick to condemn me?" Jefferson looked away from her. "That's not your way," Miss Willie counseled. "You're better than that."

"Maybe. We'll see."

She shook her head. "You're just angry now. Think about it. You'll see that anything you do will just ruin what you've already won. Mr. Bott will have to admit he was wrong."

"I don't care what he thinks, not anymore."

"But I care what he thinks about you. I care a great deal. Think about it, Jefferson."

Jefferson did think about it, but he didn't change his mind. He wanted revenge in a terrible way. I had never seen him so angry, and I suppose in a way his anger rubbed off on BB and me. We had been content to watch Mr. Bott squirm during Jefferson's interrogation, but that was not enough for Jefferson. He wanted blood—in a real way.

The last day of school Jefferson divulged his plan to BB and me. More interested in the fun and excitement than the revenge, we consented. That night we each made arrangements to spend the night at BB's place. BB borrowed his dad's old pickup truck and Jefferson brought two twenty-two rifles, and we went hunting.

Jackrabbits were plentiful around Snowflake. That night with BB's headlights glaring and Jefferson's two rifles popping, we bagged seventeen rabbits. At three o'clock in the morning, we drove to Mr. Bott's place and, with malicious cunning, scattered rabbits over his lawn, his porch, and his driveway and hung them from his trees. In the midst of our grisly gift, we posted a hand-written sign: "Dear Baby Bosko, This is a token of our undying appreciation. We hope you like rabbit stew. Most affectionately yours, the Baby Bosko Bott Booster Club."

With our gruesome work complete, we retreated to BB's back-yard, where our sleeping bags were laid out. Sleep escaped us, though. We spent the remaining hours of the morning in anticipation of Mr. Bott's early-morning discovery.

At six-thirty, watching furtively from the cover of BB's shrubs, we saw Mr. Bott amble onto his porch in his pajamas to pick up the morning paper. He surveyed the carnage in his yard. We had expected a violent paroxysm of rage, but he seemed inordinately calm; in fact, he seemed almost amused. After a moment he re-entered the house. We watched in a state of stupefaction, feeling cheated. Mumbling our utter perplexity, we crawled into our sleeping bags and slept.

It was almost noon when we awoke. The first thing we did was to peek through the shrubs toward Mr. Bott's yard. Every rabbit was gone! It wasn't until that afternoon when we passed Miss Willie's place that we learned what had happened. Miss Willie didn't greet us. She merely motioned for us to come to her.

"I have some boxes of garbage in the back," she announced. "Would you dispose of it?"

"Sure," we said, and walked around to her backyard. There, lying in the shade with a buzzing swarm of flies hovering above them, were four boxes of rabbits with our sign lying conspicuously on top.

Slowly we retreated to the front of the house. Miss Willie didn't say anything. She ignored us completely. "Where'd you get those?" BB asked meekly.

"Maybe a better question is, where did you get them?"

"How'd they get here?" Jefferson queried, shamefaced.

"I brought them."

"You didn't pick them up, did you?"

"Yes, and it was a dirty, messy, demeaning job. I was sickened by the blood, by the smell, by the act itself. And what did it prove? That you could come up with the cruelest, most vicious and detestable of pranks? Perhaps you did it so people would remember you. Will they remember that you were the first to score ninety-nine percent on Mr. Bott's test?" She shook her head. "That is forever forgotten, supplanted by a memory of slaughtered rabbits, killed on whim to upset one man."

"It was just a joke," BB said.

"Seventeen slaughtered rabbits on someone's front steps is no joke," she snapped. "Was it a joke, Jefferson?"

Jefferson shook his head.

"But you didn't have to pick them up," I said. "You didn't do it. We were the ones to get blamed. It was our necks. If you knew who did it, why didn't you come and get us?"

"It was my word of honor."

"Huh?"

"I promised to pick them up."

"Why?"

"Because I trusted you. After you left my room yesterday, Mr. Bott stopped by. You know, he was actually impressed with what you had done. I think in his own odd way he was even proud. Do you know what he said to me?" We shook our heads. "He said, 'You know, Miss Willie, I think I've misjudged those boys. I knew they had potential, at least I thought they did, but I didn't know if they would ever get at it.' Then he shook his head and said, 'It's too bad all this had to happen. I wish we had understood each other better. I think we could have had a good year. Now, well, now I think I've really upset them. They're not ones to let things like this pass. They'll probably want to retaliate.'"

Miss Willie was silent for a moment. "I assured him that you were better than that. I said I would personally take responsibility for anything you might do to Mr. Bott." Her eyes bore into each of us, and then she said, making no attempt to mask her anger, "Now, please take those rabbits and go."

None of us said anything as we hauled the rabbits away, but when we were finished Jefferson said, "Let's go apologize to her. That's the least we can do."

"She probably won't talk to us," BB cautioned. "She was mad."

"We've got to try."

We crossed the street and knocked on the door. Miss Willie was a long time in coming, and when she did, she opened the door without inviting us in.

"Can we come in?" Jefferson mumbled. She thought for a moment and then nodded. Stepping aside, she indicated with a wave of her hand that we should sit on the sofa. She waited for us to speak.

"We wanted to tell you we're sorry," Jefferson began. He looked down at his hands. "We didn't want . . . I guess we just . . ." He groped for the words without finding them. "We're sorry," he finally mumbled. "I guess in a way Mr. Bott was right about us."

No one spoke for several minutes. Finally Miss Willie said, "I was very disappointed. I can't deny that." We nodded ruefully. "Your rabbit trick," she said quietly, "was characteristic of three boys, boys who I thought had become men. Perhaps Mr. Bott has been unfair. I thought you could show him that you were men, better and bigger men than he."

She dropped into the overstuffed chair and began tracing the Indian blanket design with her finger. "I was very angry. I felt responsible. I thought I had taken you so far. I felt let down, as though it were a failure on my part." She dropped both her hands on the arms of the chair. "I've wanted to make you men. But I'm seeing now that that is a journey you must make on your own. Perhaps I, or someone else, can point out the way, but you are the ones who must travel the distance." She seemed pale and exhausted. I felt sorry for her. She smiled, but the effort seemed to pain her. "I'm not angry anymore. I'm sorry I was so brusque."

"We won't do it again," I promised.

Miss Willie leaned back in the chair so that she was staring up at the ceiling. "There's more to it than that." She thought and then said, "I guess it's a matter of integrity. Integrity isn't something that's acquired in a moment. It's not something that one merely covets and then has. We spend a lifetime in pursuit of it, but if we ever choose to give it up or sell it, for whatever reason, whether it be expediency, pleasure, or revenge, we lose the entire thing, and to gain it back there is a terribly exacting price to pay, much more than the original price. The three of you had begun your purchase. I hated to see you throw it away on some foolish prank, something so unworthy of you."

"We can make it up," I insisted.

"We're sorry," Jefferson repeated. "We're going to try harder. We'll show you. Next year when you come back we'll show . . ."

"Jefferson," she cut in sadly, "did you ever stop to think that there might not be a next year? There's just now."

"But we'll show you," Jefferson insisted.

"Jefferson, it's something you show yourself. That's where I was wrong. I wanted you to show me, to show everyone. But that's not the way. It's part of that inner peace I told you about. Each person makes his own quest. Other people don't give you integrity or character, nor can they take it away. It's something personal."

After our visit with Miss Willie we strolled down to the church lawn and lay back as dusk settled over the town. We were there several minutes pondering in silence. Then Jefferson interrupted our musings. "It's my fault. I was the one that brought the whole thing up."

"We went along with you," BB countered.

"Yeah," I added. "Like Miss Willie said, you can't pass the buck to anyone else. We're just as guilty as you."

There was another extended silence. "If we want to make it right," Jefferson said, "we'll have to go to Mr. Bott."

"To Bosko?" I said. "Nothing happened to him. Miss Willie was the one who got stuck with the mess. We don't owe Bosko anything."

Jefferson stood up. "I owe him something. I'm going to pay up. I'm going there Monday morning to apologize. I'm going to offer to work for him."

"Work for Bosko? What for?" I protested.

"So I can make up for what we did last night. Maybe that's not the right way, but that's what I want to do."

"He'll work you all summer and still say you're not even," BB said.

"Then I'll work all summer."

"I thought you were working at your uncle's store," I said.

"That'll have to wait. This is more important to me now."

"Well, we don't have to do that," BB growled. "I'm not doing anything for that old buzzard."

"This is just my way," Jefferson explained. "You might feel different."

"You're just trying to impress Miss Willie," I accused.

"She'll never know. I won't tell her. Like I said, this is something I feel I have to do."

"Well, we're not going to do it," I muttered. And yet, even then I knew we would. Jefferson was right. We owed a debt. As much as I loathed paying it, I knew we would never have complete peace until we had paid up. But it was surely hard admitting it that Saturday night.

Sunday when we went to our meetings none of us said much. We didn't mention Mr. Bott or Jefferson's resolve, but we did a lot of reflecting.

Monday morning, shortly before eight, all of us, without prior arrangements with each other, converged at Mr. Bott's place.

"You two don't have to do this," Jefferson said as he saw us coming to join him.

"Yes we do," BB snapped.

"Do you think you have exclusive rights to a clear conscience?" I asked.

We knocked on the door and Mr. Bott answered it. He was just finishing his breakfast. He nodded in greeting but did not speak or invite us in.

"We came to say we're sorry for Friday night," Jefferson said evenly.

"I'm sorry too, but Miss Willie cleaned it up for you."

"We know, but it wasn't her mess," I explained, looking down at Mr. Bott's shoes. "She cleaned it up, but it should have been us. We want you to know we're sorry."

Mr. Bott gave a short grunt that evolved into a hoarse laugh. "Saying you're sorry is easy. Did she put you up to this?"

"No one did," Jefferson replied.

"You came over on your own?"

We nodded.

"Your parents send you?"

"We came over here on our own," BB protested. "No one else knows we're even here."

"It's something we thought we had to do," I explained. "We want you to believe us when we say we're sorry."

"That might have been easier to believe a few days ago," Mr. Bott said, his face coloring with anger. "Your rabbit trick was without a doubt the lowest kind of prank I've heard of, even from you. For a while there I thought you might have come around, but after Saturday morning . . ." He shook his head. "Well, I won't deny it. I was upset. I'm still upset. And I was furious that Miss Willie was the one to clean up after you. I'm not sure who sent you here, but I'm not impressed. This doesn't change anything. In fact, I'm not sure anything you could do around here would change how I feel about your behavior over the weekend, or the whole school year, for that matter. I'm afraid it would just be a waste of time for everyone concerned."

A nerve center seemed to explode inside of me. I wanted to shout something in his face and walk off. He didn't deserve an apology. He didn't even want one. He was as bad as we had ever suspected—if not worse. I glanced at BB. His eyes were burning and his jaw was clamped tight. Jefferson saved us, though.

"We figured you might feel that way," Jefferson replied quietly. "That's why we came this morning, to show you that we really mean it. We'll work for you, for nothing. We'll work as long as you think we should, until we have made up for Friday night's mess."

"How many days are you willing to work?" he smirked.

"As long as you think."

"All summer?"

"If you think we should."

Mr. Bott laughed and picked at his teeth with his tongue. "You boys really are ambitious." He looked around. "I suppose if you want to feel sorry, I can give you something to make you feel sorry. Follow me."

Behind Mr. Bott's house were some old sheds that had been horse stables years before, but the horses had left long ago, and the sheds had become dumping grounds for the Botts. He motioned for us to follow him inside.

"I want these cleaned up," he said, pointing to the accumulation of junk. "Most of the stuff we'll take to the dump. Some of it I'll save. Take everything out, clean the sheds out, and put the good stuff back. I'll get my neighbor's truck to haul the junk off." He put his hands on his hips and grinned. "That ought to make you sorry. Any questions?"

We shook our heads and began. I don't think Mr. Bott realized how much had piled up in those sheds over the years. There were cobwebs and layers of dust everywhere. We dragged out boxes of everything from old books to rusty scrap iron. There were stacks of yellowed newspapers and magazines. Soon the air was hazy with dust from our work, and our noses and eyes were full of dirt. BB and I grumbled and complained, cursing Mr. Bott for submitting us to this torture. We were convinced he would have never cleaned those sheds had we not come along.

By the end of the day the sheds were empty, the contents stacked haphazardly about, but most of our work was still ahead of us. We went home, tired, dirty, and irritable. As we were parting company, Jefferson remarked to BB and me, "If you guys don't want to come back tomorrow, that's fine. I can finish." We shook our heads and went home grumbling.

The next day we were back cleaning out the sheds. We had thought that a simple sweeping would do it, but a lot of the dirt was caked on the floor and walls, and we had to scrape it off. Mr. Bott came out and pointed out what needed to go back inside and what needed to be hauled off.

By the end of the second day, the task was complete and I felt certain that we had made ample restitution. Had it not been Mr.

Bott's sheds, I would have probably felt immensely proud of our work, because we really had brought about a tremendous transformation. Those sheds actually looked nice. I'm sure Mr. Bott was even impressed, but he gave no praise nor showed the least bit of interest in what we had done.

BB and I felt that the sheds finished our obligation, but before we left for home that second day, Jefferson turned to Mr. Bott and inquired, "What would you like us to do tomorrow?"

Mr. Bott pulled on his ear and looked about his place. "I'm not sure any of this is proving anything," he muttered. "Cleaning a hundred sheds isn't going to erase the rabbits from my mind or from my neighbors' minds."

"We'd like to try," Jefferson said. "Maybe this isn't the way to do it. It's all we know, though. If you know of a better way, we'll do it."

Mr. Bott shook his head.

"Then if it's all the same to you, we'd like to do this. What else could we do for you?"

For a long while Mr. Bott looked at us. I couldn't tell what he was thinking. You never did know what was going on inside his head, but it did seem as though the anger was gone from his eyes, replaced by a shadow of disbelief. But he gave us another task.

Behind the Bott house and in front of the horse sheds was a weed-infested lot that extended clear through the block. It was about one hundred feet wide. That day it looked much wider. It was spotted by unpruned fruit trees struggling to survive amid the weeds and trash. It was obvious that the lot had never meant much to Mr. Bott. Since he'd moved into his home five years earlier, he had never tried to clean up the lot or do anything else with it.

"I want to get this little orchard back into shape," he explained. "I'll probably put in a garden down at this end nearest the house and try to get those trees in shape so that they can give something more than shade to the weeds and grasshoppers. What you boys could do is rake up all these dried weeds and gather all the trash—cans, papers, whatever—and burn them. Dig around the trees. Going down the right side is an irrigation ditch that needs to be dug out and cleaned. You up to all that?"

Jefferson nodded. BB and I just stared, unable to believe that Mr. Bott would actually have the audacity to make such a request.

"Are you going to do it?" BB asked Jefferson as we were walking home that evening. Jefferson nodded. "He's just being ornery. He's just trying to make us crack. It's not fair."

"You two don't have to do it," he said tiredly. "I told you that before."

"He'll keep us there all summer," I protested, trying to inject some reasoning into the discussion.

"I already told him I'd stay for the summer if he wanted."

Shaking our heads in disgust, BB and I left Jefferson, not at all certain we would accompany him to Mr. Bott's place the next day, but the next morning, with rakes, shovels, and hoes over our shoulders, we returned to our self-inflicted agony.

The sheds had seemed like an insurmountable challenge, but they were insignificant in comparison to the lot. The task was immense, and to add to our distress, what had appeared as an average, cluttered lot emerged as one choked with years of weeds and clogged with hidden mounds of trash and debris. We attacked the weeds and trash with youthful energy, but after a couple of long, laborious hours, our zeal waned. We were making little impression on the tangled jungle of neglect. To add further to our distress, the sun was hot, the air was dry, and bugs buzzed about our heads. Soon our hands were spotted with blisters, and our backs and arms ached from pulling on rakes and digging with hoes and shovels.

In the afternoon, with sweat dripping from our brows, and our hands and arms scratched from pulling papers and cans from the currant bushes that grew along the north side of the lot, BB and I began to grumble loudly and deride Mr. Bott. He was the reason for our agonizing labors, and we tried to outdo each other in our derisive descriptions of him. We thought up new names for him and poked fun at his idiosyncrasies. We planned a string of ingenious revenges. Mr. Bott would pay for our miseries.

Jefferson remained silent throughout our derogatory tirade, but finally he turned on us and said, "Look, if you don't want to be here, then go home. Who are you doing this for anyway?" We stared at him without answering, but not mistaking the warm rebuke in his voice. "No one's making you stay, so if you want to, leave. But if you're going to be here, stop your griping and start working."

"What difference does it make to you?" BB snapped. "What are you trying to prove? We've done our work."

"You're just putting in time. It doesn't mean anything to you."

"What's it supposed to mean? He's never going to let us go. Who're we trying to impress?"

Jefferson straightened up and looked us both full in the eyes. "I'm not trying to impress anybody," he said evenly. "I've just done a lot of thinking about what Miss Willie said." He paused and bit down on his lower lip. A sudden emotion washed over him, and he struggled to take control of his voice. He looked down so we couldn't see the emotion churning inside of him. "I guess I want to prove something to myself. I have to prove this to myself, not to Mr. Bott. And that's important to me."

"What are you trying to prove?" I demanded, irritated that unlike BB and me, he was unwilling to condemn Mr. Bott.

"I want to prove . . . I guess I want to prove that I'll work for something that I think is right, even though it's hard. I'm not going to give up, because if I do I won't be hurting Mr. Bott. I'll be hurting me. It's that . . . well, maybe I have to hurt, hurt bad, and still keep working because I made a commitment."

"But why?"

"Because we were wrong. Miss Willie was right. We had almost proved we'd changed and then we threw it away. I thought the rabbits were funny at first and then . . . well, then I got to thinking. I didn't feel good like when I passed Mr. Bott's test. The rabbits didn't mean anything. It just tore everything else down."

"But what does cleaning Bosko's lot prove? So we made a mistake. We admitted it. Does that mean we should slit our wrists or stay out here and rot till old Bosko decides to let us go?"

"Maybe. If I can convince Mr. Bott, then I'm back where I was. Maybe better than I was because he's never been convinced."

"Then you're doing it to impress Bosko."

Jefferson shook his head. "No, I'm doing it for me. I'm proving this to me." His voice cracked and he stopped; then with poignant emotion he burst out, "And nothing is going to stand in my way— not you, not Mr. Bott, not this lousy patch of weeds. Nothing! I'm going to keep working till he has to come out and say, 'Jefferson Judd, I believe you. I believe you really are sorry for what you did and you have made everything up.' Now, maybe you two don't feel the same way. I was the one that made the commitment, and I'm going to keep it, and I want to ask you two to do one thing for me. If you want to badmouth Mr. Bott, then do it by yourselves. I'm going over there to work. I don't want to just go through the motions. If I'm always tearing him down, I can't feel good about him, and I want to feel good about him. I have to feel good about him if any of this is going to make any sense."

Jefferson took his shovel and rake and left BB and me. He started cleaning the ditch along the side of the lot where he was unable to hear what we said. But BB and I weren't talking. For a while we just stood there staring at Jefferson and refusing to admit there was any validity to what he had said. We were irked by his holier-than-thou attitude. We didn't want to believe he was right, because admitting that, we had to commit ourselves to the lot just as Jefferson had done. I had never contemplated a sacrifice of that magnitude. Nothing had ever meant that much to me. I resented Jefferson's attitude because it made me feel so small, so in- adequate. And at the same time I was jealous. In a way I wanted to feel what Jefferson was feeling; and yet, it terrified me to think that the only way I could feel that was to commit myself as strongly as Jefferson had done.

As I watched Jefferson work, I was reminded of his inordinate obsession to study for Mr. Bott's biology exam. BB and I had never been committed like Jefferson. He had pulled us through. I knew then that Jefferson had experienced a real change, the kind of change Miss Willie had talked about. I didn't want to be left behind. I knew that I too had something to prove, not to Mr. Bott or to Jef- ferson or anyone else.

As I pondered my discovery, I began to poke halfheartedly at the dry ground with my shovel, and slowly that evolved into a weak kind of work. That's when I noticed that BB was doing the same thing, and I could see that some of the same thoughts were going through his mind.

We were at a crucial crossroads. We could pick up our tools and leave Jefferson to his quixotic quest, turning our backs on the commitment we had had a glimpse of, or we could stay and work with the same zeal and determination that Jefferson had demonstrated. There was no middle ground. We could not hide in Jefferson's shadow, going through the motions, hoping that in some small way we might derive a wholesome benefit. It was total commitment or total abandonment.

I thought of Miss Willie. I sensed that she had been working to prepare us for this one decision, and that if I made the wrong choice, nothing else mattered. Knowing Spanish and English, having a few social graces, being at ease on a dance floor, improving my GPA—none of those things had any lasting significance unless they were coupled with this frightening commitment.

I knew then I would stay. I had to. And that was the miracle of it all. Even now I find it almost impossible to believe that the three of us—just barely sixteen and emerging timidly from our adolescent cocoon—made that kind of decision. Whenever I reflect on that moment of crisis, I experience a unique detachment, as though I am viewing someone else. And yet, I know it happened, not because it is feasible or natural but because that one momentous decision has had such an impact on my life.

"Come on, DJ," BB said. The two of us walked over to Jefferson. "All right, Jefferson, this is our project as much as yours. What happened last Friday was our doing too, even though you thought it up. And even though you thought about coming to work for Bos . . . I mean, Mr. Bott, it's our responsibility too. We want to work with you. And we'll stay. I guess we'll stay the summer."

"Are you sure?" Jefferson asked, wanting us to join him but unable to determine whether we were with him completely.

"You're not the only one that's got something to prove," I growled, trying to hide the tremendous excitement that was bursting inside me. "You don't have a corner on any of the great virtues, so move over and let us join you."

"We better start back at the far corner," BB said. "The one by the sheds."

"I did that this morning," Jefferson responded.

"Well, it looks crummy," BB barked. "It's a lousy job. If I'm going to stay here all summer, I'm at least going to do a good job."

Mr. Bott's lot became our personal crusade, our trademark, a reflection on us as individuals. We were no longer content to merely clean it to pass Mr. Bott's inspection.

By Friday the lot was almost finished. There was still another full day's work ahead of us, but the lot was transformed.

An hour before we were to quit for the day, Miss Willie came to visit us, carrying a two-quart bottle of ice lemonade. She examined the cleaned sheds and surveyed the lot. The three of us stopped working and leaned on our shovels while she made her inspection.

When she was finished looking around, she walked over to us and handed us the jug. "I forgot the cups," she explained, "so you'll just have to drink out of the bottle."

Within a few minutes we had drunk every drop of lemonade and were sucking on the last ice cubes.

"How does it look?" BB smiled with satisfaction. "Looks a little better, doesn't it?"

She nodded. "I talked to your folks." We didn't respond. "They don't know what you're up to." We looked at the ground. "They asked me, but I couldn't tell them anything." She stared at us without smiling. "What made you do it?"

"We wanted to," I said simply.

"It was something we all decided—on our own," Jefferson added. "We wanted Mr. Bott to know we were sorry, that we would do what we could to make things right with him."

"And has he responded to your gesture?" she asked.

BB grinned. "Well, he's given us plenty to do, so I guess he's responding in a way."

She heaved a sigh, and there was a little of the fire in her eyes that we had seen the Saturday before. "How long are you going to keep this up?"

"Until he's satisfied," BB answered, suddenly serious.

"He'll have you working here all summer," she said.

"If we owe him that, I guess we'll give it to him," Jefferson commented.

"You've more than proved yourselves." Her anger was simmering. "It doesn't matter what he thinks."

"But it's how we think that matters," Jefferson said. "That's what you told us. I guess we're making a kind of truce with ourselves. It's what we decided to do. What we have to do."

"Why, that greedy old man," she burst out in frustration. "The tyrant! He's just taking advantage of your willingness. You'll never change his mind. He's too bullheaded to see anything. He's a cruel, poor excuse for a man."

We were all quiet for a moment. We had never heard Miss Willie speak in a deprecating way of anyone. Then Jefferson said timidly, "Miss Willie, we don't say anything bad about Mr. Bott anymore." Her mouth dropped open a little. "It's just something we decided," he said, jabbing his shovel at a dirt clod. "If we're going to do this—and we are—it makes our work easier if we feel good about him. I guess it's something we learned from you."

We all lowered our eyes, feeling embarrassed to reprimand Miss Willie. She turned her back to us and we thought she was going to walk away, but she just stood there for a moment without saying anything; then she turned and faced us. Her eyes were brimming with tears, the first we'd ever seen. We had never had a woman like Miss Willie cry in front of us. We didn't know if we had hurt her, and we certainly didn't know how to remedy the situation. We felt utterly helpless.

Miss Willie finally smiled and wiped at her tears and said, "I want you to know that I've never been so proud of anyone as I am of the three of you. I don't care what anyone says, you are the finest, most wonderful young men I know. There is more courage and integrity here than . . ." Her voice began to quaver, and she bit down on her lip before continuing. "And if Mr. Bott doesn't see it, then he's a blind old man." She turned and left us.

We would have taken on a whole city of vacant lots just to have Miss Willie stand there with tears in her eyes and tell us how proud she was of us.

The following day we had our biggest surprise. As we were finishing the lot, burning the last piles of weeds and trash and digging about the last of the trees, Mr. Bott came out and inspected our work. We were about to gather our tools together and leave when he approached.

"You've done good work, boys," he began. He was actually humble. "Very good work." He pulled out his checkbook and said, "I'd like to pay you."

"We didn't do it for pay, Mr. Bott," Jefferson stated flatly.

Mr. Bott nodded. "I know, but I'd like to pay you just the same."

"It wouldn't be the same if we was paid," BB said. "You see, we did it for another reason."

"We wanted you to know us this way," I added.

"I guess none of us has understood each other very well," Mr. Bott commented. "We've never really seen each other. We've just seen rumors." He took a deep breath. "I've probably said some unfair things about you boys. After watching you work out here, though, I know you're different. I guess there aren't three boys in all Snowflake that would do what you three have done. I accept your apology. I should have accepted it sooner. I hope you'll accept mine now. That's why I want to pay you."

"But that would ruin it," Jefferson protested. "We didn't do it for the money. We owed a debt. We paid it. Now we're even."

"Maybe not. Maybe you paid your debt, but I didn't pay mine. You've grown up out here, haven't you?"

We nodded.

"Well, I've done some growing up too, in a different way. One part of being a man is being able to apologize, even when it's hard. Right?"

We nodded again.

"Another part of being a man is being able to accept an apology, even when it's hard. I've accepted yours. And believe me, after Saturday morning I thought that would be the last thing I'd ever do. I didn't want to. I really didn't. I guess I didn't want to admit to myself that you were big enough to apologize. I have accepted the apology. You worked for me to prove you were sincere. Now I'd like you to accept mine by accepting your pay. You've earned it. It really isn't much on my part. Not compared to what you've done."

We shook our heads.

"I'll tell you why," he continued, ignoring our refusal. "Most of this work was just orneriness on my part. I was pretty sure you were sincere when you came the first morning. I don't know if I could have done that. But I was angry, angry that you had plagued me all year in class and then actually had come up with some of the highest scores on my final exam. You completely confused me. I didn't know what kind of boys you were. Then after the rabbits I didn't care. I just wanted to get back at you, maybe like you wanted to get back at me after I accused you of cheating. But Miss Willie prevented that. She cleaned up the mess and you were free. I couldn't take my mind off you all weekend. I had some very harsh thoughts about you. And then there you were on my doorstep, apologizing. I was baffled and irritated by the possibility that I was wrong again. I didn't want to believe that. I didn't want to change my impression of you another time. I guess I suspected that if I let you stay and work there was the possibility that . . . well, that maybe you were all-right boys."

Mr. Bott glanced toward the stables. "When you cleaned those sheds the way you did, there was no longer any doubt on my part. I knew what kind of boys—no, not boys, men—I knew what kind of men you were. But I was still angry, maybe because you were forcing me to see that I had been wrong about you, that everybody had been wrong about you, that Miss Willie was the only one who had ever been right about you. Because of my stubborn pride I told you to clean the lot too, but you had already proved your point by then. So you see, all of this work you've been doing since Tuesday didn't prove you were men of your word. I already knew that. I was doing that out of meanness. Then I realized you were going to stay until the meanness left."

Mr. Bott looked at each of us. "That's why I'd like to at least pay you for the work on the lot. I wouldn't feel right about you working all those hours for me, thinking that you were doing one thing when you were really doing something else. Will you take it—for my peace of mind? That way you're accepting my apology like I accepted yours."

We looked at each other. The battle had been won. We knew it, and we felt good. We had passed the biggest test of all. The victory was ours to keep. Not allowing Mr. Bott to feel good about himself would only make our triumph sour.

"We didn't do it for money, Mr. Bott," Jefferson said, "but if it will make you feel better—and that would be the only reason we would accept—then we'll take it."

Mr. Bott smiled, relieved. "I guess I should warn you that schoolteachers don't pay the greatest wages. I wish I could pay you what you were worth; I'm sorry that I can't. I also hope you won't be scared away from me in school. I know you didn't get a very good impression of me this year. None of us had a very good impression of each other. Maybe another year we can change that."

Mr. Bott made us each a check for forty dollars and we went home. It was strange that two weeks earlier the most important thing to us would have been the forty dollars, but on that Saturday afternoon the thing that meant the most was that we had proved ourselves, that nothing was beyond us. We knew then that so many things that had always seemed difficult, if not impossible—school, missions, college, professions—were within our grasp. The money was secondary.

# Chapter Twelve

THE FOLLOWING TUESDAY AFTERNOON Miss Willie was preparing to leave Snowflake. While she cleaned her house, the three of us doctored up her Ford and helped her cram and squeeze a mountain of things into the old bomb.

As we were stuffing the last of the boxes in and grunting to close the trunk, Miss Willie came out to check our progress. "Save me a little room on the back seat," she cautioned.

"The back seat is full," Jefferson panted.

"I still have a suitcase and a box of dishes and pans. And my night bag. And there might be some odds and ends."

"Miss Willie," Jefferson groaned, "you don't have more?"

"Oh, I can pack it all right. You've done the hard part."

"But there's no more room," BB cried, looking inside the car. "Did you come to Snowflake with all this junk?"

"You'll have to sit on your suitcase," I said. "That or just leave some of your stuff here over the summer."

"Yeah," Jefferson said, lighting up. "Why don't you just leave some of it here?"

She shrugged. "Do you think the Ford will make it?"

"I quit making predictions about this old jalopy," BB lamented. "I know one thing. It would sure stand a better chance if you left half of this behind. Won't Brother Reeves let you leave at least part of it over the summer?"

"The back tires look a little low, don't they?" she observed.

"Not bad. We'll check them, though. Do you think he will?"

"Will what?"

"Let you leave some stuff."

She hesitated. "No."

"Where will you stay next year?"

She didn't answer. The three of us looked at each other. "You are coming back, aren't you?" BB asked.

She pressed her lips together for a moment and then sighed. "No," she whispered.

The three of us were shocked into silence. Our startled expressions asked a hundred questions.

"I've been meaning to tell you," she said. "I just didn't know when. Or how." She wrapped her arms around herself as though there were a sudden chill. "For some time now I have been debating about next year. I made a final decision last week."

My breath was snatched away. An emptiness exploded inside of me, the void growing until I was overwhelmed, unable to grasp Miss Willie's staggering announcement.

Miss Willie continued haltingly. "Snowflake has been a lifesaver." She shook her head. "No, not just Snowflake." She swallowed and took a deep breath. "Sometimes you have to move on. Not because you want to, but because . . ." She smiled ever so faintly and shrugged. "Just because."

"But why?" Jefferson inquired hoarsely. "I mean, don't you like it here? Isn't Snowflake kinda like home?"

"You've made it home. All of you."

"Then why not come back?" I asked.

She thought for a moment. "Why did you leave Mr. Bott's lot last week?"

"We were finished."

"All of us finish sometime. Now I must go back. What I have left to do I can't do in Snowflake. But going back will be easier for me."

"Does going back to Salt Lake worry you? Frighten you, like it used to?" I asked.

Miss Willie breathed deeply. "No," she answered, "not anymore. I think being in Snowflake, with you three, has purged the fear and worry."

"So there's nothing more to worry about back there?" I asked, relieved.

She gazed across the street at two boys pulling a battered, rusty wagon down the sidewalk. "Sometimes the problems don't ever go away," she replied. "We just lose our fear of them and learn to face them. You've all learned many things during the past year." We nodded. "And I've learned to face and accept the inevitable without fear and worry. And in the process I've been rewarded with peace and hope. I couldn't ask for more."

"So you don't plan to come back?" BB asked. She shook her head. "Why didn't you tell us? I mean, earlier. Why did you wait till now?"

"I guess I hate all good-byes," she explained sadly. "Especially when they might be for . . . for so long." She swallowed. "I wanted you to remember me here, the way we've been. I want you to remember these months as happy times."

"You would have told us?" BB asked, worried. "Wouldn't you?"

She hung her head.

"You'll probably get to see Ross," BB pointed out with a sudden burst of enthusiasm. "He's up there. Who knows? He might bring you back. You do like him, don't you?"

"He's very nice."

"You're nice, very nice! What's wrong with two nice people getting together?"

She laughed. "Don't become matchmakers. Sometimes two nice people are going in two different directions."

"What time will you leave tomorrow?" Jefferson asked.

"Early."

"You won't leave without telling us good-bye?"

"We have something for you," BB said, grinning sheepishly. "Just a little something to remember us."

"I won't go until you come."

"Promise?"

"Promise."

"Even though you hate good-byes?"

"I'll wait."

The next morning before the sun was up, the three of us were waiting by the old Ford, holding a large gift wrapped in brown paper sacks. When Miss Willie came, we held it out to her.

"Sorry about the wrapping job," Jefferson said. "You didn't ever show us how to wrap presents. But if you decide to come back next year, we'll sure learn."

There were tears in her eyes as she accepted our proffered gift. "You shouldn't have done this."

"Don't get too excited. You haven't seen it yet," BB grinned. "Don't expect a Shakespeare library."

"We used Mr. Bott's money," I explained. "We figured you deserved it."

"My, it's heavy!" she grunted as she held it. We smiled with anticipation. Slowly she pulled the paper away, revealing a bright-red metal box. "What is it?" she asked, her brow wrinkled in puzzled expectation.

"Open it!" we all called out.

She lifted the lid and looked inside, then gingerly pulled out a wrench and a screwdriver. "I don't quite understand."

"It's a tool box," I said. "If you're going to be a mechanic on the side, you need tools. You can't always be borrowing BB's. Unless you stay."

The puzzled expression vanished and she began to laugh. "Just what I—"

"Just what you always wanted and needed."

"What'll I ever do with them?"

"They'll help you keep this rattling junk pile together until you get to Salt Lake. And if you happen to meet any damsel in distress, you might stop and give her a hand."

"Because gentlemen are scarce," she giggled. "Otherwise she might be there a long time."

"That's almost a hundred dollars' worth of tools," BB said,

shaking a finger at her, "so don't go give them away or sell them for a couple of bucks thinking you got a good deal."

"I don't know . . ."

"And, Miss Willie," BB interrupted, "when we see you again, if those tools are as shiny as they are now, we'll know you haven't appreciated the sacrifice we made in Mr. Bott's lot."

"I'll cherish them forever," she assured us with a misty gaze. She gave us each a warm hug, our very first from her, climbed into her old Ford, and, with her red tool box sitting next to her on the seat, drove away.

Long after her Ford had disappeared into the early-morning shadows, we stood silently in front of Miss Willie's house and stared longingly down the road through a hot mist of tears.

I thought my heart would break that day. The only other time I had felt such a devastating emptiness was when my mother had died. I knew there was no way I could explain my feelings to anyone, not even to Jefferson and BB. Though I was sure they would understand, I sensed that the mere verbalization of my emotions would crush me. I just wanted to be alone where I could ponder, reminisce, and even weep.

All of us must have felt the same, because we soon separated without a word to each other, found spots of seclusion, and braced ourselves for a world without Miss Willie.

It was a while before we could bear the pain of each other's company. At first it was too much for us to be together, because that togetherness was too acutely reminiscent of those days with Miss Willie. Then three weeks later we received a letter: "Dear BB, DJ, and Jefferson, I have been meaning to write ever since I returned to Salt Lake, but you know how things pile up and time is gone before you know it.

"I made it home all right. I didn't even need to use your tools— thank goodness! I prayed instead. I have practiced my faith and prayers more than I have my auto mechanics. And the old Ford seems to respond better. It wasn't that I was afraid to change a flat tire. That would have been easy. But you forgot to teach me to unpack the car to get at the spare. That would have slain me for sure. If you come to Salt Lake you can teach me.

"Although I made it home without a hitch, the next morning one of my tires was flat. And I changed it! All by myself! I've already tried your tools out. I knew I couldn't write this letter until I had. Actually, that's why it has taken me so long to write this letter. Now my mother actually thinks I'm a mechanic. I tightened the screws in the rear door and I changed the oil. BB, guess what I remembered to have under the car? You know, changing the oil really isn't all that messy once you get the hang of it. I wonder where I got the distinct impression that it was.

"I saw Ross the other day. So you won't die of curiosity, there were no commitments made. Just a friendly visit. We haven't changed directions, though.

"This fall I will be teaching at my old high school. I am excited, but I wish I had three of my old students with me. I miss Snowflake, the peace and quiet there. I miss our visits together. Write and let me know how you all are. I won't be content unless you tell me every little thing. Love, Miss Willie."

The letter suddenly made Miss Willie seem close again. We read it countless times. But even though the letter drew us to Miss Willie, we experienced an eerie premonition about the future. It was nothing we could explain, nothing we ever discussed. It wasn't until much later that we even understood.

## Chapter Thirteen

THERE WAS A TERRIBLE SENSE OF LOSS in watching Miss Willie drive away, but at the same time there was an enigmatic fulfillment, a pervasive tranquillity. We felt older, not just in time, but in genuine maturity.

The realization came forcefully that Miss Willie's fortuitous arrival was much more than mere happenstance. Because of her we were now stepping from the bumbling uncertainty of adolescence onto the inviting but awesome threshold of adulthood. She had found us teetering at the pivotal point of our youth. Left to our own caprices and passivity, we might have tumbled into the undistinguished rut of the commonplace, but she had diverted the tide of our own mediocrity and pointed us upward.

Afterward we felt a strange power within us. It was almost frightening. It wasn't something we discussed with others. It wasn't even something we mentioned among ourselves. But it was there, and each of us knew that the other two felt it as well.

With the stirrings of our modest maturity came a loss of youthful recklessness. We were more serious now. We knew where we were going, and after the miracle of Miss Willie, we knew we would arrive.

The months passed and we hoped that Miss Willie would change her mind and return to Snowflake, even for a short visit. We talked of visiting her in Salt Lake, but while we were in high school those dreams never materialized. We invited her to our graduation, but she was ill at the time and unable to come.

Though we went our different ways after graduation, we were destined to reunite in Snowflake at the end of that year to be ordained elders and to wait for our mission calls, which came right after New Year's.

It was only appropriate that we were all scheduled to enter the mission home the same day in February. Had we gone in on different days, chances are we would have never made that last visit to Miss Willie.

The day before we were to enter the mission home, we left our families at the motel, took BB's car, and drove up on the East Bench in search of Miss Willie. We didn't have to drive far before we were thoroughly lost in a baffling maze of streets, avenues, drives, and parks. We began to laugh, remembering Miss Willie's first days in Snowflake. It wasn't until that moment that we realized how utterly ludicrous had been our "grand tour."

When we finally did pull up to the curb in front of her house, we ached with excitement. Though we were no longer infatuated boys struggling to stir up a romance, an old romantic flame was rekindled. Climbing from the car, we perused our reflections in the windows, adjusted our ties, put every hair in place, and then marched to the door, trembling with anticipation.

Our countenances sagged momentarily when an older woman opened the door. We looked at the house number and then out into the street. "Is this Madison Drive?" I asked, wondering if we were still lost.

Suddenly the woman's face broke into a smile. "You're the boys from Snowflake," she declared, swinging the door wide. "I think I would have recognized you even without the yearbook pictures. Kathy will be so happy."

"Then this is where Miss Willie lives?" Jefferson asked.

She nodded. "I'm Kathy's mother. I've heard so much about you. When she came back, all I heard was DJ, Jefferson, and BB. It was the longest time before I realized anyone else lived in Snow-flake."

"Is she here?" BB asked.

"She's upstairs. I don't think she's asleep. Come on up."

Mrs. Willie led us up the stairs and pushed open a door. Miss Willie was sitting up in bed reading. I don't know what we had expected. Certainly not what we found. The thought had never occurred to us that Miss Willie was seriously ill. It seemed inconceivable that she could be anything but vibrantly alive and well.

I almost didn't recognize her. She was pale and emaciated. She couldn't have weighed more than ninety pounds. Her cheeks were sunken, and the bones in her hands and arms protruded with shocking detail. Her hair was pulled up under a scarf on her head.

The book she was holding dropped and she stared in disbelief, but soon the old familiar smile touched her lips, and the warm, gentle eyes sparkled with recognition and welcome.

After our initial stuttered greetings, we were silent. We stood awkwardly staring and fidgeting, unable to grasp the reality of what had transpired in the two and a half years since Miss Willie had left us.

"You didn't ever tell us," BB whispered.

Miss Willie sank into the two pillows that were propping up her frail weight. She shook her head and closed her eyes. "I tried. I hinted," she whispered. "This was something I couldn't share very well." She opened her eyes. "To say it was like saying good-bye. You know how I feel about good-byes."

"What is . . ." I groped for the words, wanting to know but incapable of verbalizing what was so devastating.

"Cancer," she said simply.

"How long?" I shook my head. "I mean, how long have you known?"

"Oh, some time now."

"This is what you were running from," BB observed quietly.

"Maybe running was the wrong word. It wasn't like I could ever escape. It was with me. But I've done quite well, considering." She smiled. "At least I've fooled the doctors."

"And why . . . Snowflake?" Jefferson said hoarsely. "I mean, if you knew why . . ."

She breathed deeply. "Everyone here knew. At least many knew. I could see the pity and the fear in their eyes. I couldn't stand it. I didn't want to live with that. I didn't want to die every time I looked someone in the face. I prayed. Oh, how I prayed. I pleaded with Him to give me time and something important to do. I wanted to be completely alive. Even for a little while. I went to Snowflake and met you three. There I lived. That was His miracle to me."

She closed her eyes and breathed deeply for several minutes as though her few words had exhausted her. "When I saw you out in Mr. Bott's lot, determined to succeed, I knew you had come of age. I knew my work was finished and I had to come home and face . . ."

"And you couldn't tell us?" Jefferson asked, the hurt in his voice poignantly clear.

"I wanted you to know me alive, with nothing else hovering above me. But had I been able to tell anyone, it would have been you."

She smiled at us from the depth of her pillows. "There are so many exciting things to talk about," she said, changing the subject. "What have you been doing? You'll have to tell me everything, starting with what brought you to Salt Lake."

"We're missionaries!" BB beamed, Miss Willie's enthusiasm contagious. "You told us you wouldn't have anybody but an RM."

"That isn't the reason we're going," I said, "but we did think of you. You're the one who got us thinking about it."

"Where?"

"BB to Chile, Jefferson to Brazil, and I'll be in Mexico. Even though I don't have any relatives from there like BB does. I guess it was just easiest to ship me across the border."

"Our Spanish paid off, though," Jefferson remarked. "If we learn it well enough, we'll tell everyone you were our teacher."

"If we slaughter it," BB laughed, "we'll tell them Miss Paine is to blame. Hey, and speaking of Miss Paine, get this. We finally took her for English. We didn't work up enough courage until we were seniors, though. Guess what?"

"You discovered that Shakespeare doesn't write westerns or play pro football."

"That too," he laughed, "but she wasn't half bad. We even liked her. In fact, she was about the best teacher we ever had. There was only one better. The rumors were just a lot of talk. Bad talk mainly."

"Straight A's too," Jefferson added. "In fact, we were on the principal's list as seniors. When I told my Uncle Roy, he thought the principal's list was the high school's version of the FBI's ten-most-wanted-men list. He fell off his chair when I told him what it really was."

"And we took Mr. Bott, as juniors and seniors," I injected. "I don't know why we ever hated him. He helped us with everything. Oh, and you never heard a guy brag like him."

"About us," Jefferson almost shouted. "Imagine that."

"And for graduation he sent us a card. He wrote, 'To the Baby Bosko Bott Booster Club from the Baby Bosko himself.'"

"And now you're missionaries."

We nodded.

"And after that?"

"Jefferson still thinks he'll be a doctor. BB's going to be a CPA if his dad will let him out of the garage. I kind of like English. I'd like to teach at a small college maybe."

"And do you still dance?"

We laughed. "Not with each other," Jefferson said. "Sometimes we asked a girl. We always tripled, though. I don't think I could go on a date unless BB and DJ were with me."

"Did you take one girl among you?"

"No, but we did have to call each other's girl. We never did get to where we could call for ourselves."

"We still haven't found anyone as good as the girl we first dated in Snowflake, but we haven't given up hope. If she's not married when we get back, we still might ask her. All three of us. Just like old times."

Miss Willie laughed. "And she'll probably accept."

"Did you ever realize how much . . . well, that we were . . ."

She covered her mouth with her hand and shook with laughter. "The thought occurred to me," she managed to say between giggles. "You know you weren't very good at hiding it."

"Did it ever scare you?"

"Never. A lady is never scared in the presence of a gentleman. Never, never in the presence of three."

We all began talking at once, laughing and calling back the memories that were such an integral part of our past. I don't know when it happened, but suddenly in the midst of our reminiscing there were tears in our eyes. We were flooded with an overwhelming emotion as we realized that those cherished days were forever slipping away from us.

"Everything is going to be all right," Jefferson choked. "You can do anything. You're the one who told us that. After our missions we're going to come back here and we'll talk and laugh and nothing will change because you'll always . . ." His words were muffled and lost in a sorrowful gasp.

The tearful smile faded from Miss Willie's face. For several minutes no one spoke. "We all run a race," she finally commented. "Some of the races are short; some are long. Whichever race we run, we run the very best we can. Sooner or later, though, we come around that last turn. We see the finish line, but we keep running just as fast and with just as much fortitude as we ran the rest of the race. We can't stop. We can't hesitate. The finish is there for all of us."

"But it doesn't mean there's not a chance," he insisted.

"I believe in miracles," she said, smiling knowingly. "I've had my share, but I won't be selfish and ask for more."

"But you can't just . . ." Jefferson couldn't finish the sentence.

The room was quiet again. "I used to have one regret," she confessed. "I wanted to have a family." Her eyes sparkled with tears and her chin quivered. "If I could have sons, I'd like three just like you." She dabbed at her eyes. "I guess you'll have to be those sons."

"You got Jefferson and me easy," I said, trying to laugh but failing. "We're orphans, remember? But you'll have to adopt BB. He's got a mom."

"Two moms don't hurt anybody," BB said quickly.

We didn't want to leave. The minutes ticked away, but we lingered as though our presence would keep prowling death at bay. The hardest thing we ever did in our lives was to leave Miss Willie and drive back to the motel. Never had we bid farewell with such finality. We knew the devastating truth. Tears came easily that day, and we were unashamed.

I was in Mazatlán, Mexico, when I received the final news. I remember the day so well. I had been in Mexico only three months, but President Holmes had called that morning transferring me to a dirty, dead little town called Guasave. It was the hole of the mission. It had been over a year since anyone had been baptized there. Not only was I being made a senior companion for the transfer, but President Holmes had asked me to serve as branch president. At first I thought it was a mistake. I was still so green. I had even argued with him, insisting that I was not ready for such a challenge. I wanted desperately to refuse, but in the end I reluctantly consented to go.

The elders' quarters in Mazatlán was close to a beautiful beach. Drowning in my own helplessness, I stared out at the waves rushing onto shore. Filled with a frustrating hopelessness, I wanted to succumb to a deluge of tears.

Then Sharon's letter arrived: "We just returned from Salt Lake. BB's mom and dad and Jefferson's Aunt Betty and I attended Miss Willie's funeral. It was . . ."

The letter dropped. I had known that that letter would come sooner or later. Earlier I had wondered if I would shed tears again. But there were none. Instead of tears came memories, and the memories brought confidence. Strangely enough I was filled with a warm, reassuring calm, a quiet hope. I recalled what BB had said after our first evening with Miss Willie. He spoke of a feeling presaging success, a feeling inspired by Miss Willie. I was consumed with that feeling now.

I knew then I would go to Guasave and be branch president. I would teach and baptize, not once but many times, and through the impending struggle I would remember and be grateful for the marvelous miracle of Miss Willie.